Philip José Farmer was born in 1918. A part-time student at Bradley University, he gained a BA in English in 1950. Two years later he shocked the sf world with the publication of his novella *The Lovers* in *Startling Stories*. This won him a Hugo Award in 1953; his second Hugo came in 1968 for the story *Riders of the Purple Wage* written for Harlan Ellison's famous *Dangerous Vision* series; and his third came in 1972 for the first part of the acclaimed *Riverworld* series, *To Your Scattered Bodies Go*. Leslie Fiedler, eminent critic and Professor of English at the State University of New York at Buffalo, has said that Farmer 'has an imagination capable of being kindled by the irredeemable mystery of the universe and of the soul, and in turn able to kindle the imagination of others – readers who for a couple of generations have been turning to science fiction to keep wonder and ecstasy alive'. Philip José Farmer lives and works in Peoria, Illinois.

By the same author

The Lovers
Doc Savage: His Apocalyptic Life
Lord Tyger
Strange Relations
Tarzan Alive
Time's Last Gift
Traitor to the Living
The Stone God Awakens
Flesh
Behind the Walls of Terra
The Image of the Beast
Blown
A Feast Unknown
The Gates of Creation
The Maker of Universes
Night of Light
A Private Cosmos
The Wind Whales of Ishmael
The Lavalite World
Jesus on Mars
Dark is the Sun
The Unreasoning Mask
Inside, Outside
The Alley God

The *Riverworld* series

To Your Scattered Bodies Go
The Fabulous Riverboat
The Dark Design
The Magic Labyrinth
Gods of Riverworld

Riverworld and other Stories

PHILIP JOSÉ FARMER

Dayworld

GRAFTON BOOKS
A Division of the Collins Publishing Group

LONDON GLASGOW
TORONTO SYDNEY AUCKLAND

Grafton Books
A Division of the Collins Publishing Group
8 Grafton Street, London W1X 3LA

Published by Grafton Books 1986

First published in Great Britain by
Granada Publishing 1985

Copyright © Philip José Farmer 1985

ISBN 0-586-06631-4

Printed and bound in Great Britain by
Collins, Glasgow

Set in Times

All rights reserved. No part of this publication
may be reproduced, stored in a retrieval system,
or transmitted, in any form, or by any means,
electronic, mechanical, photocopying, recording or
otherwise, without the prior permission of
the publishers.

This book is sold subject to the condition that
it shall not, by way of trade or otherwise, be
lent, re-sold, hired out or otherwise circulated
without the publisher's prior consent in any
form of binding or cover other than that
in which it is published and without a similar
condition including this condition being
imposed on the subsequent purchaser.

To my latest grandchild, Thomas José Josephsohn, born March 25, 1983. May he live to be old and be always as bright, friendly, outgoing, cheerful, curious, and healthy as he is now.

My thanks to Father James D. Shaughnessy of Peoria for his counsel and stimulating ideas re future popes. Any opinions and conclusions herein about seven simultaneous popes are, however, my responsibility, not his.

Author's Preface

The basis or springboard for this novel is my short story 'The-Sliced-Crosswise-Only-On-Tuesday-World.' This took place in AD 2214 (old style) or NE 130 (new style): NE stands for New Era, and NE 130 indicates the one hundred and thirtieth year after the official beginning of the 'stoner' society.

The events of *Dayworld* occur in AD 3414 or NE 1330. Thirteen hundred and thirty years have passed since the start of the New Era, NE 1.

Though there are twelve hundred years between the events of the short story and the novel, only seven and a half generations (arithmetically speaking) have been born. The reason for this will become apparent during the course of the novel.

In the future, the USA will have to adopt the metric and twenty-four-hour time systems. I use the present systems for the convenience of the American reader.

Some contemporary English words have different meanings in the New Era culture. These changes should be obvious.

Do not be confused because some of the male characters have female names and some females have male names. Times change; customs die.

The protagonist of *Dayworld* is an outlaw, a daybreaker. He lives by the horizontal calendar.

For an explanation of the horizontal and vertical calendars, refer to the illustration on the next page.

The calendar is 'vertical,' not our present-day 'horizontal' calendar. Our calendars present the seven days of the week as if we moved through time horizontally. Sunday precedes

Monday, and Monday precedes Tuesday, and by the time we have reached next Sunday, we have stepped off onto another horizontal chronological path.

The New Era or 'stoner' society uses a 'vertical' calendar. Reason: One-seventh of the world's population lives on only one day of the week. To put it another way, six-sevenths of the world's population is in a 'stoned' or 'suspended-animation' state for six days of each week. Sunday's people live on Sunday only; Monday's, on Monday, and so forth.

At the end of one passage of Earth around the sun, a Sunday citizen has lived only fifty-two days. If born in, say, NE 100, that person has been on Earth two hundred years by NE 300. But that person is not quite twenty-nine years old in physiological development. If that person has been on Earth for six hundred years, he or she is not quite eighty-six years old in terms of ageing.

The stoner culture greatly reduces the demand for food and goods, amount of pollution, and living space required. If the global population is, say, ten billion, then, on each day, only a little over one billion, four hundred and twenty-eight million, five hundred thousand people are eating food, drinking, using space, and adding trash, junk, and waste matter for disposal.

The New Era government decreed a new calendar for two reasons. One, it wanted to make a clean break with the past. Two, it made sure that each day's population would not be cheated out of its full quota of days per year because of the different days of the months as set by the Gregorian calendar. The summer solstice, which occurs on or near June 21, arbitrarily became the first day of the year, and that day was designated as Sunday.

The year was divided into thirteen months of four seven-day weeks. The end of the year was followed by a *zero* or *lost* day to ensure that there were three hundred and sixty-five days in the year. During leap years, an extra zero or

NEW ERA (VERTICAL) CALENDAR
NE 1330 (OLD STYLE AD 3414)

UNITY, FIRST MONTH

SUNDAY	MONDAY	TUESDAY	WED'SDAY	THURSDAY	FRIDAY	SATURDAY
D1-W1	D1-W1	" "	" "	" "	" "	" "
D2-W1	D2-W1	" "	" "	" "	" "	" "
D3-W1	D3-W1	" "	" "	" "	" "	" "
D4-W1	D4-W1	" "	" "	" "	" "	" "

VARIETY, SECOND MONTH

SUNDAY	MONDAY	TUESDAY	WED'SDAY	THURSDAY	FRIDAY	SATURDAY
D5-W1	" "	" " *CAIRD'S DAY*	" " *TINGLE'S DAY*	" " *DUNSKI'S DAY*	" " *REPP'S DAY*	" " *OHM'S DAY*
D6-W1 *ZURVAN'S DAY*	" " *ISHARASH-VILI'S DAY*	" "	" "	" "	" "	" "
D7-W1	" "	" "	" "	" "	" "	" "
D1-W2	" "	" "	" "	" "	" "	" "

FREEDOM, SEVENTH MONTH

SUNDAY	MONDAY	TUESDAY	WED'SDAY	THURSDAY	FRIDAY	SATURDAY
D4-W4	" "	" "	" "	" "	" "	" "
D5-W4	" "	" "	" "	" "	" "	" "
D6-W4 *CHRISTMAS*	" " *CHRISTMAS*	" " *WHOSE DAY?* *CHRISTMAS*	" " *CHRISTMAS*	" " *CHRISTMAS*	" " *CHRISTMAS*	" " *CHRISTMAS*
D7-W4	" "	" "	" "	" "	" "	" "

D1-W1 means Day-One of Week-One or the first day of the first week of the year. D3-W4 stands for the third day of the fourth 'vertical' week, etc.

lost day was added. Everybody except a minimum number of firefighters, police, administrators, and so on was kept in the stoned state.

The citizens would, of course, refer to two different types of time. Objective time, that is, time as measured by the annual circling of the Earth around the sun and Earth's spinning, would be termed obyears, obmonths, and obweeks. Subjective time, that is, the actual number of days, weeks, months, and years a person has lived, would be subdays, subweeks, submonths, and subyears.

The names of the months are, in order of succession, Unity, Variety, Joy, Hope, Comradeship, Love, Freedom, Plenty, Peace, Knowledge, Wisdom, Serenity, and Fulfilment. These are also the Thirteen Principles upon which the New Era society is supposedly based.

Tuesday-World

Organic Commonwealth of Earth
North American Ministering Organ
Manhattan State
Manhattan total population: 2,100,000
Manhattan daily population: 300,000
Greenwich Village District
House on corner of Bleecker Street
and Kropotkin Canal (formerly the
Avenue of the Americas)

VARIETY, Second Month of NE 1330
D5-W1 (Day-Five, Week-One)

Time Zone 5, 12:15 AM

1

When the hounds bay, the fox and the hare are brothers.

Today, Jeff Caird, the fox, would hear the hounds.

At the moment, he could not hear anything because he was standing in a soundproof cylinder. If he had been outside it, he still would have heard nothing. Except for himself and a few organics, firefighters, and technicians, he was the only living person in the city.

A few minutes before entering the cylinder and closing its door, he had slid back a small panel in the wall. Behind the control panel in the wall recess was a tiny device he had long ago connected to the power circuits. He had voice-activated the device, thus ensuring that 'destoning' power would not be applied to the cylinder he now occupied.

Though power was absent, the city monitoring computer would receive false data that power had been turned on in his cylinder.

His cylinder or 'stoner' was like those of all other healthy adults. It stood on one end, had a round window a foot in diameter in the door, and was made of grey paper. The paper, however, was permanently 'stoned,' and thus was indestructible and always cool.

Nude, his feet planted on a thick disc set in the middle of the cylinder, he waited. The inflated facsimile of himself had been deflated and was in the shoulderbag on the cylinder floor.

The figures in the other cylinders in the room were nonliving things whose molecules had been electromagnetically commanded to slow down. Result: a hardening throughout the body, which became unbreakable and unburnable, though a diamond could scratch it. Result: a lowering of body temperature, though it was not so low that it caused moisture to precipitate in the ambient air.

Suddenly, in one cylinder in the room and in hundreds of thousands of others in the silent city, automatically applied power surged from the discs and through the statuelike bodies. Like a cue stick slamming into a group of billiard balls, the power struck the lazy molecules of the body. The balls scattered and kept on moving at the rate determined by Nature. The heart of the destoned person, unaware that it had been stopped, completed the beat. Exactly fifteen minutes after midnight, the people of Tuesday's Manhattan were no longer uneatable and unrottable pumpkins. For the next twenty-three hours and thirty minutes, they could be easily wounded or killed.

He pushed the door open and stepped into a large basement room. He bent slightly from the waist, causing the ID badge hung from a chain around his neck to swing out. As he straightened up, the green disc surrounded by a seven-pointed star settled back against his solar plexus.

The sourceless light had come on when destoning power had been applied. As he did every Tuesday morning, he saw the shadowless light-green walls, the four-foot-wide TV strips running from ceiling to floor, the thick brown carpet with a swirling green pattern, the clock strip, and twenty-three cylinders and coffin-shaped boxes, the 'stoners.' Twenty frozen faces were framed by the round windows. Twelve seniors (adults) in the vertical cylinders. Eight juniors, young children, lying horizontally in the boxes and facing the ceiling.

A few seconds after he had left his stoner, a woman stepped out of hers. Ozma Fillmore Wang was short, slender, full-breasted, and long-legged. Her cheekbones were broad and high on her heart-shaped face. Her large black eyes had slight epicanthic folds. Her long hair was straight, black, and glossy. Large white teeth shone when she flashed a wide-lipped smile.

She wore nothing except her ID disc-star, lipstick, eye shadow, and a great green grasshopper painted on her body. It was standing up on its back legs, and her black-painted nipples formed the centres of the black staring eyes. Sometimes, when Jeff was making love to his wife, he had the feeling that he was coupled with an insect.

She came to him, and they kissed. 'Good morning, Jeff.'

'Good morning, Ozma.'

She turned and led him into the next room. He reached out to pat her egg-shaped buttock, then withdrew his hand. The slightest encouragement would inflame her. She would want to make love on the carpet in front of the unseeing witnesses in the cylinders. He thought that it was childish to do this, but she was, in some ways, childish. She preferred to call herself childlike. OK. All good artists were childlike. To them every second birthed a new world, each more astonishing and awesome than the previous. However . . . was Ozma a good artist?

What did he care? He loved her for herself, whatever that meant.

The other room contained chairs, sofas, tables, a Ping-Pong table, an exercising machine, a pool table, TV wall strips, a door to a bathroom, and a door to the utility room. Ozma turned just outside this door and went up the steps to a hall. On their left was the kitchen. They turned right, went down a short hall, and turned right to the steps. The upstairs held four bedrooms, each with a bathroom. Ozma preceded him into the nearest bedroom, which lit up as they entered.

At one end of the large room, by some shuttered windows, was a king-size bed. At another wall, by a large round window, was a table with a large mirror. Nearby were shelves holding big plastic boxes containing brushes, combs, and cosmetics. Each box bore the name of its owner.

Along one wall was a series of doors with name-plaques. Jeff inserted a point of his ID star into a hole in the door bearing his name and Ozma's. It slid open, and a light came on, revealing shelves holding their personal-property clothing. From a shelf at eye level, he picked out a crumpled ball of cloth, turned, placed a section between his thumb and first finger, and snapped the ball. It unrolled with a crack of electrical sparks from its hem and became a long, smooth Kelly-green robe. He put it on and tied a belt around his waist. From another shelf he took two socks and a pair of shoes. After putting these on, he sealed the tops of the shoes with a firm pressure of fingers.

Ozma straightened up from her inspection of the bedclothes.

'Clean and done according to specifications,' she said.

'Monday's always been good about house duties. We're luckier than some I know. I only hope Monday doesn't move to another house.'

She spoke a codeword. A wall sprang into light and life, a three-dimensional view of a jungle composed of gigantic grass blades. Presently, some blades bent, and a thing with bulging black insect eyes looked at the two humans. Its antennae quivered. A hind leg raised and rubbed against a protruding vein. Grasshopper stridulations rang through the room.

'For God's sake,' Jeff said. 'Tone it down.'

'It soothes me to sleep,' she said. 'Not that I feel like sleeping just now.'

'I'd like to wait until we've had a good rest. It's always better then.'

'Oh, I don't know,' Ozma said. 'Why don't we give it a scientific test? Do it before sleep and after and then compare notes?'

'That's the difference between forty and twenty-five. Believe me, I know.'

She laughed and said, 'We're not a December-April

match, darling.'

She lay down on the bed, her arms and legs spread out.

'The Castle Ecstatic is undefended, and its drawbridge is down. Charge on in, Sir Galahad, with your trusty lance.'

'I'm afraid I might fall into the moat,' he said, grinning.

'You bastard! Are you trying to make me mad again? Charge on in, faint-hearted knight, or I'll slam the portcullis down on you!'

'You've been watching reruns of *The Knights of the Round Table*,' he said.

'They turn me on, all those violent men on their big horses and maidens ravished by three-headed ogres. All those spears thrusting. Come on, Jeff! Play along with me!'

'I seek the Holy Grail,' he said as he eased down. 'However, it's more like the Holy Gruel.'

'Can I help it if I overlubricate? You keep this up, and I'll paint you brown and flush you down the toilet. Don't spoil it for me, Jeff. I have to fantasize.'

He thought, Whatever happened to good old unimaginative sex? But he said, 'I've just taken a vow of silence. Think of me as the mad monk of Sherwood Forest.'

'Don't stop talking. You know I love it when you talk dirty.'

Fifteen minutes later, she said, 'Did you apply for a permit?'

'No,' he said, breathing hard. 'I forgot.'

She rolled over to face him. 'You said you wanted a child.'

'Yes. Only . . . you know I had so much trouble with Ariel. I wonder if I really want another child.'

Ozma stroked his cheek gently. 'Your daughter's a wonderful woman. *What* trouble?'

'Lots after her mother died. She got neurotic, too dependent. And she's very jealous of you, though she has no reason to be.'

'I don't think so,' Ozma said. 'Anyway . . . trouble?

What trouble? Have you been holding out on me?'

'No.'

'We'll talk about it during breakfast,' she said. 'Unless you'd like to talk about it now. You know, I thought for sure that you wanted a child. I had some misgivings myself. I am an artist, and I should give my all to my art, excluding of course what I gladly give to you. But a child? I wasn't sure. Then –'

'We've been through that,' he said. He mimicked her low husky hint-of-gravel-grinding voice. ' "Every woman is an artist in that she can produce a masterpiece, her child. However, not all women are good artists. But I am, I am. Painting is not enough." '

She hit his arm with a tiny fist. 'You make me sound so pompous.'

'Not at all.' He kissed her. 'Good night. We'll talk later.'

'That's what I said. But . . . you'll apply today?'

'I promise.'

Though they could have sent in their application via TV strip, they had a much better chance of acceptance if he used his connections as an organic (a euphemism for policeperson, who represented the force of the 'organic' government). He would talk face to face with a superior official of the Reproduction Bureau for whom he had done some favours, and the application would not go through regular channels. Even so, it would be a subyear before the Bureau's decision came through. Jeff knew that they would be accepted. Meanwhile, he could change his mind and cancel the application.

Ozma would be angry if he did, which meant that he was going to have to think of a good excuse. However, many events could happen before the day of wrath.

Ozma went to sleep quickly. He lay for a while, eyes closed but seeing Ariel's face. The immer council had already rejected his request to initiate Ozma. He had expected that, but he had thought that Ariel would be accepted. The daughter of immers, she was very intelligent and adaptable, highly qualified to become an immer. Except . . . she had shown some psychic instability in certain matters. For that reason, the immer council might reject her. He could not deny that the council had to be very cautious. But he was hurt.

Sometimes, he wished that Gilbert Ching Immerman had not discovered the elixir or chemical compound of whatever it was that slowed down ageing. He also wished that, since the elixir *had* been discovered many obcenturies ago, Immerman had made the discovery public. But Immerman, after some agonizing, had decided that the elixir would not be good for humankind as a whole.

As it was, the stoner society eliminated many generations that would have been born if the stoners had not been invented. It took a person one hundred and forty objective years to reach the physiological age of twenty. Thus, six generations were lost every one hundred and forty years. Who knew what geniuses and saints, not to mention the common people, were never born? Who knew how many people who might have led the world in scientific and artistic and political progress were missing?

Immerman had thought that the present situation was bad enough. But if the existing slowing-down of living and of birth was increased by seven, then the loss would be even greater. And this global society, the Organic Commonwealth of Earth, would become even more static and would change even more sluggishly.

Whether Immerman's decision was ethically right or wrong, he had made it, and its result, the secret immer family, was living today.

Immerman had not, however, been selfish in keeping the secret for himself, his descendants, and those initiated into the family. The immers would be hidden rebels against the government. In a slow and subtle revolution, they would infiltrate the upper and middle echelons of the commonwealth. Once they had enough power, they would not change the basic structure of the government. They did not want as yet to abandon the stoners. But they did want to get rid of the constant and close monitoring of the citizens by the government. It was not just irksome; it was degrading. It also was not necessary, though the government claimed that it was.

'Only by being watched may you become free' was one of the government's slogans often displayed on the strip shows.

At the age of eighteen subyears, Caird had been told of the immer society by his parents. He had been studied by the council, weighed in the balance and found more than satisfactory. He was asked if he wanted to become an immer. Of course, he did. Who would turn down the opportunity of a much longer life? And what intelligent youth would not want to work for greater freedom and for an eventual position of power?

It was not until some subyears later that he realized how anxious his parents must have been when they revealed the secret of the immers. What if, through some perversity, their son had refused to join? The immer council could not allow him to live, even though it was unlikely that he would betray the family. He would have been taken away in the dead of night and stoned, then hidden where no one would ever find him. And that would have grieved his parents.

When Caird had realized that, he had asked his parents what they would have done if he had rejected the offer. Would they have turned against the immers?

'But no one has ever refused,' his father had said.

Caird had not said anything, but he had wondered if there had been people who had turned down the offer and no one except those immediately involved had known of it.

At nineteen, Caird had been approached by his uncle, an

organic whom Caird suspected might also be on the Manhattan immer council. Did his nephew wish to become a daybreaker? Not just the ordinary type of daybreaker, a common criminal, but one who would be protected and helped by the immers. He would have a new identity on each day, he could have many professions, and he could carry messages verbally from one day's council to the next when recorded messages were dangerous.

Entranced, eager, the youthful Caird had said that he certainly would like to be a daybreaker.

2

Thinking of this, Caird finally fell asleep. And he was in a chapter of a serial dream, though he had never been in this cliff-hanger before. He was sitting in a room that he somehow knew was part of the long-abandoned sewer system buried by the first great earthquake to level Manhattan. This room was just off the middle of a huge horizontal sewage tunnel blocked at both ends but accessible by rungs down a vertical shaft. A single unshaded light bulb, a device not used for a thousand obyears, lit the room in archaic fashion.

Though the light blazed harshly, it could not keep at bay the dark mists rolling in from every side. These advanced, then retreated, then advanced.

He sat in a hard wooden chair by a big round wooden table. He waited for others, *the others*, to enter. Yet he was also standing in the mists and watching himself seated in the chair.

Presently, Bob Tingle walked in as slowly as if he were moving through waist-high water. In his left hand was a portable computer on top of which was a rotating microwave dish. Tingle nodded at the Caird in the chair, put the computer on the table, and sat down. The dish stopped turning, its concave face steady on Caird's convex face.

Jim Dunski seemed to float in, a fencing rapier in his left hand. He nodded at the two, placed the rapier so that it pointed at the Caird at the table, and sat down. The blunt button on the rapier tip melted away, and the sharp point glittered like an evil eye.

Wyatt Repp, a silvery pistol-shaped TV camera-transmitter in his left hand, strode in. Invisible saloon batwing doors seemed to swing noiselessly behind him. His high-heeled cowboy boots made him taller than the others. His sequined Western outfit glittered as evilly as the rapier tip. His white ten-gallon hat bore on its front a red triangle enclosing a bright blue eye. It winked once at Caird and was thereafter fixed lidlessly on him.

Repp sat down and pointed the machine at Caird. His first finger was curled around the trigger.

Charlie Ohm, wearing a dirty white apron, stumbled in with a bottle of whisky in his left hand and a shot glass in the other. After sitting down, he filled the glass and silently offered it to Caird.

The Caird standing in the fog felt a vibration passing up from the floor through the soles of his feet. It was as if an earthquake shock had touched him, or thunder was shaking the floor.

Then Father Tom Zurvan strode into the room as if the Red Sea was parting before him. His waist-long auburn hair waved wildly like a nest of angry vipers. Painted on his forehead was a big orange *S*, which stood for 'Symbol.' Bright blue was daubed on the end of his nose. His lips were painted green, and his moustache was dyed blue. His auburn beard, which fell to his waist, sported many tiny blue butterfly-shaped aluminium cutouts. His white ankle-length robe was decorated with broad red circles enclosing blue six-pointed stars. His ID disc bore a flattened figure eight lying on its side and slightly open at one end. The symbol for a broken eternity. In his right hand was a long oaken shaft that curled at the upper end.

Father Tom Zurvan stopped, leaning the shepherd's staff against his shoulder, and formed a flattened oval with the tips of the thumb and first finger of his right hand. He passed the long finger of his left hand three times through the oval.

He said loudly, May you speak the truth and only the truth.'

Grasping the staff again, he walked to a chair and sat down. He placed the staff on the table so that its curling end was directed towards Caird.

'Father, forgive me!' the Caird sitting at the table said.

Father Tom, smiling, made the sign again. The first time, it had been obscene. Now, it was a blessing. It was also a command to unloose verbally all pent-up wild beasts, to spill your guts.

The last to enter was Will Isharashvili. He wore a green robe slashed with brown and the Smokey Bear hat, the uniform of the Central Park ranger. Isharashvili took a chair and stared at Jeff. All were staring at the Caird at the table. All their faces were his.

A chorus, they said, 'Well, what do we do now?'

Caird woke up.

Though the air-conditioner was on, he was sweating, and his heart was beating faster than it should.

'Maybe I made the wrong decision,' he muttered. 'Maybe I should have stayed in one day, maybe I should have been only Jeff Caird.'

Presently, the faint noises of street-sweeping machines lulled him back to sleep.

Sitting at the breakfast-room table, Caird could see the picket-fenced backyard through the window. In one corner was a utility shed; in another, the garage; in a third, the garden. A small one-room building of transparent plastic, a studio, was in the centre. Thirty feet to its east was a large apple tree. It bore fruit, but bypassers who had not heard of Ozma might have wondered what kind of a tree it was. Ozma had painted every apple with a different design, though viewed together the designs made an aesthetically pleasing whole. The paint would not wash off easily, but it was edible, and a bowl full of the fruit was on the table now.

Ozma had agreed with Jeff that he could decorate the

kitchen. He had arranged the walls so they glowed with four paintings by T'ang Dynasty artists. He liked the Chinese quality, the quiet and eternal look with the human figures always far off, small but important, not the masters but an integrated part of the mountains, the forests, the cataracts.

Though Ozma had more Chinese ancestry than he, she did not particularly care for them. She was an outré and outrageous Westerner.

She had turned on the recorder in the corner to find out if Wednesday had left any messages. There were none, so it could be assumed that Wednesday had no complaints about the cleanliness or order of the house.

Their breakfast was interrupted by the front doorbell. Ozma, clad in a knee-length robe so thin that she might as well not have worn it, answered the bell. The callers were, as expected, Corporal Hiatt and Private First Class Sangalli. They wore green caps with long black visors, green robes on which were the insignia of the Manhattan State Cleaning Corps and their rank-stripes and good conduct medals, brown sandals, and yellow gloves.

Ozma greeted them, made a face at their boozy breaths, asked them in, and offered them coffee. They refused, and they plunged into the dusting, washing, waxing, and vacuuming. Ozma returned to the table.

'Why can't they come later, while we're gone?'

'Because they have a quota, and because that's the way the bureaucracy set it up.'

Jeff went upstairs, brushed his teeth, and rubbed on the whisker-removing cream. The face in the mirror was dark, the long dark hair in a Psyche knot. The hazel eyes brooded under heavy brows. The nose was long and slightly hooked, and the nostrils flared. The jaw was heavy. The chin was round and cleft and stuck out.

'I look like a cop,' he muttered. 'And I am. But not most of the time.'

He also looked like a big dark worrybird. What's to worry about? Besides being caught? Besides Ariel?

He showered, put underarm deodorant on, went into the bedroom, and donned a blue robe decorated with black trefoil figures. Clubs, the same symbol used on a pack of cards. He was the joker or perhaps the knave of clubs. Or both. He did not know who was responsible for this organic symbol, but it probably had been some bureaucrat who thought he was being subtle. The organics, the cops, had the real power, clubs.

He picked up his over-the-shoulder bag and walked downstairs. A strip by the front door glowed with a message. Ozma wanted him to stop by her studio before he left.

She was inside the transparent one-room building and sitting on a high stool. She put her magnifying glass down on the table when she heard him enter. The grasshopper she had been looking at had been stoned to keep it immobile while she applied paint to it. Its antennae were yellow; its head, pale orange; its body, bright purple with yellow crux ansatas; its legs, jet black. A mauve paint, which had the properties of one-way glass, covered its eyes.

'Jeff, I wanted you to see my latest. How do you like it?'

'The colours don't clash. Not by modern standards, anyway.'

'Is that all you can say? Don't you think it'll make a sensation? Doesn't it improve on nature? Isn't it true art?'

'It won't make a sensation,' he said. 'My God, there must be a thousand painted grasshoppers in Manhattan. Everybody's used to them, and the ecologists are complaining that you're upsetting the balance of nature. Preying insects and birds won't eat them because they look poisonous.'

'Art should please or make one think or both,' she said. 'Sensation is for inferior artists.'

'Then why'd you ask me if they'd make a sensation?'

'I didn't mean the sensation of startlement or outrage or just novelty, of course. I meant the sensation of recognition of something aesthetic. The feeling that God is in His heaven, but it's the human on Earth that does God one better. Oh, you know what I mean!'

'Sure,' he said, smiling. He turned her head and kissed her lips. 'When are you going to start on cockroaches? They're so God-ugly. They need beautification.'

'Where would I get one in Manhattan? I'd have to go to Brooklyn for them. Think I should?'

He laughed and said, 'I don't think the authorities would bless you.'

'I could sterilize the roaches before I let them loose again. But, really, are cockroaches ugly? If you adopt another frame of mind, think in a different category, look at them from the religious point of view, they're beautiful. Maybe, through my art, people would come to know their true beauty. See them as the living jewels they are.'

'Ephemeral classics,' Caird said. 'Short-lived antiques.'

She looked up and smiled. 'You think you're being sarcastic, but you may be telling the truth. I like those phrases. I may use them in my lecture. Anyway, they're not so ephemeral. I mean, the insects will die, but my name will go on. People are calling them *ozmas*. Didn't you see the seven o'clock Art Section of the *Times*? The great Sam Fang himself called them *ozmas*. He said . . .'

'You were sitting there with me when we saw it. I'll never forget how you giggled and carried on.'

'He's usually a jerk, but sometimes he's right. Oh, I was so ecstatic!'

She bent down to apply the near-microscopic end of her brush. The black paint was over the spiracles, the openings in the exoskeleton which passed air to the tracheae, the breathing tubes that went to the insect's internal organs. A chemist at Columbia University had developed for her the paint that permitted entrance of oxygen to the spiracles.

Caird looked at the stoned praying mantis at one end of the table and said, 'Green is quite good enough for it, for God, and for me. Why, as it were, gild the lily?'

Ozma straightened up. Black eyes wide, mouth twisted, she said, 'Do you have to spoil it for me? Who gave you a certificate as an art critic, anyway? Can't you just enjoy my joy and keep your ignorant opinions to yourself?'

'Now, now,' he said hastily, reaching out to touch her shoulder. 'You're the one that says you should always tell the truth, hide nothing, let the emotions be trigger-happy. I *am* happy because you're happy in your work –'

'Art, not work!'

'Art. And I'm happy that you're getting so much public recognition. I apologize. What do *I* know?'

'Well, let me tell you something, cop! I've learned a lot from my study of insects. Do you know that the highest forms of insects, the bees, wasps, and ants, are female societies? The male is used only for fertilization.'

'Yeah?' he said, grinning. 'What's that supposed to signify?'

'You just watch it, buster! We women may decide that entomology has the key to the future!'

She burst into laughter, squeezed him with one arm, the other hand holding the brush attached to a very thin hose attached to a machine on the table. He kissed her – her anger came and went like heat lightning, nothing permanent or hurtful about it – and went to a strip on the wall. He voice-activated it and asked for their schedule. He probably needed a reminder more than anybody in Tuesday.

He and Ozma were to go to an artists' party at 7:30 PM. That meant two hours or more of standing around drinking cocktails and talking with people who were mostly phonies. There were, however, a few he would enjoy talking to.

He had a luncheon engagement with Anthony Horn, the Manhattan organic commissioner-general. He doubted that they would talk much about police business. She was an immer.

There was also a note to see Major Wallenquist about the Yankev Gril case. He frowned. The man was a Monday citizen. What was Gril's name doing on the MCOD file?

He sighed. Yankev Gril. He did not even know what he looked like, but he would find out today.

3

After kissing Ozma good-bye, he got a bicycle, one of six, out of the garage. As soon as it had rolled a few feet, its squeaking told him that Monday's occupants had neglected to lubricate the pedal mechanism. He cursed softly. He would make a recording to chew Monday out, but the omission was no big thing. He'd get an OD mechanic to attend to it. He was not supposed to do that, but what was the use of being a detective-inspector if he did not have his little perks?

No. That would not be right. Anyway, he'd be damned if he'd ride all the way to work on the irritating and attention-getting vehicle. He returned to the garage and got another bike. This one squeaked, too. Swearing, he took out a third, the last of the adult-size, and rode out of the garage. When he saw Ozma bent over with laughter, he shouted, 'Straighten up! You look like a cow! And put a robe on!'

Ozma, still laughing, gave him the finger.

'What a relationship we have,' he muttered. He went past the white picket fence along Bleecker Street and turned the corner onto the bike path along the canal. Two men fishing from the walk looked up as he passed them. Caird rode on. As usual, there were many pedestrians illegally on the path. Some of them saw his OD badge, but they moved only to get out of his way and some did not do that.

Time for another sweep, he thought. Not that it would do any good. The pedestrians would have to pay only a small fine. Ah, well. His daughter Ariel, the historian, had told him that Manhattanites had always paid little attention to traffic rules. Even in this law-abiding age, there were so many misdemeanours that the organic officers usually ignored most of them.

The air had cooled off a little during the night but was beginning to warm up. A fifteen-mile-per-hour wind behind him, however, helped his pedalling and cooled him somewhat. The sky was unclouded. It had not rained for twelve days, and the thermometer had surged past 112°F for eight of them. He kept on pumping, zigzagging to avoid walkers. Now and then, he glanced at the canal, ten feet below street level. Rowboats or foot-pumped pontoon craft or small barges pushed by small waterjet tugs moved up and down the canal. The houses along the wide path were mostly two-storey dwellings of various architecture with here and there a six-storey apartment building or a two-storey community general store. In the distance to his right was the enormous building known as the Thirteen-Principles Towers, the only skyscraper on the island. Its centre was on the site of the last Empire State Building, torn down five hundred obyears ago.

Jeff Caird had passed twelve canal bridges when he saw a pedestrian sixty feet ahead of him drop a banana peel on the pavement. Jeff looked around. There was no organic officer in sight. Maybe it *was* true that the organics were always around except when you needed them. He would have to write out this ticket himself. He looked at his wristwatch. Fifteen minutes to report on time. He was going to be late. But, if he was performing a duty, he would be excused.

He braked to a stop. The litterer, a short thin pale man – the shortness and paleness were in themselves causes for suspicion – was suddenly aware that a cop was near him. He froze, looked around, then grinned. He removed his huge brown coolie hat, revealing an uncombed pale brown thatch.

'It sort of slipped out of my hand,' he whined. 'I was

going to pick it up.'

'Is that why you walked away from it?' Caird said. 'You are now approximately twelve feet past it and the waste barrel by the wall.'

Caird pointed at the TV strip on the wall.

NO LITTERING
LITTERING IS UNAESTHETIC
UNSOCIAL
UNLAWFUL
REPORT ALL CRIMES TO TC CHANNEL, 245-5500

Caird kicked the bike parking-stand down, opened the bag in the basket over the front wheel, and removed a Kelly-green box. He raised the attached screen on its top and said, 'ID, please.'

Holding the unbitten banana in one hand, the man lifted a chain from around his neck. Caird took the chain and the metal seven-rayed star-on-a-disc attached to it. He inserted a ray point into the slot in the box.

The screen displayed:

DOROTHY WU ROOTENBEAK
CZ-49V-#27-8b*-WAP412

Caird glanced at the personal history and pertinent data that rolled on the screen after the name and ID number. Rootenbeak had four priors, all misdemeanours for slobbishness, though none for littering. Neither the history nor the present offence justified Caird in having a sky-eye satellite zero in on Rootenbeak.

The man edged closer so he could see the screen. 'Give me a break, officer!'

'Did you give your fellow seniors a break? What if one had slipped on the peel?'

'Yeah, I'm sorry. I wasn't thinking. Look, officer, I've

got a lot on my mind. I got a sick child and a wife that drinks, and I been late a couple of times without a good excuse – so they said. What do they know? My mind was on my troubles. You got troubles, ain't you? Maybe you don't, being an organic and all that. But I got them. Everybody got them. Give me a break. I won't do it again.'

Caird spoke into the front section of the box, asking for the file department. A complete update on Rootenbeak flashed on the screen. This included the fact that Rootenbeak had used the same excuses to other officers as he had to Caird. Also, Rootenbeak had no children, and his wife had left him three weeks ago.

'I'm going to be late again if you don't let me go now. I can't afford another credit cut. I ain't making enough now. We just barely get by.'

The state guaranteed that nobody just barely got by. Rootenbeak knew that Caird had checked out his story, yet he was lying. And he knew that being caught in a lie would cost him at least another credit.

Caird sighed. What made *them* do it?

He should know. He was a far bigger criminal than Rootenbeak, who was, actually, a committer of misdemeanours, not of felonies. But Caird believed, at least he told himself that he believed, that there was a difference between him and other criminals. A qualitative difference. Also, if he let Rootenbeak go because of a misplaced sense of empathy, he would put himself in danger. Moreover, the discarded peel, besides being offensive, *was* dangerous.

And I'm not hurting anyone.

No, not yet. But if I were caught, many would be hurt.

He took a camera from the bag, held it between two fingers, sighting with one eye through the tiny magnifying glass in the centre, and squeezed. A second later a photograph slid out. He inserted that into another slot in the R-T box. The screen displayed that the photograph had been transmitted and was recorded in the files. It also confirmed that the culprit was indeed Rootenbeak. Caird read the ticket for Rootenbeak into the box. A few seconds later, the screen flashed that the charges had been recorded at files and on the culprit's ID disc.

Caird handed the disc to Rootenbeak. 'I'll give you a break,' he said. 'You won't have to appear immediately at court. You can go after work. Put that peel where it belongs and get going.'

Rootenbeak's face matched his whine. It was long and narrow with a thin drooping nose, close-set small watery blue eyes, a short jaw, and a chin that had failed to bud in the womb. His shoulders were slumped, his hair was uncombed, and his robe was torn. Caird expected only servility from the slob. He certainly did not expect what happened next.

Rootenbeak put the chain of his ID badge around his neck and started to walk off, his eyes downcast. Suddenly he wheeled, screaming, the ferret face changed into a wildcat's, and pushed an old woman who had just come between him and Caird. Propelled by the woman, Caird fell back into the bicycle, knocked it over, and fell down on it. He yelled with pain as the end of the pedal drove against his spine. Before Caird could get up, Rootenbeak had jumped into the air and come down with both sandaled feet on Caird's chest. The air oofed out of his lungs, making it impossible for him to yell with pain as the pedal drove again into his back.

Rootenbeak grabbed the bars, yanked the bicycle up and ran it towards the edge of the path. He stopped and let it go over into the canal. Caird's R-T box and the bag went with the vehicle.

Caird had his breath and his strength back. He roared with anger, rose, and charged. Rootenbeak turned as if to run, then dropped to one knee, spun, and grabbed Caird's outstretched hand. Rootenbeak fell backwards, his foot came up, planted itself in Caird's stomach, and Caird went over and into the water. He missed striking the edge of a rowboat by an inch.

When he came up spluttering, more from rage than from swallowed water, he saw Rootenbeak's jeering face above.

'How do you like that, pig!'

Other faces were lined up along the edge of the path. Caird yelled at them to hold Rootenbeak for him. The faces disappeared.

'You're ignoring your organic duty!' Caird roared, but there was no one to hear him except the two grinning men in the rowboat. They helped him in and took him to the steps below the West Twenty-third Street bridge. By the time he got to the path, Rootenbeak was gone. Caird phoned in to the precinct via his wristwatch and arranged for divers to recover his vehicle, bag, and R-T box. He walked the rest of the way to work.

The precinct station on East Twenty-third Street and Womanway occupied one-fourth of the six-storey building that formed the whole block. Dripping and scowling, Caird strode down the entrance walk lined on both sides by the uniformed and stoned bodies of officers who had died in the line of duty. All were in upright, lifelike poses, though some had not been very upright in life. The one closest to the entrance, standing on a six-foot granite pedestal, was Abel 'Bloodhound' Ortega, Caird's mentor and ex-partner. Caird usually said good morning to him, a ritual which some of his fellow officers thought morbid. Now he strode past Ortega's body without a glance or a word.

Caird walked by the desk sergeant without acknowledging his greeting. The sergeant called after him, 'Hey, Inspector, I didn't know it was raining! Haw, haw!'

Ignoring the stares, Caird left the big admittance lobby and went down a hall. Near the end, he turned right into the locker room. After opening a locker, he chose one of a dozen robes, took it out, and hung the wet robe on a hook.

He rode an elevator to the third floor and entered his office. The screen on his desk told him what he already knew. He was to call Major Ricardo Wallenquist at once. Instead, he made his verbal report to the computer and then had the Rootenbeak file displayed. The culprit's last known address was an apartment at 100 King Street. Caird called two foot-patrolmen in that area and asked them to check out the apartment. He was told that had been done five minutes ago. Rootenbeak had not come home nor had he gone to work.

Which meant that he probably was not going to do so. Having assaulted an officer, his first known felony, he was probably headed for the 'minnie' district near Hudson Park. People living on the minimum guaranteed income, those who for some unfathomable reason disdained work, tended to congregate there. They were also inclined to take in criminals and hide them. Now and then the organics raided the area and swept up a few of the wanted. It was time for another search.

Caird had coffee brought in. While sipping the hot liquid, he cooled off. Finally, envisioning his dunking, he began laughing. There was something funny about the scene even if he was the one humiliated. If he had seen the incident in a movie, he would have thought it laugh-provoking. And he had to admire Rootenbeak to some degree. Who would have expected a whiner, a sniveller, a nothing, to erupt like that?

Tracking him down was a routine better left to the patrolmen. He switched off the display and started to tell the strip to call Wallenquist's office. Then he remembered that he was to apply for a reproduction licence. Just as he was going to code in the propagation department of the Population Bureau, the face of Ricardo 'Big Dick' Wallenquist appeared on a wall strip.

'Good morning, Jeff!'

Wallenquist's fat red face beamed.

'Morning, Major.'

'You saw my message?'

'Yes, sir. I had some prior duty. I was just going to . . .'

'Come up to my office, Jeff. Now. I've got something interesting. No run of the mill, no distilled-water bootlegger. I'd rather be face to face.'

Caird stood up. 'Right away, Major.'

Wallenquist made a big thing of the personal touch. He deplored communication through electronics. It was too impersonal, too aloof. 'Barriers go up then, man! Wires, waves, screens! You can't really know a person or like him or get him to know you and like you if you're talking through machines. You're just ghosts then. What we need is flesh and blood, man. Touch and smell. Electricity can't transmit nuances or soul. Can't send you the proper signals. Only face to face, nose to nose can do that. God knows we've lost too much humanity. We must preserve it. Flesh to flesh, eye to eye. Touch and smell.'

All very fine, Caird thought as he went up on the elevator. The trouble was that Wallenquist was an onion-fiend. Ate them for breakfast, lunch, and supper. And he insisted on getting as close as possible to the person he was talking to.

Wallenquist's office was twice as big as Caird's, which was the way it should be. The major, however, was only one-fourth larger than his lieutenant. Six feet and seven inches tall, he weighed two hundred and eighty-seven pounds. Ninety of that had to be excess fat. The Health Department was after him, of course, but he had enough connections to keep its attention from being more than a minor nuisance. No subordinate bureaucrat was going to tackle an organic major head-on, and the Health Department supervisors were rather lax about getting rid of their own lard. It was the person without power, the little guy, who had to toe the mark in this officially classless society.

Thus it had been and would be.

The major rose from his huge padded chair when Caird entered, and he shook hands with himself. Caird shook his own hands.

'Sit down, Jeff.'

Caird took a chair. Wallenquist came around the crescent-topped desk and sat on its edge. He leaned far forward until he seemed to be in danger of toppling off. Like Humpty-Dumpty, Caird thought. But that big egg did not eat onions.

Grinning, Wallenquist said, 'How's the wife, Jeff?'

For a second, Caird felt sick. Had Ozma done something unlawful?

'Fine.'

'Still painting those insects?'

'Still.'

Wallenquist boomed laughter and slapped Caird's shoulder.

'Isn't that something! I don't know if it's art, but it's sure good publicity. Everybody knows about her. I heard about the party given in her honour.'

Caird relaxed. The major was just going through his warming-up routine. Nose to nose, eye to eye, flesh to flesh.

'How's the daughter? Ariel . . . uh . . . Mauser, isn't it?'

'Fine. Still teaching at East Harlem University?'

Wallenquist nodded; his jowls flapped like sails.

'Good, good. Party, heh? Anyone I know?'

'Perhaps. It's one of those arty events. The host is Malcolm Chang Kant, the curator of the Twentieth-Century Museum.'

'I've heard of him, of course. But I don't move in those circles. It's good that you do. An organic should know people outside his field.'

You'd be surprised how many I know, Caird thought.

He continued the ritual by asking about the major's health and that of his wife, two children, and three grand-children.

'Fine, couldn't be better.'

Wallenquist paused. Caird had turned his head away until he was looking at the major from the corners of his eyes. He moved his head then to look directly into his eyes and received the full blast.

'I got a make-your-ears-prick-up case,' the major said. 'A *daybreaker*! Ah, I thought so! That woke you up, heh?'

He punched Caird lightly on the arm. 'I'll supervise, of course, but I'm letting you have all the fun. You're a damned good man, by God, and what's more, I like you!'

'Thanks,' Caird said. 'I . . . get along fine with you, too.'

'I know my people. If I do say so myself, I got a knack for bringing out the best in the best. You're a real bloodhound, Jeff.'

4

The major got off the desk, much to Caird's relief, went behind it, sat down, and activated a wall strip behind and to one side of him. Wallenquist spun his chair to look at it.

'This isn't any run-of-the-mill daybreaker.'

Three views of a clothed adult male from head to toes and at different angles appeared. Below these came three views of the same man unclothed. The two stared, fascinated, at the circumcised organ. Caird had never seen one in the flesh and had viewed few photographs of them. It was exotic but ugly and Old Stone Ageish.

The head and shoulders, full-face, of the same subject followed. His red hair was long, and he wore a green skullcap. The bushy red beard underlined a strong broad face with small green eyes, a broad and short nose with flaring nostrils, and very thin lips.

YANKEV GAD GRIL
MONDAY SENIOR

His code-identification flashed. It moved up and was succeeded by codes of his earprints, eyeprints, fingerprints, footprints, voiceprints, normal skin-odourprints, bloodtype, skull and skeleton X-ray and sonograms, brain topography and waveprints, hormone balance, hair and blood and genetic prints, exterior dimensions, intelligence quotient, psychic quotient, social quotient, and gait classification.

Wallenquist told the strip to roll the file more slowly. After a few seconds, Caird said, 'Hold it! Allergic to shellfish! Orthodox Jews don't eat shellfish!'

'Aha!' the major said, his tone indicating that he had just seen a great light. 'This Jew does! Did, I mean. Just once. See . . . he got dizzy and broke out in hives. See there. He said it was a judgement of God on him!'

'Nobody's perfect,' Caird said.

'Ah, but, by God, humankind will be perfect!'

Yes, Caird thought. Next year we meet in Jerusalem. The second coming of Christ occurs any moment now. The proletariat will govern, and the state will eventually wither away.

'As you can see,' Wallenquist said, 'he seemed to be an exemplary citizen, aside from being religious. Then, poof!' Wallenquist threw his hands up. 'Houdinied! Didn't come out of his stoner yesterday. His colleagues at Yeshiva investigated, of course – he has no family – and his stoner was empty. No messages, nothing to indicate what had happened.'

Wallenquist bent down close to Caird. 'That means that he's in Tuesday. Right now!'

Caird got up from the chair and began pacing back and forth. 'Yankev Gril,' he said. 'I know the man.'

'You know him? But . . .'

'You didn't read all the file. He played chess with other days via recordings. I was one of his opponents. I knew his name only, and, of course, this is the first time I've seen him. But I'm the champion chessplayer of Manhattan; I got seventh place in the Tuesday World Champion Matches and twelfth in the All-Days matches. Gril was eleventh in the All-Days.'

'Really?' Wallenquist said. 'I don't go for the game myself. When I think that you could go fishing instead . . . Anyway, I'm proud of you because you're a champion, even if it's just in chess. The whole department's proud of you.'

He came up close to Caird, but Caird wheeled and walked away. When he was as far away from the major as he could get, he turned and stopped. 'You're not thinking of giving me a temporal passport?'

Wallenquist approached him. 'Oh, no. That's not necessary. Besides, it takes too much red tape to get one. Since you know something about him, have played chess with him, you're the one who should chase him today. Devote most of your time to his case.'

'Well, either he's just moved to this day or he's breaking all the days. Why? Find the motive, find the man.'

'Excellent,' the major said, rubbing his hands together. 'I know how to pick them.'

Caird slipped by Wallenquist, who had come nose to nose. 'Can I get permission to voice-interview his Monday colleagues?'

'I'll put in an application, but it'll take some time to get a yes or a no.'

'Application' reminded Caird of Ozma's demand.

'I'll get right on it, Major,' he said, heading for the door. 'Unless you've got something else for me.'

'Damn it, man, I don't like talking to the back of your head!'

Caird stopped, turned, and smiled. 'Sorry, Major. Overeager, I guess.'

'Quite all right, my boy. Always happy to see my men full of zeal. Not too much of that nowadays.'

'Anything else, sir?'

Wallenquist waved his hand. 'Just keep me informed. Oh, yes, I saw on your schedule . . . you're lunching with the commissioner-general?'

Envy? Indignation?

'Yes, sir. The commissioner and I grew up together in the same neighbourhood, went to the same schools. We like to get together now and then to talk about old times. Besides, we're related. My first wife was her cousin.'

'Oh, well. I wasn't prying.'

The major looked at two strips that had lit up at the

same time. 'Busy, busy. Run along. Have a good time at lunch. Be sure to give my best regards to the commissioner. Only, report on what you've found out about Gril – what the hell kind of a name is that, anyway? – report before lunch.'

Jeff gave the major a salute, which wasn't noticed. Wallenquist was looking back and forth at the strips, unable to decide which was the most important. Caird went back to his office and asked a strip for Gril's latest move.

The chessboard, sixty-four alternating green and red squares, eight horizontal lines of eight squares each, and the eight green and eight red pieces, appeared on the strip. The game had begun with Green, Yankev Gril, making the first move: 1 BL-WC-4. That is, the first move took Green's World Councillor's Block Leader to the fourth vertical square from World Councillor's position. Red, Jeff Caird, had made his first move by putting his World Councillor's Block Leader to his World Councillor's Four square.

Green's second move was BL-WC SG. Or 03. That is, he had moved his Organic Officer to World Councillor's State Governor's third square out.

Caird remembered that, when he had made this move, he was thinking that an early twenty-first-century chessplayer would not have been puzzled long if he had been watching this game. He would have caught on quickly that the white and black squares had been changed to green and red. The Kings had become World Councillors; the Queens, Superorganic Directors; the Rooks, Intraorganic Coordinators; the Bishops, State Governors; the Knights, Organic Officers; the Pawns, Block Leaders. If the hypothetical early chessplayer had any knowledge of present government set-ups, he would have surmised that the changes in the game were for political reasons and that they were superficial.

Caird studied the board for five minutes, though he was nagged by the feeling that he was neglecting duty for pleasure. Also, he could not keep from wondering where Gril had been when he had made his last move.

He told the strip to make a BL-WC or 04 move. He did not know if the refugee Gril would ever see the latest development. He hoped that he would. They were playing a dangerous but stimulating contest of simultaneous attack and defence. Both their World Councillors were open to, as a master had once put it, 'flailing blows from all directions.'

That was also true of their real-life situations.

Caird had several matters to deal with before he could get to the Gril case. There was a raid planned for next Tuesday on the Tao Towers, an apartment building on West Eleventh. According to an informant, some tenants there were not only smoking tobacco but selling it. There were always people who desired harmful things even after seven generations of education and conditioning.

The poor, contrary to what Jesus had said, were no longer in society. At least, the poor did not have to be poor. But the perverse were still here. One born every hour.

The raid on the minnie district in search of Rootenbeak would take place inside an hour. Caird was not going to be there in person. He left that up to Detective-Inspector Ann Wong Gools, but he would be in constant VA (video-audio) contact.

He asked for and, after a ten-minute wait, got the results of the satellite sweep for both Rootenbeak and Gril. There were three sky-eyes up there taking photographs of the Manhattan and neighbouring areas at three different angles. The computers had sent holographs of the culprits to the central base, and there the graphs of the two were compared with the faces of Manhattanites in the streets or on housetops. So far, the results were nil. That was not unexpected, since Gril and Rootenbeak had only to wear wide-brimmed hats and keep their faces down to avoid these being photographed. However, all wearing such hats had been tracked by the sky-eyes, and the buildings they entered had been noted. Unfortunately, the Organic Department did not have enough personnel to follow up the leads. Only central Manhattan addresses could be investigated, and that was going to take much time.

It was not difficult to get fake IDs if you knew where to go. Rootenbeak seemed to be the sort who would know. Gril, though, was a scholar and a recluse. What would he know of the underworld? Nothing – unless he had been planning his daybreak for a long time and so was well-prepared.

Caird put Rootenbeak on mental hold and considered Gril.

Find the motive; find the criminal. A fine dictum, except that he was not looking for suspects. He knew who the culprit was.

Monday had opened Gril's bio-data to Tuesday, but Caird could not interrogate Gril's associates and intimates. That was up to Monday. About all he could do was to have the data transmitted to all organics' R-T boxes so that they could see them while looking for Gril. The sky-eyes, of course, would also be scanning the streets for anyone resembling Gril. Caird did not think that Gril would be foolish enough to venture forth on the daytime streets. He also might have cut his hair and shaved his beard, though that had little chance of deceiving the sky-eyes. The ID Department had probably sent out photos based on what Gril's shaven face would look like.

Gril's file had some interesting personality bio-data, especially the item that he was the last Yiddish speaker on Earth. He was also an authority, in fact, *the* authority, on an ancient writer named Cerinthus. Two of Gril's studies on him were in the World Data Bank. Caird had asked for a summary of data on Cerinthus, though more from curiosity than hope that it would give him any clue.

Cerinthus was a Christian who had lived circa AD 100. Born a Jew, he had converted to Christianity but was generally regarded as a heretic. Saint John was supposed to have written his Gospel to confute Cerinthus' errors. Very little had been known about him until the discovery of a manuscript in the south of the state of Egypt three hundred obyears ago. He had founded a short-lived sect of Jewish Christians with Gnostic leanings. Though a Christian, the only New Testament book he had accepted was Matthew's Gospel. Cerinthus had maintained that the world was created by angels and that one of these had given the Jews their law. But that law was imperfect. He also held to circumcision and the Jewish Sabbath.

'Sounds as crazy as the rest of them,' Caird had muttered when he had turned the display off.

Another strip glowed with orange letters, and a buzzer sounded loudly. It bore a reminder from Ozma to make out the reproduction permit. Caird turned off the Gril data and went to a desk computer. He had filled in only four lines of the form on the strip before him when another strip began flashing. Rootenbeak had been sighted in the Hudson Park district.

Caird put the application form on hold. He called the woman who had sent the message, Patroller-Corporal Hatshepsut Andrews Ruiz. She was standing before a transmitter strip on the wall of a building but parts of her were obscured. Some minnie had probably thrown mud or something worse on the strip. Behind her on the sidewalk were three organics, privates first class. One was holding a small camera and panning it up and down the street. Caird asked for its POV, and the street appeared on the wall strip by the one showing Ruiz. The woman who had turned Rootenbeak in was standing near Ruiz and was holding a large sack of groceries.

Ruiz saluted and said, 'The witness, Benson McTavish Pallanguli, 128 . . .'

'I'll get that from the computer,' Caird said. 'What happened?'

'The witness had just come from the West Clarkson Street Food Dispensall with a sack of groceries with a bunch of bananas on top.'

Caird had started to tell her to skip that, but the reference to the bananas changed his mind.

'The suspect, Dorothy Wu Rootenbeak, who has been positively identified by Pallanguli, walked by her. As he did so, he reached out and tore a banana from the stalk on top of the sack carried by Pallanguli. Rootenbeak thereupon ran down the street –' Ruiz pointed west '. . . until he came to the corner of Greenwich and West Clarkson. The suspect, according to Pallanguli and two other witnesses, thereupon turned left, still running, and proceeded down Greenwich Street. He entered the block building designated as GCL-1.'

Caird had a street map displayed on a strip so he could see the exact path taken by the fugitive. By now he also had points of view of two patroller-operated cameras in front of the building into which Rootenbeak had gone. The sergeant in charge, Wanda Confucius Thorpe, was just going through the doorway. He held in his right hand an electrical prod. Three organics, also armed with prods, were following him.

Caird radioed Thorpe and asked him if the building was surrounded. The sergeant, a faint tone of resentment in his voice, replied that he had arranged for this – of course. One of the cameras showed Caird two orange-and-white cars pulling up to the curb outside the door. Caird called the cameramen on the other two sides of the building and got a complete picture of the operation. The building occupied the whole block, but between it and the sidewalks was a yard with an uncut lawn, many dandelions and other weeds, and many palm trees and sycamores. No doubt, the block leader had gotten official reprimands from the state, followed by orders to clean the yard. But the minnie leaders were often as uncouth and rebellious as their flock.

The building was about forty objective years old, constructed when Nautical Design was all the rage in the Bureau of Architecture. Its upper sides curved outwards, ending in a flat top. This and one tapering end and the three-storey penthouse made it resemble a twentieth-century aircraft carrier. The rooms on the outside wall at the top floor had windows in the floors so that the tenants could look straight down into the yard.

Rootenbeak might be in one now, staring down at the organics.

Caird tingled with excitement. It had been three months since he had been in on a hunt. And now he had two in one day.

He asked the computer to clump all references to bananas in Rootenbeak's file. This was flashed almost immediately on a strip. After reading it, he called Ruiz and asked her to ask Pallanguli if she knew the man who had snatched her bananas. The corporal did so with Caird watching and listening to the two. The dark woman's expression changed a little and then was replaced by indignation.

'No, I never saw the stiff before, and if I ever see him again I'll put a banana in him where the sun don't shine.'

Ruiz had plugged in the woman's ID before questioning her. Caird was running it off now after instructing the computer to expand and make orange any references to Rootenbeak. After a few seconds, a paragraph swelled and began flashing. Caird stopped its rollup to read it. Pallanguli had been Rootenbeak's neighbour on the fourth floor of a Dominick Street apartment building three objective years ago.

He sighed with exasperation. Pallanguli must know that that would be in her file, yet she had lied. Was she just stupid or perverse? It made no difference. She must be brought in for questioning. But he would have bet thirty credits that her story was made up. Rootenbeak had asked her for help and gotten it. Moreover, he had gotten two other minnies to give a false story. Instead of turning left and running south and then entering the building, he had turned right and gone . . . where? Someplace close to but outside the police net.

That is, unless he was subtle enough to calculate that the person in charge would think of this and so he had, instead, actually entered the building. No. There was too much danger of outsmarting himself.

Caird would have called off the apartment search if he had been one hundred percent sure that he was right. He did ask for more personnel to widen the net and to send organics into nearby block buildings. He was told that he could get no more than ten people.

Caird glanced at the strip with its flashing APPL ON HOLD! No time for that now. The application for permission for Ozma to have a child by him would have to be transmitted later.

Another message appeared on a strip. It was from the commissioner-general's secretary, asking him if he could move the luncheon date up to 11:30 A.M. He replied that he could. The strip displayed: RCVD & TRMD.

His request for satellite data re the search for Rootenbeak came in then. Usually, he got it within ten minutes. Today, for unexplained reasons, the channels were clogged. Caird studied the pictures and then called the Hudson Park substation for more personnel. He wanted ten more foot organics but was told that none would be available for several hours or more.

'Why not?'

'I'm sorry, Inspector,' the sergeant said. 'But we have a

particularly gory murder on Carmine Street. Two victims, a woman and a child.'

Caird was shocked. 'That makes two murders in Manhattan this subyear, and the second month isn't over yet. My God, there were only six all last subyear!'

The sergeant nodded solemnly. 'It's become an epidemic. Social rot, sir, though the terrible heat is a contributing factor.'

After Caird had quit talking to the sergeant, he sat and scowled. The organic force could have been much larger and he would not now be lacking personnel if every organic was not required to get a Doctor of Philosophy degree in criminology. But, no, every candidate had to pass a psychological test (which was also a subtle ideological test), which eliminated five out of ten. After this, the candidate studied for six subjective years at West Point. Then, if the candidate could survive the rigorous discipline and get a *B* average in the courses, he or she became an Organic Department foot-patroller, zero class.

Ah, well, he could only work with what he could get. By three this afternoon, according to the weather-strip report, he could no longer depend upon the sky-eyes. A heavy overcast would cut off their view.

5

When eleven o'clock came, Rootenbeak still had not been observed or caught. Caird worked for a few minutes at other duties before leaving the building. A station-pool robot car took him up Womanway Boulevard to Columbus Circle and up Central Park West to West Seventy-seventh Street. The John Reed Community Block Building occupied all of the Number 100 blocks of Seventy-sixth and Seventy-seventh streets, including the enclosed streets. Just north of it was the Museum of Natural History. Caird got out of the car just off the third-level ramp. The car moved slowly away and disappeared down the west ramp. He walked into a huge lobby decorated this year in Mycenaean Mode. Golden Agamemnon masks smiled at him from the walls, ceiling, and floor. In the middle of the lobby was a fountain holding a statue of Ajax defying the gods. A yellow fluorescent jagged lightning bolt of plastic reached halfway down from the ceiling towards the arrogant and doomed Achaean. This piece of statuary had been selected by some bureaucrat who thought that it would subtly put across a moral. If you were stupid enough to resist the government, you were fried.

However, despite one-hundred-percent literacy and free life-long education if you wanted it, nine-tenths of the viewers had never heard of Ajax, the first human lightning rod, and most of the others did not care about him. The moral was lost, and the art was, Caird thought, tacky.

He went up a pneumatic elevator to the top floor and got off at the entrance to the Zenith Restaurant at 11:26. He told the maître d' that his reservation had been made by Commissioner Horn. The maître d' tapped three keys; the screen displayed Caird's face and some lines of bio-data.

'Very well, Inspector Caird. Follow me.'

The Zenith was very elegant and select. Six musicians on a podium played softly, and the conversation was in low tones. That is, it was until Anthony Horn rose from her table to greet him. She strode towards him, arms out, her orange-and-purple robe flapping in her wake. 'Jeff, darling!'

The other diners looked up or flinched or both as her voice boomed out. Then he was enfolded in silk, perfume, and abundant flesh. Looking down her breasts was like looking along the curve of twin planets from forty thousand feet up. He did not mind having his face pressed against them, even though it was undignified. For a brief moment, he was happy and secure in the bosom of the Great Mother Herself.

She released him and smiled, showing big white teeth. Then she turned and led him by the hand to the table in the meateaters' section. She was six inches higher than his six feet three, though her high heels accounted for four of the inches. Her shoulders and hips were broad; her waist, very narrow. Her golden hair was piled high in a coiffure shaped like an eighteenth-century tricorn hat, all the fashion just now. Huge golden earrings, each inset with the Chinese ideogram for 'horn,' dangled from small close-set ears.

They sat down, and she leaned against the table, her breasts extending like two white wolfhounds eager for release so they could chase the prey. Her big deep-blue eyes connected with his. In a much lower tone, she said, 'We have a big bad problem, Jeff.'

His eyebrows rose. He said, softly, 'The government's found out about us?'

'Not yet. We . . .'

She stopped what she was going to say because the waiter, a tall, turbaned, bearded Sikh, had appeared. They were busy ordering drinks and looking at the printed menus for a while. The Zenith was too elegant to display the menus on wall strips. When the waiter had left, Horn said, 'You know about Doctor Chang Castor?'

He nodded. 'He hasn't escaped?'

'Yes, he has.'

Caird grunted as if he had been hit in the solar plexus, but just then the waiter brought his wine and Horn's gin, and two minutes later, a folding table and two trays with dishes of food. It did not take long to fill an order. The food was precooked anywhere from last Tuesday to two subyears ago, stoned, and so kept in perfect state. Destoned, it only needed warming and putting on the plate.

They chatted about their families until the waiter left. Caird jerked a thumb at the waiter's back.

'He's an informer?'

'Yes. I used my connections and a code I'm not supposed to have to identify the informers here. The place isn't bugged, though, and there are no directional mikes. Too many bigshots eat here.'

She cut into her steak and chewed on a small piece. 'I . . . it's not just that you're an organic and we can work through you. It's much more personal . . . involved . . . for you.'

After swallowing the meat, she sipped at her gin. The moderation told Caird that she was deeply shaken. Any other time, she would have half-emptied her tall glass before the food was served. Obviously, she was afraid of dulling her wits.

Chang Castor was an immer and a brilliant scientist, head of the physics department at the Retsall Advanced Institute. He had always been eccentric, but, when he had begun showing signs of mental sickness, the immer organization had acted at once. It had framed him so that he seemed to be much more mentally unstable than he really was at the time. He had been committed to an institution that, though owned by the government, was secretly controlled by immers. There, Castor had quickly slid into deep psychotic quicksand in which it seemed that he would stick until he died. Fourteenth-century medical science, for all its advances, was unable to pull him out.

Caird remembered a lunch with Horn at another place when she had told him that Castor believed that he was God.

'He's an atheist,' Caird had said.

'Was. Well, in a sense, he still is. He says that the universe was formed through sheer chance. But its structure is such that it finally and inevitably, after many eons, gave birth to God. Himself, Castor. Who has now ordained matters so that there is no such thing as chance. Everything that happens from the moment his Godhood was crystallized – which also happened by chance, the last time that chance existed in the universe – everything that happened from that moment is fixed by him. Capital Him, by the way. He insists on being addressed as Your Divinity or O Great Jehovah.

'Anyway, he says that there was no God until he came along. So he divides cosmic time into two eras – BG, that is, Before God. And AG, After God. He will tell you the precise second when the new chronology began even if you don't ask him.'

That conversation had taken place three obyears ago.

Anthony Horn said softly, 'God hates you.'

Caird said, 'What?'

'Don't look so confused and guilty. By God I mean Castor, of course. Castor hates you, and he's out to get you. That's why I had to call you in on this.'

'Why? I mean . . . why does he hate me? Because I was the one who arrested him?'

'You got it.'

The whole operation had been immer-directed and

immer-controlled. Horn, a lieutenant-general then, had given him private orders to take Castor into custody. Caird had gone to the neighbourhood of the Retsall Institute. By chance, or so it seemed, he had been handy when the frame had been put into action. Two other immers had smashed up the laboratory but blamed it on Castor. By then the victim was raving and had attacked the two because of his fury at the put-up job. Caird had taken him to the nearest hospital as organic routine required him to. But, shortly thereafter, the courts having been advised by Dr Naomi Atlas, also an immer, Castor was transferred to the Tamasuki Experimental Psychicist Hospital on West Forty-ninth Street. Since then, no one had seen him except for Atlas and three first-class nurses. Only Atlas was allowed to talk to him.

'It could have been someone else,' Horn said. 'Anyone who arrested him. It was your bad luck to be the one.'

She sipped at her gin, put the glass down, and said quietly, 'In a way, he's a Manichaean. He's split the universe into good and evil, just as he split time. Evil is the tendency of the cosmos to revert to chance in its operations. But chance has to be directed . . .'

'How in hell could chance be directed?'

Horn shrugged. 'Don't ask me. Who am I to question God? You don't expect conventional logic from a crazy, do you? Castor has no trouble reconciling his schizophrenic contradictions. In that, he's far from being alone. What matters is that he thinks. In his divine wisdom and perception, he knows that you are the Secret and Malignant Director of Chance. He refers to you as Satan, The Great Beast, Beelzebub, Angra Mainyu, and a dozen other names. He's said that he will find you, vanquish you, and hurl you howling and with utter ruin and complete combustion into the deepest pit.'

'Why wasn't I told about this before?'

'Don't look so indignant. People will notice. Because

there was no need for it. You know we try to keep all communication at a minimum. I was the only one to hear about Castor from Atlas, and that was at parties or social functions and not much was said about it then.'

Tony was silent for a moment. Then she leaned forward again and spoke even more softly.

'The orders are to stone him and hide the body if it's possible. If not, kill him.'

Caird gave a slight start, and he sighed.

'I knew it would come to this someday.'

'I hate it,' Tony said. 'But it's for the common good.'

'Of the immers, you mean.'

'Everybody's. Castor is hopelessly insane, and he's dangerous to anyone who gets in his way.'

'I've never killed anybody,' Caird said.

'You can do it. I can do it.'

He shook his head. 'Our psych tests showed that we could, but they're not one hundred percent accurate. I won't know until I either must do it or can't do it.'

'You will. You'll catch him, and you'll do what must be done. Listen, Jeff . . .'

She put one hand on his and stared into his eyes. He stiffened.

'I . . .'

She cleared her throat.

'I got the decision on . . . Ariel . . . from the council today. I'm sorry, really sorry, Jeff. But . . .'

'She's been rejected!'

She nodded. 'They say she's too unstable. The psych projection is that she'd be burdened with too much social conscience. She'd break eventually and confess all to the authorities. Or, if she didn't, she'd have a mental breakdown.'

'They don't really know, they don't really know,' he murmured.

'They know enough. They can't take the chance.'

'There's no use appealing right now,' he said harshly. 'Not in a case like this. Tell me. Was the decision final or will they reconsider in five years? After all, Ariel's only twenty. She could mature.'

'You can try again then. The psych projection, however . . .'

'That's enough,' he said. 'Are you finished?'

'Please, Jeff. It's not that bad. Ariel will be just as happy if she isn't an immer.'

'I won't, but I suppose that doesn't matter. They reject Ozma and now Ariel.'

'You knew that might happen when you became one. Everything was laid out for you.'

'Is that all? You're done?'

'Kill the messenger who brings bad news. Come on, Jeff!'

He patted her hand. 'You're right, I'm wrong. It's just that . . . I feel so bad for her.'

'And for you.'

'Yes. May I leave now?'

'Yes. Oh, Jeff. Don't cry!'

He pulled a tissue from his shoulderbag and wiped the tears.

'I think you want to be alone for a while, Jeff.'

She rose, and he got up from his chair. She preceded him, since her rank was higher. When she stopped so the data clerk could put the bill into her ID star, he went on, saying softly, 'I'll see you, Tony.'

'Don't forget to report,' she called after him.

He asked through his wrist radio for an organic-car ride back to the station. Told he would have to wait twenty minutes for one, he flagged down a cab. So it would cost him a few credits. After he got in, though, he wished that he had waited. He was losing the battle to hold back more tears; he could have let loose in the unchauffeured vehicle.

By the time he arrived at the station, he was dry-eyed.

He went to his office and reported to Wallenquist, who was curious about his meeting with Horn but did not dare ask too many questions.

Gril had disappeared as completely as if he had slipped down into the ancient abandoned subway-sewer system. Which he might have done. Ten patrollers and a sergeant were searching for him now in the deepest known area beneath Yeshiva University. So far, they had found only a bashed-in human skull, which did not look fresh, some huge rats, and two almost unreadable lines in twenty-first-century spelling on a wall.

I HATE GRAFFITI
I DO TOO AND HIS BROTHER LUIGI IS A REAL PRICK.

Rootenbeak had escaped like a rabbit into a briar patch.

His relief, Detective-Inspector Barnewolt, came in at three. Caird brought her up to date, and they talked for a while about the efforts by the young to bring back into fashion the wearing of trousers.

'I don't like them,' Barnewolt said. 'The kind of pants they're wearing, they're too tight, too form-fitting. I tried on some, and they made me feel embarrassed. I don't know. There's something immoral about them.'

Caird laughed, and he said, 'Wednesday, I hear, has been wearing pants for some time now, both young and old.'

Barnewolt shrugged. 'Well, you know how those people are.'

6

Caird rode his bicycle home, checked in on Ozma at her studio, found her painting a wasp, and went into the house. After watching a news report – nothing new – he went into the basement and worked out on the exerciser. He showered and put on a white sheer blouse, an orange waistband, a removable white neck-ruff, and an emerald-green kilt. When Ozma came in, he had her paint his legs yellow. His curled-toe ankle-high shoes were crimson. After they ate, he put on some lipstick and selected a wide-brimmed hat with a high conical top sporting a crimson artificial feather.

Ozma wore a white cap with a long red bill, factory-grown eagle feathers dangling from holders in her earlobes, green eye makeup, green lipstick, rouged cheeks, a loose sheer blouse, a shimmering green hooped skirt that reached to her ankles, sequined red stockings, and Kelly-green high-heeled shoes. Many finger rings and a scarlet umbrella completed her ensemble.

'Where's yours?' she said.

'My what?'

'Your umbrella.'

'The weathercaster said it wasn't going to rain.'

'You know what I mean,' she said. 'Umbrellas are obligatory for evening wear.'

'I suppose it'll make you unhappy if I don't take one.'

'Not unhappy. I'll just feel embarrassed.'

'And you're the wild unconventional artist,' he said. 'Very well.'

At seven, they left the house, each carrying a big shoulderbag, and they got into a taxi. By the time they arrived, the huge museum lobby was packed with guests, all holding cocktails or stronger drinks, standing in close groups and chattering or wandering from group to group. The phatic lines of communion, as a twentieth-century anthropologist had called them, were functioning well. Everybody was talking and nobody was listening.

After greeting their hosts, Caird and Wang joined a gaggle of Goalists. Bored by them, Caird went to a pride of Pressurists and Ozma to a soup of Supernaturalists. The latter group was not painters interested in the hereafter but a new school which insisted that its subjects had to be shown realistically not only on the exterior but also on the interior. Thus, one side of the faces of their human subjects would show what the eye saw. The other half was slices of the *deeps*, as they called it, the skin removed, the skull removed, the brain shown, the inside of the brain shown, and the back-brain a shadowy presence.

Caird could not see any merit or value in Supernaturalism, but he did not argue with Ozma about it. What did he know of art? Besides, it made her happy, though there were times when he got tired of her talking about it.

At ten-thirty, the party was just reaching its climax. Ozma had been induced to paint her host. He stood nude in the middle of the lobby while she improvised the designs. Caird, far back in the crowd, wondered if she would somehow make the host look like a grasshopper.

'There's a call for you, Inspector,' a waiter said. 'The strip near the door as you go into the Absolute Zero Room.'

Caird thanked him and went through the doorway indicated into a vast dark-blue and very cold room containing many stoned ice-sculptures. The strip just around the corner showed the face and torso of Commissioner-General Anthony Horn.

'I'm sorry to pull you away from the party, Jeff.'

'Don't be. What is it?'

She swallowed and said, 'Naomi Atlas has been murdered.'

Lightning seemed to leap within his brain. He wanted to say, 'Castor did it?' but there was always the possibility that the line was being monitored.

'Her body, what was left of it, was found fifteen minutes ago in the bushes in the yard outside the apartment section of the building. I want you . . .' She swallowed again, her face spasmed, and she said, 'I want you to come up here and take charge. At once. Find out all you can before midnight, and report your findings to me. I've put you in charge because you're the murder expert in Manhattan. Colonel Topenski isn't too happy about it, but he'll cooperate or I'll have his ass. I told him so.'

'I'm leaving now,' Caird said.

'A patroller car will be waiting for you at the main entrance. I'll give you more details on your way up.'

Caird went into the lobby, forced his way, though apologizing, through the crowd, and said, 'Ozma! Hold it a minute.'

She stopped applying yellow paint to the host's buttocks and said, 'What's the matter, Jeff?'

'I've been called in on a case. It's very urgent.'

He spoke to the host. 'My sincere regrets, but duty calls.'

'Of course. What is this about?'

'That's organic business, though you may see it on the news.'

He walked to Ozma, kissed her cheek, and said, 'I'm sorry. You'll have to go home without me. I may be kept so long I'll have to use an institute stoner. I'll be home in the morning.'

She smiled and said, 'A policeman's wife is not a happy one.'

In the car, he called Horn. There was a delay of two

minutes before her face appeared on the screen on the back of the front seat. He said, 'Fill me in.'

There were no suspects as yet, and neither he nor Horn could mention Castor. She had at the moment no facts to add to what she had told him in the museum. He knew from her tone that she might have more to tell him when they were alone.

The yard was bright with the big lamps the organics had set up. Caird muscled through the spectators, showed his badge and ID star, and was admitted into the work party area. He saw Horn at the same time she saw him. She gestured for him to come to her under the big sycamore. She rose from the folding chair as he approached and held out her hand to him. She gripped his strongly and said, softly, 'She's over there.'

Over there was understatement. Atlas was all over, her head under a bush, a leg nearby, and the other leg stuck into a bush, an arm hanging over a branch, and the limbless torso propped up against a tree trunk. Entrails festooned another bush. Blood had stained the grass and soaked into the earth in the area marked off by string.

Caird clamped his teeth together and sucked in breath. It had been seven obyears since he had seen such grisliness.

Caird looked around. Without the lamps, the place would have been rather shadowy. Even so, pedestrians must have been strolling on the sidewalk not fifty feet away.

'The ME says that she died exactly sixty-three minutes ago,' Tony Horn said. 'The body was found by a sixteen-year-old boy who was taking a shortcut through the yard to the door. From what we've been able to determine so far, Atlas had gone to a party given by Professor Storring. You know him, of course.'

Caird nodded. Storring was also an immer, but he had met him only three times.

'Atlas has lived alone since she broke up with her husband,' Horn said. 'Two submonths ago, I believe. However . . .'

She hesitated and looked around. Then she held out her other hand, opened her fingers, and gave him a folded piece of paper.

'It's from Castor. I found it stuck to my door when I left my apartment after I got the call about Atlas. My God, he was right outside it immediately after he butchered her! It's a wonder he didn't try to kill me, too. But he's putting it off, wants to torture me, the sadistic bastard.'

Caird opened his shoulderbag and put the paper in it.

'What does it say?'

'God – Castor refers to himself in the third person – announces proudly the death and dismemberment of God's enemy, Doctor Naomi Atlas. God also prophesies the death and dismemberment of all his enemies, notably and firstly Commissioner-General Horn and Detective-Inspector Caird. There will be other announcements naming those who will die as surely as the stars are set on their courses by God. He signed it with one name. God.'

'God!'

'You'll have to get him,' she said. 'You'll have the best opportunity. I think he'll daybreak, and if he does you'll be travelling along with him and you can personally notify the immers in each day. They can help you.'

He nodded and said, 'Castor doesn't know my other identities, does he?'

'He shouldn't, but who knows what investigations he made? He always was nosy.'

'Do you have anyone watching for Castor near my house?'

'Oh, yes. Two organics, immers.'

'I wasn't going back tonight, but I think I'd better. Castor might want to hurt me by doing something . . . hell, doing something! . . . killing Ozma! He could destone her, drag her out of the stoner, and butcher her before Wednesday came out. Maybe he wouldn't care if they did. He could kill them, too!'

Her voice shook. 'This is terrible. It's so terrible that I have to warn the other days that another Jack the Ripper may be loose. I can't tell them who it is, of course. They'll have a lot of personnel looking for him, and . . .'

'They won't know whom to look for,' Caird said. 'Officially, we don't know whether it's a man or a woman who did this, one or two or more people. Have they found footprints?'

'Yes. Those of about twenty different people. No instruments, no knives or saws.'

'He probably dumped them in the canal.'

Colonel Topenski joined them, and the three talked. If the colonel resented Caird's being given command, he did not show it. After summing up what he had found so far, no more than Horn had told Caird, Topenski took Caird over the string-surrounded area. All photographs and laboratory work had been done by then, and their footprints would not confuse the situation. Caird felt sick when he got close to the parts of the corpse, but he did not throw up. He listened while the colonel, who seemed unaffected, pointed out various things that Caird could see for himself quite well. At a quarter after eleven, the pieces were bagged by the lab personnel and taken away. They would be stoned at the morgue, and, later, destoned for extensive analysis.

Patrollers and detectives had been sent out to question everybody in the neighbourhood they could before midnight. The desk workers at the local precinct would also be calling up many in the neighbourhood. They would report whom they had made contact with so that the foot personnel would not duplicate efforts. Even so, only a few of the possible witnesses would be questioned before midnight.

'We've made sure that no escapee from Tamasuki has done this,' Colonel Topenski said. 'They're all accounted for, all locked up.'

'That's good,' Caird said. What was not so good was that it was possible that someone might notice the recording of Castor's transfer. If that were followed up, then Horn would be in deep trouble. Eventually, so would Caird and all immers.

Caird looked at his watch. He said, 'I have to get back home, Colonel. I live in Greenwich Village.'

'Why don't you use a stoner here? There are plenty in the precinct house, only two blocks away.'

'My wife isn't feeling well.'

One more lie to cover up many.

'Perhaps she could stone early and go to the hospital next Tuesday.'

'Thanks for the suggestion, Colonel, but I know her. She'll want me to be there with her.'

Topenski shrugged and said, 'Ah, well. We don't have much time left, and what'll we do with it anyway?'

'Not very much,' Caird said. He started away, then stopped. 'Well, yes, there is something we can do right now and so save time when we get going in the morning. We're dealing with a homicidal maniac. I think I'll put in a request for arms for the investigating personnel.'

Topenski bit his lip, then said, 'This situation really seems to call for extreme measures. I think the general will agree. She's over there.'

Caird hurried to catch Horn, who was just about to get into an organic vehicle. She stepped back out when she heard him call and turned towards him. Caird gestured that she should join him. She understood that he wanted them to be out of earshot of the others. After hearing his suggestion that weapons should be requisitioned, she nodded.

'Of course, I'll have to justify it to the governor and the

organic council. If they balk, I'll show them recordings of the scene of the crime and take them to the morgue.'

'Can you get away with orders to shoot to kill if necessary?'

'Yes . . . only . . . the murderer has to be identified first. And the other days may not want to issue an order to shoot. At least not until they have ID.'

'As for us, we must drop any plans for stoning and hiding him. What if he were found and destoned? No. We must kill him.'

'It's the right decision, hard as it is,' Caird said. 'Anyway, I suspect we'll have no choice. He's probably got a gun or will get one. We'll have to kill him if only in self-defence.'

'Yes, but I'll have to follow routine and order the armed personnel to warn him first.'

'I know. I just hope I get to him first.'

He looked at his watch. 'I need a weapon right now. Just in case Castor should be in my neighbourhood when I get home.'

Horn went into the car and turned on the rear seat strip. She was giving her order before he got settled in beside her. The driver took the car off as fast as the electric motor would take it, orange lights flashing, siren wailing. The traffic was thin; most people were home and getting ready to stone. By the time the few blocks had been covered, the sergeant in charge at the precinct had opened the armoury. Caird and Horn went in past the organics lining up to receive their arms and got the sergeant to wait on them immediately. Rank had its privileges.

Caird put his weapon in his shoulderbag, said, 'Until tomorrow, Tony,' and hurried out to the car. The driver, delighted at being permitted to speed, took the car at its top velocity of forty miles an hour. Horn had arranged that the signal lights would be green for them all the way to the house on Bleecker Street. Caird did not know what excuse she might have to give for this special treatment, but he was sure that she would think of something reasonable.

Five blocks from his house, Caird told the driver to turn off the siren. If Castor should be in the house, he should not be frightened away. On the other hand, it might be better if he were. He might be prevented from doing whatever he might have in mind – if he was there.

At Caird's order, the driver slowed the car down during the final block and stopped it two buildings from Caird's house.

It was 11:22 PM.

Caird got out of the car and said, 'You can go now. There's an emergency stoner shelter at 200 Bleecker. You have eight minutes, plenty of time, to get there.'

'Yes, sir, I know,' the driver said. 'Good night, sir.'

Caird said good night and watched him drive off. He walked towards his house. The two guards were gone, of course. There were no lights in the house. This might mean that Ozma had decided that he was staying in an emergency shelter or in an extra stoner in a precinct station. She could already be in her cylinder. Or . . . someone else had turned the lights off and was waiting for him.

That someone could only be Castor. He would know that the front room light would come on as soon as Caird's ID tip entered the front door slot. Castor might have turned the light off with the manual switch, but then he would know that Caird would suspect that something was wrong.

Instead of going onto the front porch, Caird walked along one side of the house, the weapon in one hand, a flashlight in the other, looking for signs of breaking and entering. He saw nothing suspicious, and the back door was locked. He went to the other side and moved slowly, looking for signs of entry there. Nothing. As he walked back to the rear, the lights in the house began flashing, and he could hear, faintly, the siren moaning inside it.

It was now 11:30.

All over the city, all over this time zone, in every inhabited building, lights were flashing and sirens were moaning. And so were the street lights and sirens.

The seniors and the juniors now had less than five minutes to enter their stoners before power was applied to them. If they had not gone into them by now, and most had, because of life-long conditioning, they should hurry, hurry. Never mind if they had to go to the toilet. Never mind if some were in the midst of having a baby. Never mind what. Get into the stoner.

Those cylinders with closed doors would automatically get the power. Those with open doors would not. From 11:30 to 11:35 PM was a grace period. A citizen could still get into one and close the door and be stoned sixty seconds later. After that, no power until next Tuesday at fifteen minutes after midnight, and that was destoning power, which had a field quite different from the stoning power.

The lights and the sirens lasted for sixty seconds and would be the last warning of three. At 11:00, when Caird had been travelling south on the Manhattan streets, the lights had blinked and the sirens had whooped. Fifteen minutes later, the second citywide warning had occurred.

Before the lights in the house had darkened again, Caird was at the back door and had inserted the ID tip in the slot. He had the door open before the warning was over. If Castor was inside, he would not be able to distinguish the entry warning light from the others. But, as soon as the warning lights quit, he would see the flashing orange light above the door in the front room. And he would know that someone was entering the back door. Unless Caird got in in time to close the back door.

He did so, and the hall and front room lights went out. The kitchen light stayed on, though it no longer blinked. He walked down the hall with his weapon set at maximum charge. The hall lit up as he left the kitchen, the light of which went dark. Castor, if he were here, would see the light and know that someone had entered.

The light should also be on in whichever room Castor was. Castor, however, would be intelligent enough to have overridden the automatic light with the manual switch. But he must also know that if Caird went into a room and the light did not go on, then Caird would know that it had been manually turned off.

Caird told himself that he should not get spooked and shoot at anything that moved. It was possible that Ozma was still up. On the other hand, Caird did not want to give Castor a break by hesitating too long.

He stood listening. The house was silent, except for his subjective impression that it was breathing and also straining to hear something. Weapon held ready, finger on the button, he resumed walking. He passed the sliding closet doors on his left and a bathroom door and children's bedroom on his right. All the doors were shut. Since Castor could be behind any of them, Caird kept looking back.

He was also sharply aware that Castor could approach him from the rear through the kitchen. The dining room door opened onto the kitchen. Castor could come from the dining room and circle behind him.

The big front room lit up. He looked up the dark stairs to his right at the end of the hall. Then he put his hand over the bottom steps. The stairwell sprang into illumination. No one was there, and no shadowy face was looking from around the corner at the top of the steps. There were no signs of forced entry, and it was highly unlikely that Castor could have used some electronic means to get in. On the other hand, how had he gotten out of the Tamasuki institute?

He looked behind every piece of furniture in the front and dining rooms. Then he went through the kitchen again and down the long hall. He walked up the steps and went into the bathroom and two bedrooms there and looked into every closet.

It was midnight when he entered the basement. Fifteen minutes to go. The game room and the utility room and the PPC, the personal possessions closet, were empty of human though not of insect life. A big daddy-longlegs scuttled towards a refuge under the pool table. He would have to leave a recording for the cleaning squad when he had time for less important matters. No. The squad was not responsible for such matters. He would have to attend to a possible web under the table himself come next Tuesday. It was his turn to see to the minor cleaning.

He looked through the porthole of Ozma's cylinder. Her eyes looked lifelessly into his. Most people closed their eyes before power came on. Ozma had the crazy idea that her unconscious could see what was going on in the room, and she did not want to miss out on a thing.

He was happy with relief though still sweating from fear. Actually, the strain was not over yet, but that which he felt now was minor. It would become major if he did not get going.

He went to the cylinder which bore a plaque with his name and ID data. He put his shoulderbag on the floor, opened it, and took from a compartment a small flesh-coloured object attached to a small cylinder. After opening the stoner door, he set the object and cylinder on the stoner floor. He turned a dial at the end of the cylinder. The object unfolded, swelling, and ballooned into an air-inflated and full-sized replica of himself.

He pinched the big right toe of the replica, pulled the small compressed-air cylinder from the valve in the toe, and screwed a cap onto the valve. He dropped the cylinder into a compartment of his shoulderbag. His neck-chain with the attached ID star came off his neck and was put on the dummy's. Though they weighed less than an ounce, they were heavy enough to topple the dummy forward. However, steel balls glued inside the feet of the replica compensated for the weight. The replica would not lean until its face was pressing against the window.

He took the Wednesday ID from the bag and dropped the neck-chain over his head and onto his neck. He picked up the gun, which he had placed on the floor, and stuck it between the waistband and his body. He placed the bag on the stoner floor and closed the door. Inside the great cylinder was what had so far always passed as the relatively molecularly motionless body of Jefferson Cervantes Caird.

Soon enough, it would be stoned.

Blowing a kiss to Ozma as he left, he ran upstairs, opened the front door, closed it, sprang over the railing at the end of the front porch, and hastened under the trees to the east fence. Leaped over the white picket fence with a hand on it. Ran across the yard and under the trees. Up the front steps of the big building with many white columns that looked so much like Scarlett O'Hara's mansion. Stopped at the front door to insert one tip of the ID star into the hole. Saw the light come on in the apartment lobby. Pushed in on the door and let it swing shut. Sped across the lobby to the wide staircase and up it to the second floor. Ran down the thickly carpeted corridor to Number 2E. Inserted the star tip again and entered the apartment living room. Raced down a narrow hall to the stoner room and darted to the left through a doorway. Fourteen cylinders here, much more closely spaced than in the basement of the house he had just left.

Ten minutes after midnight.

Never had he cut it so close. Never again would he have to, he hoped.

7

Wednesday's wife stared unseeingly at him through her window. He turned away from her to his own cylinder, which faced hers across a narrow aisle. It bore a plaque with the name ROBERT AQUILINE TINGLE. His own face looked at him through the window. Its door should have been locked since there was someone – no, some thing – inside it, and it should be unlocked only from the inside. Caird, however, had arranged that it could be opened.

At the moment, he could do nothing with the air-inflated dummy. He ran from the room to the shower room, removing the gun and taking off the sash and blouse on the way. In the shower room, he punched a button, and the water began gushing at a preset pressure and temperature. The rest of his clothes came off, and he stepped under the water and began vigorously soaping himself. There was not time to do a thorough cleansing of the makeup; he stepped out while there were still paint streaks on his legs. He rubbed off these with a towel and then threw the towel into the hamper. He would dispose of that later, though the chances that his wife would see it were small. Taking another towel, he began rubbing himself, only to stop with a muttered exclamation. He reached over and punched the button to stop the shower.

His hair was still too wet, but he did not have time to dry it completely. After putting the second towel on top of the first in the hamper, he picked up his Tuesday clothes, balled them, and put them under the towel. When he had the opportunity, he would hide the clothes and towel in his personal possessions closet or destroy them.

Naked except for the neck-chain and ID star and holding the gun, he ran down the hallway and into the stoner room. Eighty seconds to go. He could get into the cylinder and try to find room beside the hard and unsqueezable replica or he could pretend that he was just coming out of the cylinder. The second action seemed more perilous. The microsecond that destoning power went on, his wife would probably open her eyes. She would see that the door was closed. Unless he stood in front of the window of his stoner until she had gone away, she would see that other face in the window. Even if she did not see it, she would wonder why he had gotten out of his cylinder before she did. And he would have a hell of a time explaining why he kept standing in front of the cylinder window.

'Choices of equal misfortune,' he muttered.

Cursing, he opened the door and sidled in, bent over. Ten seconds to go. His foot hit the stoned shoulderbag on the floor, and he said, 'Ouch!' After dropping the gun, he leaned hard against the cold and heavy dummy. It fell away from him, stopping when the side of its head hit the cylinder. He crowded in front of the dummy and straightened up. Anyone looking in would see part of it behind him.

Three seconds to go before destoning power struck. It would have no effect on him since he was not stoned. Maybe he could pull this off.

Perhaps it was the sight of his wife, recalling the one he had just left, that stabbed a panicky thought through the other panics. 'Oh, my God! I forgot to complete the licence application! Ozma will kill me!'

Wednesday-World
VARIETY, Second Month of the Year
D5-W1 (Day-Five, Week-One)

8

Nokomis Moondaughter, a long-legged brunette of medium height, stepped out of the cylinder. She wore a clinging scarlet ankle-length robe slashed with black. Her thinness and sharply angled face made her look like a ballerina, which she was. She stopped just outside the cylinder door and narrowed her eyes.

Caird knew that she was wondering why he was still standing in the cylinder. He gave up his intention to 'carve,' as he called the process, the persona of Bob Tingle. That would have to come later; no time for it now. Just now, he must keep her from seeing the dummy.

He pushed the door open, bounded through the doorway, and closed the door behind him quickly. Bounding again, he grabbed Nokomis and lifted her in his arms. Whirling, he danced down the hall.

'What are you doing?' she cried. 'What's gotten into you?'

He set her down in the kitchen and said, 'I love you, and I'm so glad to see you! Is that so hard to understand?'

She laughed, then said, 'No. Yes. Usually, you slouch out like some rough crotch-scratching beast who's lost his way to the bathroom. You're grumpy until you've had your coffee. Don't you think you should put some clothes on?'

'Yes, you're right. It's too early for the sight of naked me.'

He leaned down and kissed her lips. 'Shall we have coffee and talk a while? Or should we sleep first?'

She narrowed her dark eyes, and something settled over her face, what he called the suspiration of suspicion. It was like the mist formed on a mirror by a breath. Suspiration of suspicion.

'How could you forget?' she said. 'You know I slept for six hours before getting up for stoning. You told me you took a nap for an hour or so while I was sleeping. You woke up just as I did. Or so you said. You never go to sleep right after a nap. Why do you want to sleep now?'

As Bob Tingle, he would have remembered what he had told her. But he was still Jeff Caird, desperate after yesterday's events and jittery with the present urgency. The dummy. He had to deflate it.

He told himself to smooth out the rippling inside himself. Press it down with a quiet and cool mental hand.

'I'm not Tik-Tok,' he said. 'I don't run on wind-up machinery. Now and then, I use free will. Or call it whim. Or indigestion.'

'You certainly didn't act sleepy and tired when you sprang out like a jack-in-the-box.'

Before he had married her, he had known that she was a radar set sensitized only to nonroutine phenomena, a TV channel with a wavelength of near-paranoia. She even suspected the weathercaster's motives when rain came instead of the predicted clear skies. Perhaps that was exaggerating somewhat. But not much. As Jeff Caird, he would never have married her, would not even have dated her very long. As Bob Tingle, he had fallen in love with her. Just now, he disliked and resented her because of her suspicions, and he also was wondering why he had ever tied himself to this scrawny woman. No. He, Caird, had not done that. Tingle had.

The near-panic wrapped itself around him again. It was an octopus of ectoplasm seen and felt only by himself. But which self? Not just Caird. Caird would not have thought of such phrases as 'suspiration of suspicion' and 'octopus of ectoplasm.' Tingle was trying to get out, but he would never make it until Caird had a minute to go through the summoning ceremony, the ritual raising the top of Tingle's tomb, immured in his mind and making him master of this mess – he meant 'mass' – known in Wednesday as Tingle. However, Caird would never be completely gone. If he were, Caird-Tingle would be completely ineffective in his role and duties as an immer. Jeff Caird was the primary, the original.

'A jack-in-the-box!' he cried, smiling. 'How about a Bob-in-the-box? Your box!'

He picked her up and whirled again. 'Let's!'

She smiled, but she said, 'Let's not. And let me down. You know I have to practise. After that . . . I'm not frigid, you know.'

He set her down on her feet and said, 'No, you're not, but I wonder sometimes about your thermostat. OK. Anything you want, Tippytoes. Your every desire is mine. You make the coffee, and Tingle will go tinkle.'

Caird would never have said that either. Perhaps, the evocation evulsion was evitable.

I have to stop that sort of thing, Caird thought. At least, water it down. It's too much. But it's a sign that Tingle lurks on the threshold of Wednesday and might come out even if I neglected the ritual. Now, however, was no time for experimenting. Too dangerous.

'You went to the toilet just before you were stoned,' Nokomis said.

Choi-oi! How did Tingle put up with her?

He was glad that he had not voiced the exclamation. Wednesday did not know it, since its main ethnic flavouring in Manhattan was not Chinese but Amerind and Bengali. Hearing that, she would have pumped her suspicions to the bursting point.

'Yes, and I have to go again,' he said.

He turned and walked down to the hall to the bathroom, which was on his right. After closing the door, he sat down on the closed toilet lid. He noted that Tuesday had forgotten to replace the toilet paper; three lone sheets clung to the spool. That however, was not worth leaving a remonstratory recording for yesterday's yahoos.

He closed his eyes and sank into a noiseless and frictionless world. His image of himself as Caird hung solid, bright, and full-sized before him. Watching it with one eye, as it were, he spun the other eye, also imaginary, so that it turned inwards. That saw at first only darkness. Then, quickly, many sagging lines, grey in the black, formed. They seemed to stream from the abyss within his body, flying past the eye into the abyss above. He straightened them out until they were so tight that they hummed with tension. He increased the pressure at each end, though he did not know where their ends were, until it seemed that the lines, now glowing brightly and coldly, would snap. He hurled heat at them. The 'heat' was comet-shaped energy complexes, each of which struck a line and was absorbed, though not entirely. Some of the heat slid down or up the lines, like drippings from a candle. It was up to them which way they went. Here, in his mind, there was no gravity.

No gravy, either, he thought. Or maybe he was wrong. The drippings did remind him of hot gravy.

The lines of force were used to suppress himself and bring forth Tingle. Who, when summoned from the floor of his mind like the ghost of Samuel evoked by the Witch of Endor, would change from ghost to guest. Today's guest.

He increased the strain on the lines. They snapped and then darted wriggling and shining in the darkness. They went here and there, colliding, then coalescing, until all had touched and melted together and formed one slim, long, and glowing column. It seemed upright, that is, stretching from the darkness below to the darkness above. Now, he rotated it so that it was at right angles to its previous position, and he spun it so fast that it melted from a column into a blurry disc.

The other eye saw that the image of Caird had lost much of its brightness and had shrunk. No wonder. The heat hurled at the lines had been sucked from Caird. Now, a line, the boundaries of a trap door, formed around the image's feet. Sometimes, the image to be done away with was shot up like a rocket or rolled into a ball and hurled down an alleyway with phantom bowling pins at the far end. Today the image was to be dropped through a floor.

The second eye watched the spinning and bright white disc as its sharp edge cut a block from the darkness and then began cutting away parts of the blackness. A rough figure was left from the hewing away of the darkness, a figure that became grey as it absorbed some of the light from the disc. Which became darker as the figure gained a finer form.

When Tingle was almost perfected, the first eye gave a mental order, and the image of Caird dropped through the trap door. The lines forming the door vanished.

Now, both eyes focused on Tingle, and, as the disc became black and small, having lost its heat and worn its edge to almost nothing, Tingle floated glowing in the blackness.

Presently, the disc disappeared, and the image of Tingle was shot upwards so swiftly that its friction formed a long ghostly comet tail.

His eyes turned outwards, and he opened his lids. Bob Tingle had landed, though not without a residue of Caird. Ninety-eight percent of him was Wednesday's tenant; two percent, Tuesday's. Enough of Caird was left to remember the dummy still inflated in the stoner. What would he do if Nokomis saw it? He could not give her an explanation that would satisfy her. And he could not tell her the truth. Why had he ever gotten into this mess?

He rose from the seat and started towards the door. He stopped, grimaced, snapped his fingers, and turned back.

If Nokomis did not hear the toilet flushing, she would come galloping down the hall to find out why not. She always noticed the breaking of a pattern, the nonhappening of events that should happen unless something was wrong. He pressed the button, and, as the water roared, he stepped into the hall.

Usually, he was almost all Bob Tingle by now, though Jeff Caird would not have really dropped entirely through the imaginary trap door. Always, Caird was a speck in the eyeball, a tiny itch in the skin of the mind, not noticed by Tingle unless there was a good reason for him to be noticed. As just now, when the dummy had to be deflated. What made him even more present was that Chang Castor was loose in Wednesday – probably – and Tingle could not ignore him.

Tingle looked down the hall. He could not see Nokomis, but she might think of something to fetch from the PP closet.

He called, 'I'm going to get dressed! Anything you want from the closet?'

Nokomis said, cheerily, 'Nothing, dear! The coffee'll be ready soon!'

Nokomis would now be destoning the lox and bagels for their breakfast. After that, she'd put the bagels in the toaster. He would have to be dressed by then or she would be looking down the hall to see where he was.

He ran to his stoner, opened the door, and bent down. After he had removed the plug from the base of the dummy, he shut the door and ran to the closet marked WEDNESDAY. He said, 'Open,' and a mechanism, recognizing his voiceprint, released the lock so that he could swing the tall door out. He snatched the nearest robe, slid it over his head, said, 'Close,' and hurried back down the hall after a glance to assure himself that Nokomis was not looking after him. He opened the stoner again.

'Damn!'

The dummy was deflating too slowly.

He pressed down on it, aware of the louder hissing as the air left it. Nokomis, however, had turned on a strip. The voices should drown the hissing.

When the replica was half-collapsed, he stepped into the cylinder and closed the door. He shoved down on the dummy until it was completely deflated, then rolled it up and put it in the little bottle in the shoulderbag. The gun also went into the bag. Though he knew that Thursday's ID star was in the bag, he could not resist checking to make sure. His fingers touched the tips of the star.

He stepped out backwards and closed the door. Breathing more heavily than he liked, he walked towards the kitchen. Just before he got to it, he saw Nokomis come around the corner.

'There you are. The bagels are getting cold.'

He followed her to the balcony, where a small round table held coffee, orange juice, and the food. He sat down opposite Nokomis. There was just enough light from the street to make him and his wife seem to be in a grey limbo. The katydids and tree frogs were still singing.

He sipped hot coffee and looked at his Tuesday home. Its windows were bright, but he could see no one in it. Enough of Caird lingered for him to think briefly of Ozma, standing in the cylinder. Ozma, waiting to see him six days from now.

Nokomis, as almost always, looked lovely. Her skin was darker in this dimness than the beautiful copper it showed in sunlight. Her black hair was cut close and spotted with white dye to give it Wednesday's current 'skunky' look.

Nokomis had tried to get Tingle to spot his hair and grow a beard, which would be cut to the fashionable square shape. He had refused, though he could not give her, of course, his true reasons for not being in mode.

He thought: the clothes in the hamper. I must not forget to hide them better.

Nokomis, halfway through her second cup of coffee, perked up. She began chattering away about her role in the new ballet, *Proteus and Menelaus*. It had not opened yet, and its troubles were many.

'. . . composer is crazy. She thinks atonal music is something new. She won't listen when you tell her it was dead ten generations ago. Roger Shenachi is constipated, and every time he comes down from a grand jeté he farts something awful. I told Fred . . .'

'Fred?'

'Haven't you been listening? Pay attention. I just hate talking to myself, you know that. Fred Pandi is the big muckamuck; she wrote the story, composed the music, and did the choreography. I told her she should rewrite the whole thing around Roger, call it *Gas* or something like that, and while she was at it, she should throw out the music and write something that could at least be danced to . . .'

'I'm sure you're artist enough to overcome all that,' Tingle said. 'Anyway, since when does a ballerina, even one of your stature, have any say in –'

'Thank you, but you don't understand. I have a say in it, a big one, because I'm a committee member, as you know very well. At least, I'm supposed to be one, but the composer and the orchestra director are lovers, and they gang up on the rest of us.'

'Two doesn't make a gang.'

'What do you know about it, Bob?'

'Not much. What's this about a committee? Since when has a committee ever produced great art?'

'Oh, don't you ever listen? I told you all about it last yesterday. Or was it the day before? Never mind, I did tell you.'

'Oh, sure, I remember,' he said. 'Whose idea was that?'

'Some bureaucrat's. I'm sure the other days don't have such problems. It's just . . .'

9

Though it was not fair to let his mind wander, he could not help it. Gril, Rootenbeak, and Castor had risen from the depths like sunken ships filled with gas from decaying corpses. Never before, well, hardly ever before, had he found it hard to shut out the other days. Usually, when he was in Wednesday, he was almost completely Bob Tingle; Wednesday was sufficient unto itself. Now, the pattern and routine had been shattered. There were three daybreakers on the loose, and two could be very dangerous. Well, one could be. Rootenbeak might come across him and recognize him, but it was not likely that he would say anything to the authorities about Bob Tingle looking so much like Jeff Caird. Unless he did so anonymously via TV. Castor . . . that maniac could have been lurking nearby in the shadows and seen him running from the house to this apartment building. Or Castor might be apprehended at any moment and, as Horn had put it, spill the beans.

'Bob!'

Tingle pulled himself from his mental morass.

'Sure, I agree with you. Committees stink. But look at it this way. If you were living in the old days, you wouldn't have a thing to say about the production. This way, you might get some things changed.

'Committees are just like balloons, always up in the air, subject to the whims of the winds or of the windy, and they come down when they run out of gas. I'm telling you, the whole show's going to crash. Utterly crash! And I'll be ruined, utterly ruined!'

He sipped on the coffee and said, 'Tell you what. I am

an official at the World Data Bank . . .'

'I know that. What about it?'

'I'll find out if there's anything in the way of blackmail material that can be used against the committee members, especially against Pandi and Shenachi. You can use it, if I find any, that is, to get those two to knuckle under. Of course, I might have to dig up dirt about everyone on the committee.'

She rose from the chair, came around the table, and kissed him. 'Oh, Bob, do you think you could?'

'Sure. Only . . . doesn't the ethics bother you? It'll be . . .'

'It's for art's sake!'

'Mostly for your sake, isn't it?'

'I'm not just thinking about me,' she said. She went back to the chair and poured more coffee. 'It's the whole production. I'm thinking organically. For everybody's good.'

'I don't know that I can get enough leverage to pry the composer loose from her atonal music. Even if I could, that means a longer delay, a new score written.'

She shrugged and said, 'Who cares? It's not like the old days. We're not dependent on money.'

'Yes, and I think it'd be better if you were. However, let's not talk about that now. I'll see what I can do. Now . . . aren't you lucky to have me? Where's your gratitude?'

She laughed, and she said, 'You haven't done anything yet.'

'I've built up some credit for good intentions.'

'A contractor for the highway of hell. You don't need any excuse, you know. However, let's wait until tonight. I'm in a better mood after practice.'

'Not lately,' he said. 'You've been coming home furious and disgusted.'

'The better to work out anger and frustration then. You aren't really complaining, are you?'

He stood up. 'I never complain about anything unreal. Someday, our moods will mesh, and this apartment will explode.'

'I don't want to have to look for a new one,' she said. She kissed him again. 'What're you going to do?'

'I have a busy schedule today,' he said, 'but I'll work on the research for Project Blackmail somehow. To make sure that I have enough time, however, I should go to work early.'

'Early?' she said, her eyes widening.

'Yes, I know. It'll be dangerous. *You* can work as hard as you wish and put in long hours, and nobody frowns on you. You're an artist. But I'm a bureaucrat. If I go in early and stay late, and my fellow workers find out, they might check up on me. I can't have them find out that I'm doing unauthorized work, opening channels irrelevant to my work. I'd be in real trouble then.

'Maybe it'll be better if I just go to work at the appointed time. I'll just slough off some of my regular work. My coworkers don't mind if I'm lazy or inefficient – that makes me a regular guy, one of the old gang – and my superior won't mind if I don't get too far behind. I'm allowed an unofficial margin for lagging, you know. Just so I don't make trouble for my superior by forcing him to call me in for a reprimand.'

They finished breakfast, and Nokomis went to the bathroom. He hoped that she would not take the clothes from the hamper for washing. He did not expect her to do so, since she was quite willing to leave the washing to him. If he remembered correctly, she had done it last Wednesday and would expect him to take his turn today.

Fifteen minutes later, she came back onto the balcony. She was dressed in a white blouse and tight scarlet pants and was holding the strap of her shoulderbag.

'Oh, I thought you'd be in bed, getting ready, anyway.'

He smiled and said, 'No, I was planning how to do the

blackmailing research.'

'Good. I'm going to the gym now.'

He stood up, and they kissed briefly. 'Have a good workout,' he said.

'Oh, I will. I always do. I won't be able to meet you for lunch. The committee is meeting during lunch hour at a restaurant.'

During her absence, Tingle had activated a strip on the side of the balcony and checked their schedule. He already knew that she could not lunch with him, and she knew that he knew. But she was not one hundred percent sure that his memory would not fail him. She trusted only herself.

'I'll see you at seven at The Googolplex,' he said.

'I hope the salad is better than the last time.'

'If it isn't, we'll look for a better place next time.'

He sat on the balcony until he had seen her bicycle down Bleecker and north along the canal. As soon as she was out of sight, he rose and went to the bathroom. More than once, she had returned a few minutes after going out of the door, saying that she had forgotten something. She did not fool him; she was checking on him to make sure that he was not doing something he should not. There had been a time when he had wondered if she were an organic officer whose public role was that of a ballet dancer. His investigations through data bank channels had convinced him that she was not.

What was she then? An overly suspicious, perhaps a paranoiac woman. Not at all the woman who should be Bob Tingle's wife. But she had not shown her true nature when he was courting her, and he had been careless in not checking out her personality index before marrying her. Passionate love had blinded him, but that was Bob Tingle's nature. Tingle was likely to be carried away by emotions that Jeff Caird would never have allowed to flourish in him. Yet Caird was responsible for Tingle's nature. Caird had deliberately chosen that nature for his Wednesday role because he wanted to feel strongly – as Tingle – what Caird could feel only weakly.

However, Caird must have had some liking for Tingle characteristics, some feeling that he was missing much by being so self-controlled. So Caird, when building, perhaps *growing* was the better word, when growing the personality of Tingle, had indulged himself, the Caird self. He was paying now for that luxury because his passion for Nokomis had put him in danger. Though she was not a government secret agent, she did watch him closely. If she discovered something suspicious that was not concerned with their personal relationships, she might probe deeper. If she found something that she suspected was criminal, would she turn him in?

He did not think so, but she would be angry because he had not confided in her.

The truth was that he just did not know what would happen if she pried too much. What he did know was that Tingle should not have married her. Tingle should leave her, the sooner the better. But Tingle was still in love with her, though the high passion blazing in him in the beginning had become a middling but pleasant warmth. Moreover, if he did tell her he wanted a divorce, he would have to suffer her hurt and anger. She was very possessive and egotistic; *she* would have to be the one who did the leaving. However, she was not only a great collector of things and of some people, but also fiercely resented having to give any up. Their personal possessions closet was jammed with bric-a-brac, teddy bears, china dolls, mementoes of birthdays and of world and national and district holidays, ballet trophies, recordings of herself from birth on up to a few weeks ago, a first-place medal for the one-hundred-metre dash for Manhattan eighth-grade girls, a good conduct citation awarded when she was twenty subyears (she had never gotten one after that because of her quarrels with various members of the ballet company), and at least a hundred other items.

Tingle had tried many times to get her to throw them out. They were a pain and vexation because she insisted on getting some of them out almost every night and placing them on a shelf. Then she had to put them back in the closet before stoning time. They also made it hard for him to get to his own few possessions or even to the clothes rack.

One day, Tingle knew, his not-easily-aroused temper would take him over, and he would dump her stuff down the trash chute. And that would mean their farewell. Which, logically, from his viewpoint, should come about before her possessiveness and suspiciousness got him into trouble.

He sighed, got up from the chair, and went to the bathroom. He removed his still-damp Tuesday clothes from the hamper and hung them up to dry. Later, he would roll them up and stuff them into the shoulderbag. It would be easier and more intelligent to drop them into the chute, but he had only one outfit for partywear. To get another, he would have to turn in the old outfit on Tuesday or have a good excuse for losing it. The latter required filling out a report for the Department of Clothing Outlets.

When he got into bed, he expected that sleep would be slippery, but he got hold of it at once and slid into a throng of dreams.

Awakening when the wall-strip alarm belled, he remembered only one of the dreams that had besieged him. Father Tom's face, his own, of course, recognizable even under the wig and the fake beard, had appeared on a wall strip. The strip showed Father Tom standing on the near side of a broad, dark, and sluggishly moving river. Just beyond Father Tom was a massive stone bridge. Father Tom held in his right hand a heavy iron candelabrum with seven candles. It looked like those used in synagogues, but Tingle could not remember its name. A long bright flame was spurting from the long finger of Father Tom's right hand. Father Tom was frowning as if he could not decide which candle to light.

'This is the moment,' Father Tom said sternly.

Tingle had woken up muttering, 'Moment of what?'

He had slept for six hours, though he usually required eight. He put on shorts and went down to the basement, where he exercised in solitude on a machine. Returning to the apartment, he showered again, dressed, and drank a cup of coffee. By then the sun was strong, the city astir, and the temperature was beginning to climb towards the projected afternoon high of 112° Fahrenheit. Tingle, dressed in thin underwear shorts, a white short-sleeved shirt slashed in green and ruffled at the neck, Kelly-green bellbottom slacks, and brown sandals, his bag on his shoulder, stood once more on the balcony. He was looking at the neighbourhood for . . . for what? Doctor Chang Castor?

Which meant that he was not entirely Tingle. Jeff Caird still lived in him. He was reminding Tingle that he was supposed to contact his immer agent in Wednesday. That would have to be done from the data bank, however.

At the moment there was only one person in front of the house at the corner of Bleecker and the Kropotkin Canal. A man on a bicycle pedalling west, his back to Tingle. A big green coolie hat shaded his neck, and he wore a brown shirt and billowy green slacks. Tingle watched the man stop at the corner and turn his head to look behind him.

Tingle said, 'God!' He clenched his hands and stepped out farther onto the balcony. The face under the hat had Castor's long narrow features and rather large nose. And why was he looking so intently at the house?

Tingle shook his head and spoke loudly to himself.

'It's just your imagination! He wouldn't be dumb

enough to do *that*!'

Whatever *that* meant. Danger for Ozma?

The man turned his head, allowing Tingle a glance at his profile. It was like the vulturine face of Castor, but . . . No, it could not be Castor.

The bicycler disappeared behind the house as he went north on the canal road, appeared again, then vanished behind the next house. A man stepped out of the back door of the corner house and went to the garage. Presently, he came out with a bicycle. Tingle recognized him as John Chandra. Tingle knew well his face and that of his wife, Aditi Rotwa, having seen them through the stoner windows in the basement. He stepped back so that Chandra would not look up and see him.

Even if his neighbour noticed the likeness of his face and that of Jeff Caird's in the basement stoner, he would think only of what a remarkable coincidence it was. Tingle waited until Chandra had disappeared behind the house before he stepped out again to look for the bicycler. By then, he was gone.

'Just my nerves,' Tingle muttered.

Three minutes later, he was headed east, a part of a flow of cyclists and an occasional electric car. He had just begun to sweat when he saw out of the corner of his eye a banana peel on the sidewalk.

10

He zigzagged through the crowd, braked by the curb, kicked the stand, picked up the peel, and dropped it into a waste container. When he went back to the bike, he looked around. He did not see Rootenbeak and really did not expect to. There were other slobs besides Rootenbeak in Wednesday – *if* he was here. Nevertheless, he was shaken, and, as he pedalled away, he rebuked himself for his automatic action. He should not have stopped; he should have gone even faster.

At Thirtieth Street, he went up the ramp and rode until he came to the west side, the dark side, of the Thirteen-Principles Towers. The building, which was covered with solar panels, occupied the area bounded by Seventh, Fourth, Thirtieth, and Thirty-seventh. The main structure soared up to four thousand feet, and the thirteen towers along its perimeter added fourteen hundred feet. Tingle's office was near the top of the tower on the northwest corner at Seventh and Thirty-seventh.

After riding down the ramp to the parking room on the third subfloor, he took an elevator to the northwest main lobby. From there, he rode in the express to the level at the top of the main building. Then he took an elevator to his level in one of the towers.

While walking down the hall leading to his office, Tingle was distracted by the view through the tall and wide windows on his right. There were six mooring masts on the roof of the main building, three zeppelins socked into three masts, and a fourth glittering orange giant was easing its nose towards a mast. Tingle stopped to watch the thing of beauty and splendour.

There were powerful updrafts alongside this building, but the zeppelins came down past them into the relatively still air over the immense roof where they had no trouble manoeuvring. Moreover, they needed no landing crews to pull on ropes dropped from the ship. The pilot had at his control twelve swivable jet engines that could counterbalance any windthrusts. Slowly, the ship approached the socket at the top of the mooring mast, and then its nose was locked.

Tingle would have liked to watch the stoned passengers, safe from accidents and tedium, packed in nets, lowered to trucks. A glance at his wristwatch showed him that it was almost time for his prework briefing with his boss. He entered the office anteroom, where the secretary sat at his desk. The secretary looked pained and mournful, as if he had a hangover. Tingle breezed by him, saying, 'Good morning, Sally!'

Hearing only a grunt, Tingle called back, 'Surly, Sally?'

The secretary said, 'Good morning, Maha Tingle. Maha Paz is . . .'

'I know, I know. Eagerly, perhaps impatiently, waiting for me. Thank you.'

The office was dome-shaped and elegantly furnished, like the man behind the desk. Welcome Vardhamana Paz rose to his full seven feet of stature. His glittering many-coloured blouse and trousers strained to hold in a ball-shaped torso and mighty buttocks. Above three chins, sagging dewlaps, was a round head with a massive overhanging forehead. When he bowed and held his hands in a prayerful attitude, he gave the impression of labouring to lift his many rings. There were two on each finger, each ring bearing a massive diamond or emerald. The gold was fake, and the jewels were artificial, and Paz looked unreal to Tingle. That was probably because fat and misshapen people were so rare.

Tingle, after bowing, his hands held up before him and

pressed together, said, 'Good morning, chief.'

'Good morning, Bob.'

Paz lowered himself slowly and gently like a balloon losing hot air through a small leak. He told Tingle to take a chair, and he said, 'For others it's a good morning. For you and me . . .'

'Twinkledigits,' as he was called behind his back, waved his walrus-flipper hand. His face contorted as if he had eaten too many beans.

'I got the news about your troubles . . . our troubles . . . through our line.'

Tingle shifted uneasily and looked around the room. He would feel very stupid if he asked Paz if the room had been debugged and a scrambler was operating. Of course, it had been and was. Also, three news strips were on, the volume annoyingly loud.

Tingle moved the chair until his stomach cut into the edge of the desk, and he leaned forward.

'You heard from Tony?' he said.

'No. Someone else.'

'Rootenbeak and Gril are not my concerns, not today. But Castor . . . I suppose your informant told you how dangerous he is to us?'

His jowls flapping like sheets in a wind, Paz nodded.

'A certain high organic is looking for Castor. But he's handicapped because he can't do anything official as yet. If he had gotten official word from Tuesday that Castor was a daybreaker, he could act swiftly. But he'd have to kill Castor to prevent his arrest. We can't have him talking to the authorities.'

Though Tingle was not supposed to know the name of the man Paz referred to, he did. His data bank researches, unauthorized by both today's government and the immer council, had revealed it.

'We must find Castor,' Paz said.

'I'll work like a beaver on it,' Tingle said.

'What're you smiling about?'

'Nothing. Just a pun.'

'Pun? What pun? This is no time for levity, Bob.'

'The American beaver belongs to the genus Castor canadensis,' Tingle murmured.

'What?'

'Never mind,' Tingle said, speaking loudly. 'Chief, I'll have to set up fake time on my work-hours report. But my immediate supervisor, Galore Piecework, is too zealous. She almost always checks on my report.'

Paz frowned and said, 'Galore Piecework?'

'Gloria Peatsworth. We underlings call her Galore Piecework.'

Paz did not smile.

'I told you, Bob. Levity . . .'

'. . . is a grave matter. I know, chief. Please forgive me.'

Paz heave-sighed, and he said, 'I'll take care of Peatsworth. But . . .'

After a few seconds, Tingle said, 'You've got even worse news?'

'You're very perceptive, Bob.'

Paz sighed deeply again, and he said, 'My informant told me that there's a Sunday organic here. A Detective-Major Panthea Pao Snick. She has a temporal visa, Bob. A *temporal*!'

'And it concerns us, of course. Otherwise, you'd not have mentioned her.'

'I'm afraid so,' Paz said. 'From what my informant said – he wasn't able to get any details that would enlighten me – Snick's mission is so secret that only the commissioner-general knows what it's about. And maybe he doesn't know all. The commissioner's given orders that Snick's to get full cooperation. It sounds ominous. We have to find out what she's up to.'

'She may not be here because of us.'

Paz sighed again.

'I wish I could think so. Unfortunately, she's already asked about you. In fact, she wants to talk to you.'

It would be impossible to be all-Tingle today. Tuesday would not stay silent. It demanded that Tingle at least be Jeff Caird's agent. That was all that Tingle was going to allow himself to be. Caird had to be regarded as someone who had temporarily employed Tingle to represent him in Wednesday.

Tingle said, 'I may have to work overtime.'

'I'll authorize it. No sweat.'

Tingle grinned because Paz's face was filmed with salty water.

The reason given for overtime would be one more cover-up. Lies bred lies, and their growing weight put immense stress on what they were supposed to ease.

Paz's cough sprang Tingle from his reveries.

'Do you have anything to add?' Paz said.

Tingle rose and said, 'No. If that's all . . .?'

'Yes. If anything important comes along, notify me.'

'Of course.'

Tingle was biting his lip when he left the office. As he walked down the corridor, he felt bladder pressure. Halfway down the corridor, he turned right into a doorway above which was a sign: *P & S*. The anteroom gave onto a large room with off-white pseudomarble walls, ceiling, and floor. On his left was a long row of urinals above each of which was a strip displaying news programmes. On his right was a row of cubicles from which came the muted voices of newscasters and soap opera actors, the flushing of a toilet, and groans.

After looking along the unoccupied row, he chose a urinal in front of Channel 176. John 'Big' Fokker Natchipal, its daytime caster, was a man whom Tingle detested. Thus, while he stood there, Tingle could imagine himself urinating on the ever-egregious Natchipal. Four screens away was the channel on which the fantastically beautiful and sexy Constant Tung delivered the news. But he had given up watching her – at least, in toilets – because he usually got an erection and that made it hard (no pun intended) to pee.

However, this time his choice of station did not help him. He could hear her voice faintly, and that was enough to keep him thinking about her. While standing exasperated and frustrated, he became aware that someone was standing a few feet to his left. He turned his head towards her. She was wearing a brown jockey cap on which was a green circle enclosing a red star and a brown robe decorated with small green crux ansatas, looped Egyptian crosses. Her shoulderbag was large, green, and jammed full. Bright green shoes thrust their pointed snouts from under the hem of the robe.

She was short, about five feet eight inches high, slim, and had short black hair gleaming like seal's fur. Her face was delicate-boned, high-cheeked, and triangular. Her large dark brown eyes – also reminding him of a seal's – stared at him. Though as beautiful as Tung, she did not have the same effect on him. Her rudeness made him angry.

'Yes?' he said.

Before she could answer, a woman entered, waved at Caird, said, 'Good morning, Bob,' and disappeared into a cubicle.

'I'm sorry to disturb you here,' the woman said in a husky but rapid voice, 'I didn't want to wait outside. I don't like to waste time.'

'Who are you, and what can I do for you?' he said harshly.

Embarrassment and anger had deflated his penis, but he still was unable to urinate. He said, 'I give up,' and he zipped his pants. He strode angrily to the washbowl while the woman followed him.

She said, 'I'm Detective-Major Panthea Pao Snick. I –'

'I know who you are,' he said, looking at her in the mirror. 'My superior, Colonel Paz, told me about you. He said –'

'I know. I came into his office a few seconds after you left it.'

He walked to the hot-air blower and punched its button. She followed him, saying, 'I'm authorized to give only a minimum explanation about my mission. But I can and will demand full cooperation.'

That meant that the North American Superorganic Council was backing her. Or that she was claiming more authority than she had because she could then get full cooperation. Tingle, as Caird, had done that more than once. However, he did not intend to call her bluff, if it was one. If she was sent by the NASC, she could be investigating rumours or suspicions or, he hoped to God not, facts about the immers. But, whyever she was here, it was not just to pass the time.

Fear groped around in his guts for a handle.

11

Snick said, 'I want to talk to you privately.'

Just as the blower went off, he said, 'We can't use my work-office. I doubt you're authorized to go in there.'

He started walking towards the exit. Dogging him, she said, 'I'm not, though I could be. But that's too much trouble. I just want a few minutes where no one can hear us.'

He stopped and turned in the hall. Her big brown eyes looked into his as if she were trying to read something in them. They were very beautiful eyes, he thought, unfitted to an organic officer. Or perhaps they were appropriately inappropriate. She could throw a man off guard with them. Who could believe that there was steel behind their softness?

He told her that they could talk in a lounge just down the hall. She walked with him, her legs moving swiftly to keep up with his long and quick stride. He did not slow down. If she was so intent to save time, she could trot for all he cared. His own time was also important.

The lounge was deserted. He seated himself in a big comfortable body-moulding chair. Snick took a chair, which deflated a few inches to accommodate her shorter legs. She was facing him across a narrow table.

'Just what do you want from me?' he said. He glanced at his watch.

'Don't you want my identification?'

He waved his hand. 'Colonel Paz told me that you wanted to talk to me.'

He intended to get all the data he could about her when he got to his office, but he wished to give her the impression that he was not curious about her.

She took from her shoulderbag a small green box and put it on the table. She raised the screen, punched a button, and inserted the tip of the star on the ID disc into the box. He read the display, which showed on both sides of the screen, looked at her photo on the screen, and said, 'OK. So you're who you say you are.'

'I've been authorized to track down a daybreaker. A citizen of Monday and of Manhattan, Yankev Gad Gril. A doctor of philosophy who teaches at Yeshiva University, an Orthodox Hebrew, a chessmaster, and a specialist in the works of a first-century AD Gnostic Christian called Cerinthus.'

For a moment, he thought about denying any knowledge. Her statement had been so far from what he had expected, though he really did not know what to expect, that it had numbed him.

'*Gril!*' he said. 'Oh, now I see why you want to talk to me! I play chess with him. But my contact has been limited, of course. I don't know what he looks like, and we've never spoken to each other. Intertemporal chess competition has very strict rules.'

She nodded. 'I know. However, Gril is now in Wednesday, or at least we think he is. He's a passionate chessplayer, a fanatic . . .'

'And a great one, too,' Caird said.

'. . . and he may continue his games with you. I don't think he'd be stupid enough to do that, but his passion for it may override his good sense. He might believe that he could transmit his next move to you from a public strip and then get away quickly. I said "might," but, actually, he has a good chance of eluding the organics here. If we don't get an immediate report, we can't get a satellite fix on him.'

'You want me to report to you or the organics the moment I get his transmission? If I do?'

'Report to me. It may do no good because Gril can set up a delay in transmission and be long gone by the time you get it. But report anyway. Oh, by the way, you haven't already gotten one from him, have you?'

A trick question. No doubt, she had had Bob Tingle's calls checked.

'No, I haven't,' he said.

Unless he was under surveillance, any calls would not have been recorded in the communications base. If he had received a picture of the chess board with Gril's next move on it, he would have asked that it be stored until Gril could ask for it. Under normal conditions, Tingle's next move would then be transmitted to Gril when next Monday came. If Gril had sent his next move to Tingle, it would be stored in Wednesday's data bank and also at the Manhattan World Data Bank.

Snick would have checked on this. She also would have asked Wednesday's organic data monitors to notify her the moment that Gril made his move. Why, then, require him to report on Gril?

Was she really after something else? Was Gril just an excuse to cover up another interest, the driving interest, in his activities?

He wished now that he had confined his chessgames with Gril to just one of his roles. As it was, every day, in each persona, he had played a game with Gril. Tomorrow, Snick would follow the Gril line to Jim Dunski. She would know then that Bob Tingle and Jim Dunski were the same. Perhaps she already knew that Jeff Caird and Bob Tingle were the same.

No, that surely could not be. She would have arrested him and by now would be grilling him in the closet interrogation room. Perhaps she really was just looking for Gril.

Why, then, had a Sunday organic been chosen to track down a Monday daybreaker?

Whatever her reasons, she must not see him in Thursday. Actually, she did not have to see him in the flesh. One look at Jim Dunski's face on a data screen would be enough.

'I'm not being too curious, I hope,' he said. 'I wonder why you were sent after Gril. Why is his case so unusual? From what I've heard, daybreakers are handled by the organics of each day. I never heard of an organic using a temporal visa to go after one.'

'We have our reasons.'

'Oh, I see. None of my business.'

'My call number is a special one. X-X. Easy to remember. If Gril's game appears, you will call me at once? No delay?'

'Of course. X-X.' He grinned. 'It'll be easy. A double cross.'

Her face was blank. Either she did not get the reference or she was cool enough to ignore it.

He laughed and said, 'Yankev Gril, heh? Do you know what Yankev and Gril mean in Yiddish?'

'No. Should I?'

'Yankev is James, which could be Jimmy. Gril means Cricket. Which means that you're looking for Jimmy Cricket.'

'I suppose so,' she said. 'But I don't see anything amusing or relevant in it. Am I missing something?'

She looked at her watch, and she rose. He stood up, too.

'Just some fun, something to make life a little easier. Puns are a lubricant.'

'I think they're stupid,' Snick said. 'But they're not against the law, though if . . .'

'You had your way, they would be.'

'That's antisocial thinking. No, I wasn't going to say that.'

Whatever she was going to say stayed unsaid. She walked swiftly away without a good-bye, but she did turn her head and say, 'I may see you again, Maha Tingle.'

'Hope not,' he muttered. But he sighed. Snick was one of the prettiest women he had ever seen, a seal-fairy, but she did not stir admiration and lust in him. She scared him.

He went down the hall, inserted the ID tip into the hole in the door, and entered as it swung back. The first-shift data banker was already gone. The office was dome-shaped, twenty feet in diameter across the floor, and walled with strips from the floor to the centre of the ceiling. In the middle was a chair around which was a circular desk. A small control box sat on the desk. He lifted the flap in the desk and went within the 'charmed circle.' After putting the flap down, he sat in the chair. It could rotate so that he could see every strip, and it could be tilted back so he could read the upper displays comfortably.

He punched in a code known only to himself. The strips glowed with the data and photographs that had been on when he had quit work last Wednesday. Reluctant to put aside a project he loved, he scanned the strips for a few minutes. This was an unofficial job ordered unofficially by Paz, who had gotten his orders from his superior. Tingle was not supposed to know who Paz's chief was. But he had found out through an unofficial investigation of which Paz was unaware.

One of Tingle's characteristics was a dangerous curiosity, sometimes bordering on the reckless. The immer council would have been alarmed if it had known about it. But it had verified the stability of Jeff Caird's character, and it had not thought of the possibility that Bob Tingle was not the same person as Jeff Caird. Caird, in programming Tingle's character, had indulged himself. Yet he knew that he could not have developed certain Tingle traits if these had not existed in embryo in Caird, sternly suppressed though not aborted.

The first stage of the project was to get statistics on the number of people 'semi-permanently' stoned and put in storage for the last one hundred subyears. These had been dying of incurable physical diseases or had mental diseases not responding to therapy or were habitual criminals who could not be 'cured.' When science found the method for restoring these people to health, they would be destoned.

That was the theory. The government had issued figures about the numbers of 'abeyants,' as they were called. Paz had asked Tingle to find out if the Wednesday world government was lying. Official statistics said that 46,947,269 people had been put into abeyance as of when Tingle had started the project. Tingle, after four subyears of discreet inquiry via many channels, had found that the real number was 86,927,326. This, of course, was only those who had been semipermanentized (government jargon) in Wednesday. Tingle and Paz assumed that the other dayworlds were doing much the same and that there were approximately 609,000,000 semipermanents.

Paz had then asked Tingle to determine if any successful therapies to treat the abeyants had been developed during the past twenty subyears. This task was easier than the first. Tingle had discovered that enough various 'cures' or therapies had been published and put into practice to permit destoning at least 30,000,000 of Wednesday's abeyants. By extrapolation, 210,000,000 of the entire population.

Not one of Wednesday's 30,000,000 possibles had been destoned so that the new techniques and therapies could be used on them. Nor had any public proposals been made to do so.

'In the first place,' Tingle had said to Paz, 'it would take, at the rate of a million cured per subyear, if that could be done, thirty subyears to restore them. Meanwhile, at least 40,000 are piling up, literally, in storage. The backlog of approximately 87,000,000 will be untouched.

'There's no need to look for sinister motives in the government's neglect. It just made a promise that it can't keep. I'm sure that others have discovered what I did, but their reports have been suppressed.'

'Then all those millions might as well have died,' Paz had said.

'Not necessarily. Maybe . . . someday . . . we'll have the number of medical personnel and the system and the funds necessary to fulfil that promise.'

'Sure,' Paz had said. He had looked down at his belly and pinched the lowest of his three chins. 'And someday everybody will eat only the amount they need.'

Tingle had thought that, if all the world's abeyants were to be cured, their overwhelming numbers would be such a problem that an eighth day would have to be added to the week.

'Why do you want this information?' Tingle had said.

'Perhaps we immers can use that as a weapon someday.'

'Blackmail? Extortion? Threat?'

Paz had replied with a grin.

Now, in the last stage of the project, Tingle was 'ghosting' into biographical data records and the conversations of some high officials in both the Manhattan and the world government. A device that had been made, he supposed, in the secret laboratory of the immers enabled him to unscramble the dialogues. At first, he had been pleased with the device. Then he realized that what the immers could do, the government secret scientists could do. Which meant that the immer scramblers could be unscrambled any day now or might be right now.

He had passed the word on up via his superior, and that had resulted in the immers changing their scrambler format every few weeks.

Tingle had asked Paz about the motive behind his eavesdropping. Paz had said that Tingle had no need to know. Tingle's theory, kept to himself, was that the immer council meant to use the information as future protection for itself. Or, perhaps, it was using it now to pressure these officials for its own obscure but doubtless worthy reasons.

During his 'ghosting,' Tingle had selected and stored certain data. If he should need protection for himself, he would not be above using it.

Thinking of this, he was touched by a 'ghost' of the thought that he, Tingle, would not hesitate to use blackmail if he had to. But Caird, his Tuesday client, would have considered that dishonourable.

Looking at the strips, he was reminded that he was supposed to get coercion data for Nokomis' use. That could not be done today, which meant that she was going to be angry with him. He sighed. Snick was his number-one priority. If he had time, he could tackle the Castor problem.

He muttered, 'Castor should have been put in abeyance as soon as possible. Then we wouldn't be having this crisis.'

The immer council must have been aware of what needed doing. But the legal procedure for stoning Castor as an incurable required that he be thoroughly questioned. He might not have revealed his immer identity to the authorities, especially if he had insisted that he was God. The immer council, however, could not take that chance. It had had to keep him alive as a possibly curable mental patient.

Tingle sighed again and, whistling softly the tune of 'The Criminal Creed,' Ko-Ko's song in Gilbert and Sullivan's *The Mikado*, started work on Project Snick. The strip displays were replaced by the codes needed to break into the Sunday organic files. These were provided by an immer data bank not to be used except in extreme emergencies. Which this was. Tingle, however, had to wield them carefully, since it was possible that a security system other than the one he knew was now being used by the Sunday data bankers.

Sunday's people were all stoned – except for Snick, of course – but when they awoke on their appointed day, they would know that someone had tried to ghost into the bank. If, that is, Tingle's requests for data tripped the alarm. If this happened, he would have to cover his own electronic tracks. He might even have to wipe out the immer data bank to keep the organics from tracing it to the source.

Within fifteen minutes, Tingle had gotten from six different sources all the available biographical data re Panthea Pao Snick. After two hours of trying every safe approach and every relevant circuit, he gave up trying to get her official orders for her mission. Either they were inaccessible or she had gotten them verbally.

At least, he knew all her weaknesses. That is, all that had been recorded. From his own experience, however, he knew that she could have withheld some of them from the government psychicists. He was just going to start his inquiries into Castor when all the operating strips flashed red and the data displays faded. Startled, he spoke into the strip connected with the door. His heart was beating fast, telling him that he was not as calm as he wanted to be. He was more distressed than he had admitted to himself.

'It's me,' Paz's voice said.

The security system was set up to warn Tingle and to turn off the displays if anyone tried to talk to him through the strips or inserted a lock-tip into the door hole.

Tingle pressed a button. The door swung open. Though he knew that Paz would have warned him if he had a companion, he swung around on the chair to make sure. Paz strode in; the door swung shut.

Tingle opened his mouth to tell his chief that he had not taken as much time with Snick as he had expected. The paleness and grimness of Paz's face cut off his intention. He said, 'What's the matter?'

'The news on the organic channel! Somebody's been killed in the house next to your apartment building! I don't know, of course. It may be just a coincidence, but Castor . . .'

Tingle had risen to greet Paz. Suddenly feeling woozy, he sat back down.

Paz said, 'Hey, what's the matter?'

In that moment, Tingle had become a little less Tingle and a little more of Caird.

'Who's been killed?'

'Hell, I don't know!' Paz said loudly. 'They were just bringing out the body. I thought since you live next door . . . and Castor . . . maybe he was found there and he got killed. Or he killed someone in the house by mistake.'

Paz did not know that Caird lived next door to Tingle. It was not necessary that he have that information.

'I think . . .' Tingle said.

Paz said, 'Yes?' He looked expectantly at Tingle.

Tingle made a dismissing notion with his hand.

'Never mind. Turn the channel on. We'll wait and see. This may have nothing to do with us. There are a dozen explanations . . .'

Paz breathed in deeply several times. 'Yes. I probably jumped the gun, got spooked. It's just a coincidence. But if Castor was cornered there and killed, that's all to the good.'

The strip showed blue-uniformed organics on the sidewalk and in the street holding back the curious. Three news crews were shooting the scene. There were several patrol cars and an ambulance from the coroner's office parked near the curb. Two men were guiding a cart down the steps, its wheels moving up and down to adjust to the steps. On top of the cart, strapped down, was a green bodybag – filled.

The face of Channel 87's on-the-spot reporter, Robert Amanullah, appeared on the screen. He said, 'We've just talked to Maha Aditi Rotwa via . . .'

The strip went blank.

12

'Organic cutoff,' Paz said. 'What're they suppressing?'

Whatever the reason, other cameras were still operating. Paz ordered two other channels on, and these showed the scene from different angles. After a thirty-second delay, Channel 87 came back on. Amanullah was talking again but not saying a word about the identity of the body. This was put into the ambulance, which moved away slowly through the crowd. Once beyond the onlookers, the ambulance picked up speed but did not turn on its lights and siren. There was no hurry.

From what reporters said, someone had been murdered in the house. No details were known as yet. When the reporters got the story from the organics, they would broadcast it. Meanwhile . . . two of the cameras shifted to the East Side and other reporters took over the on-the-spot news there. Channel 87 continued its coverage, probably because Amanullah was angry at being censored.

'It's a clampdown,' Paz said. 'It may be hours before we find out.'

'Or never.'

Tingle rose unsteadily, walked to a wall and activated a strip. He asked a few questions, listened, then turned to Paz.

'You heard?'

'Yes, Rotwa lives in the house . . .'

'I . . .'

Tingle stopped. He had almost told Paz that he knew Rotwa. Or, at least, had seen her face many times through her cylinder window in the basement of that house.

The corpse could be Castor's. Or it could be Ozma's. It

could not be one of the two Wednesday occupants because the woman was still alive. If she had murdered her husband, she would have been hustled out long ago, stoned to prevent an escape attempt.

There was a code that Tingle could use to ghost into the organic records. This, however, was to be used only in red-emergency situations. Wasn't this one?

'We have to find out if the body was Castor's,' he said.

Paz frowned, thought a minute, then said, 'If he's dead, there's no hurry. We'll find out eventually.'

'I doubt that it was Castor,' Tingle said. He smiled weakly. 'Can God be killed?'

Paz stared hard at him, then said, 'You're a nice guy and a good man, Bob. But you are annoyingly facetious.'

'Facetious, right? Sorry.'

'There's her husband, coming home,' Paz said. He pointed at a strip. 'At least, I think it's him.'

Tingle recognized the man but could not tell Paz that he was right. Or should he? Wasn't it about time to reveal to Paz that he lived on Tuesday in that house? If he didn't, he could not tell Paz that he was in a painful mental squeeze because Ozma might have been killed by Castor. On the other hand, perhaps Paz should know about it. He could alert his superiors that Castor was on Tingle's trail and so was a danger to all immers.

He scanned the screens. None of the faces in the crowd was Castor's. That madman might have been tempted to hang about the scene of the crime so that he could see the body being brought out and thrill with excitement. But Castor was too canny for that. He would be long gone.

There was a writhing, a moving thing that hurt in Tingle's chest. He knew that the little animal of pain gnawing in his breast was the grief that Caird felt. As Caird's agent, however, he could feel or would only allow himself to feel the lessened grief that he, Tingle, would experience at the murder of the wife of a client.

That was what Tingle told himself. Actually, the pain was sharper than that, so much so that he was afraid that it might break through. Should that happen, he would revert, partly at least, to Caird. He could not let that occur.

He told himself, Really, I don't know that Ozma is dead.

Nevertheless, he knew.

'Well?' Paz said.

'I'm sorry,' Tingle said. 'I was thinking.'

'Does thinking hurt that much?'

Tingle forced a smile.

'Only when I laugh. Forgive me, chief. I was thinking that we have to find Castor, get there fust with the mostest as the great Bedford Forrester once said.'

'Forester? What's a ranger . . .?'

'It's an historical allusion begat by hysteria, I'm afraid. Forget it, chief. I've got all the data I could get on Snick, and I still don't know if she's really after Gril or her story's a cover-up and she's after me. I . . . we . . . will have to handle her with improvisations. I'm sure the council has taken action to deal with her. So we won't be without help.

'What's important just now is Castor. I'll go to work on him, but I don't think the bank is going to help me. Action is what we want, not data. You let me think about this for a while. If I come up with something good, I'll leave work. You can arrange an excuse, but you'd better tell me what it is before I leave.'

'That's no sweat,' Paz said, perspiration sliding down his face. He walked out, saying over his shoulder, 'Check in with me before you go, if you go.'

'Of course.'

He leaned back in the chair, eyes closed. Two minutes later, he got a call from Nokomis.

'Have you got anything for me?'

'Nothing yet, my dear. I'm swamped with urgent work.

I really don't know when I can get to the you-know-what.'

She frowned and said, 'I need the you-know-what as soon as possible. Otherwise, my God!'

She rolled her large brown eyes and grimaced.

'If it can be done, it will,' he said.

She told him that their seven o'clock dinner date would have to be changed to eight. The producer and the choreographer had gotten into a shouting contest, which had become a slapping match until they were pulled apart. Roger Shenachi, the star ballerino, had overdosed himself with a laxative and now, when he landed from a grand jeté, he became a pathetic, if laughable, spectacle as he ran off the stage.

At another time, Tingle would have been amused by all this. He told Nokomis that he had to go, and he said good-bye. Tragedy and danger were stalking him, yet he was supposed to cluck-cluck over her trivia. He knew her well enough, however, to know that if he did not get her what she wanted he would have to endure not-so-mild reproaches.

A half-hour later, after pacing back and forth in the office, he gave up on all the plans he could think of for finding Castor. What he needed was something to take his mind off the problem for a little while. Then he could attack it with a fresh attitude.

He left the office, went to the urinal, and then went into Paz's office. Paz had a huge lunch, including a large steak, spread out on the desk before him. He looked at Tingle as if daring him to comment. Tingle looked away from the food and said, 'I'm going out now. No, I don't have anything good for you. I need to exercise my body, not my mind. I'm going to the fencing gymnasium for a half-hour or so.'

'You wouldn't be doing it if you didn't need it,' Paz said. 'Very well. Only I hope you come up with something soon.'

'I like to overtake events, not have events overtake me,' Tingle said. 'But I'm afraid that just might happen. Then . . . I'll have to improvise like hell.'

'One has to be a good improviser,' Paz said through a mouthful of steak. 'But it's better not to have to. Call me every half-hour.'

Paz did not look worried; he looked guilty. Tingle bowed to him and left, thinking that his chief was too sensitive about his meat-eating. He, Tingle, did not care what Paz ate, though he wished he would not eat so much. Any day now, Paz's superior would have to ignore whatever influence Paz had used to pressure him, and she would force him to go on a diet. If that failed, he would be examined for metabolic dysfunctions and either treated electrochemically or sent to a 'fat farm.'

Tingle went on the elevator to the twentieth floor, walked down a corridor, and entered the anteroom of the fencing gymnasium. After warming up for ten minutes, he engaged in two matches with a woman and a man, neither of whom were immers or data bankers. He won both, which pleased him. But, during his shower, he began thinking again about Castor. Conclusion: Since the madman knew where he, as Caird, lived, he might also know where he, as Tingle, lived. The probability was strengthened because Tingle lived next door to Caird. Castor might have seen him coming out of the apartment building.

Since there was nothing else to do, Tingle decided to be a decoy. Though he might be wasting his time, whatever he did could be a time-waster. Castor, however, was a fanatic. Hence, he was not one to burn time as if it were incense. He would be doing whatever he could to get Tingle unless he had some crazed plan that involved mentally torturing his chief prey. Who knew what evil lurks in the hearts of men? The Shadow was not the only one; God also knew. Actually, God was The Real Shadow.

'But,' Tingle muttered, 'Castor is not really God.'

He went down to the Fifth Avenue exit, stepped out into the heat and hailed a cab. After getting in and telling the driver where to go, he inserted the tip of his ID star into the machine mounted on the back of the front seat. The driver scarcely glanced at the ID verification and credit rating displayed on the front panel. She had never been ripped off and did not expect to be.

Tingle watched a news strip on the back of the front seat. The murder at Bleecker Street was not mentioned. It was evident that the government's hand was over the mouth of the media. There would be nothing more on the news about the event unless the government decided on a cover-up story. So . . . Ozma *had* been killed, and today's authorities had decided that the public would not know about her. It might panic at the idea that another day's citizen could be destoned and killed.

He shivered with cold at the vision of what might have been done, surely was done, to her by Castor. That was Tingle's reaction, however. If he were wholly Caird, he would have vomited.

There was no point in trying to elude Snick. That would make her even more suspicious – if she suspected him. If she were not suspicious of him, she would be made so by his unroutine behaviour. He would just go to his apartment and wait for Castor. Or perhaps wander around the neighbourhood.

The cab turned east from Fifth Avenue onto Washington Square North. Tingle, sitting on the right side, looked out across Washington Square. He said loudly, 'Stop!'

Startled, the driver said, 'Huh!' She pulled over to the curb through the bicyclers. She turned around and said, 'Changed your mind?'

'We'll get going in a minute.'

Thirty feet south of the sidewalk was a large oak tree.

Under its shade were some tables and chairs, all occupied by chessplayers. One of the intent gamers was a stocky man in a black robe. His profile was aquiline, his eyebrows were enormously thick, and his red beard was long and uncut. On top of his red hair was a little black round cap called, if Tingle remembered correctly, a yarmulke.

'Gril!' Tingle said. Or was it Caird speaking?

For a minute, Tingle watched him. Gril seemed so unlike a fugitive from the law. If he was tensing for the inevitable hand on his shoulder, listening for the heavy footsteps, watching out of the corners of his eyes for the approaching shadows, he did not show it. Chess seemed to be his only concern. He watched the pieces as intently and motionlessly as a praying mantis who had just seen a caterpillar.

Tingle was surprised that Gril had escaped arrest. And then he realized why the man had been free so long. The organics would be looking for someone like Gril but not too much like him. They would assume that Gril had shaved his beard, abandoned his yarmulke, stained his face darker and put on contact lenses of a colour other than green. But crafty Gril had remained an obvious Orthodox Hebrew. His disguise was himself.

'I'll just walk from here,' Tingle said. He stuck the ID point into the hole so that he would have a record of the mileage to compare with that of the cab. If someone was tracking him, and that person questioned him later about his stopping there, Tingle would say that he had gotten out for exercise. That was the only excuse he could think of for leaving the cab. No, it was not. A chess enthusiast, he wanted to watch the players for a while. After all, he had played in Washington Square many times before. Some of Manhattan's best were there.

Tingle strolled up to a table near Gril's and watched for a while. After stopping at another table, he went to his real destination. He felt a little strange looking into Gril's small green eyes. He was not recognized, yet he knew Gril well.

Fairly well, anyway.

He could not keep from glancing up through the branches. A sky-eye, if it was watching him, could not see him or Gril now.

After a minute, during which neither player moved his pieces, Tingle walked away. He had no reason to speak to Gril. The impulse to warn him had sped away, as it should. What was Gril to him, today, at least?

He walked slowly through the shouting and screaming children at play, the mimes, the carts with nuts, fruit, and vegetables for sale, the vendors with their overhead cargo of brightly coloured balloons, the blaring soapbox orators baring their singularly singed psyches, the tumblers and acrobats, the magicians plucking rabbits and roses from the air, the unkempt and foul-mouthed barbs (Wednesday's minnies), and the always-there plainclothes organics. The latter had the indefinable but obvious – to him – expression they wore when among civilians.

Seeing them made him suddenly aware of the weight of the weapon in his shoulderbag. If he were stopped for some reason and searched . . . He shuddered. It was not wise to carry the gun with him. Yet he had to because he might find Castor.

Thinking of Castor seemed to conjure him.

Tingle faltered in his stride.

First, Gril. Now, yes, there was no doubt about it.

Castor was walking along fifty feet ahead of him on his right on a path that would meet his.

He renewed his former pace. And he faltered again.

To his left, about seventy feet ahead, also on a collision course, was a woman wearing a brown jockey cap and a brown robe decorated with green looped crosses. Her shoes were bright green.

Snick.

13

All things throughout the universe are connected, but things similar are more closely connected than others.

Tingle, Gril, Castor, and Snick were more or less tightly bound together by the unlawful acts of three of them. And here they were, pulled together in Washington Square by what might be called the law of criminal gravity. They were like planets attracted by forces that, in this case, defied the statistics of probability. All, except Gril, falling towards a common centre.

However, human beings were not unconscious forms of matter like planets. They could decide to leave their orbits.

Castor was the first to do so. Looking to his left, he saw Tingle. His eyes widened; his pace was checked. And then he ran. God does not run; He is all-powerful and fears nothing. Just now, however, He fled like a human, not like one who could float or fly or make Himself invisible or zap His enemy with lightning or a quick case of the creeping crud.

His flight was a break for Tingle. Snick had turned to watch the tall thin Castor, a bipedal gazelle running as if a cheetah were after him. Knowing that Snick would turn to see who was chasing Castor, Tingle stepped behind an oak tree. While pretending to be relaxed, a loafer leaning against the trunk, he watched the plainclothes organics. Some of them had seen Castor, but they apparently thought that he was a jogger. Gril was still at the table.

The expected shrilling from Snick's whistle did not come. The plainclothes kept their indifferent but subtly watchful attitudes. Unable to curb his curiosity any longer, Tingle peeked around the tree. Castor had vanished around one of the block buildings on West Fourth Street, south of the square. Snick had her back to Tingle, her hands on her hips, her head slightly cocked. He could visualize her look of puzzlement. Why in hell hadn't she had the conditioned reflex of all organics and pursued the man? Perhaps it was because she was on a mission and she was not going to deviate from it. The running man was no concern of hers.

He groaned. Wrong again. Snick had started trotting south on Thompson Street. Presently, she turned right on West Third Street and was hidden by the building there. She *was* following Castor.

Tingle bit his lip, looked at Gril, who was still playing chess, and stepped out from the shade of the oak. The sun wrapped a smotheringly hot blanket around him, but he felt cold inside himself. What to do? He did not want to run into Snick because he did not want to be associated in her mind with Castor. In any event, he could account for his being here. His apartment building was only a few blocks away.

He did not run, though he walked swiftly. If the organics in the square saw three people, one after the other, start running, they might be curious enough to investigate. On reaching the corner of the building at which Snick had turned on Thompson Street and West Third, he went around it, too. Neither the chased nor the chaser was in sight. When he got to Sullivan Street, he saw Snick, her back to him, going around the building on Bleecker Street. Since there was no one else on the street, he ran after her.

Before getting to Bleecker Street, he slowed down. When he got to the corner building, he stopped and peered around it. Snick, now trotting, was just rounding the corner at MacDougal Street. Evidently, Castor had gone north. Tingle ran west on Bleecker and stopped at MacDougal. He stuck his head around the corner until

Snick had turned left onto Minetta Lane. Meanwhile, he was hoping that none of the neighbours would notice him and his curiosity-arousing behaviour.

Reaching Minetta Lane, he paused long enough to make sure that Snick was not in sight. He went west until he came to the house at the end of the block. Tingle hid behind a tree, his head out far enough from the trunk for one eye to see Snick. She was still trotting, her robe sticking to her back with sweat, on the canal road. He waited until she had gone around Jeff Caird's house on Bleecker before he stepped out from the tree.

Tingle ran. The fishers, pedestrians, and bicyclists on the canal road stared at him. They must have thought he was crazy to run in this heat; they were crazy just to be out in it. Panting, sweat stinging his eyes, he stopped at the corner. Not seeing Snick, he stepped out from the fence onto the sidewalk. There she was. Entering the front of his apartment building. Castor must have gone into it. The main front and back entrances were usually left unlocked during the day. Castor had had no more trouble getting in than Snick was having.

Tingle could not believe that it was just coincidence that the man had gone into that building.

Paz had told him to call every half-hour. He was fifteen minutes late. No time to call now. But, as he started walking, he heard the shrilling from his wristwatch. He turned it off and held it close to his mouth. 'Hello.' Then he held the watch close to his ear.

Paz's voice said, 'I was worried. You didn't . . .'

'I know. Call in.'

He sketched what had happened and told Paz that he was going to follow the two into the building.

'Do you think that's wise?'

'Just now, I don't know what's wise.'

'I can get two men down there fast and have them take care of Castor,' Paz said. 'You wait outside to make sure that he doesn't leave.'

'He may be going out the back door,' Tingle said. He was running as he talked and was now alongside the building. 'I'm headed that way now.'

He stopped at the corner and looked around it. Castor was not there, which meant that he was still inside the building or that he had run out of the back and out of sight. Tingle did not think that Castor had had time to do that. Moreover, he did not believe that Castor would go out into the open again. He would be waiting for Snick.

While Tingle went up the steps to the back porch, he called Paz and told him the situation.

'I have to go in. I don't want Snick to get hurt.'

'Why not? She could be as dangerous as Castor. Let him take care of her, then we'll get him.'

'We don't know that she's after me,' Tingle said. 'Anyway . . .'

There was a pause.

'Anyway what?' Paz said sharply.

'If people . . . if there are witnesses . . . then the organics will be there almost immediately. We don't want that, right?'

'Are there people around?'

'No one at the moment,' Tingle said.

'I think it's best you get out of there. Let my people handle this.'

'Is that an order?'

Paz coughed and then said, 'No. I'm not there. I don't know exactly . . . I'm not on the spot. You have good judgement, Bob. You go ahead, do what you think the situation demands.'

'Doing,' Tingle said. 'I'm going in. Call you later.'

'Yes, but –'

Tingle had turned off the transmitter.

He pulled out his blouse, opened his shoulderbag, took the weapon from the bag, and stuck it into his belt. The bottom of the blouse covered the gun. He walked swiftly but softly down the hall to the wide curving steps leading to the second floor. The huge recreation room was empty, and no sounds from outside or inside reached him. The sweat was drying off his face under the coldness of the air-conditioning, but it seemed to be pouring out from his armpits. He stopped at the foot of the staircase and took his gun from the belt. It was heavy, weighing four pounds, and shaped like an archaic automatic pistol. In addition to the firing button, it bore two dials, one on each side just above the grip. He set its left-hand dial for a tight and narrow beam and the right-hand one for full power for the charged particles.

He started up the stairs slowly, listening intently for any sound from above. Before he got to the top step, he crouched down. He raised his head quickly above the last riser but only far enough so that his eyes were level with the floor of the hall. He held the gun barrel up, its tip just by the lobe of his left ear.

The hall was empty.

He could wait outside the door of 2E until Snick or Castor came out. He did not know that either was in there, but he assumed that they were. He could be wrong. Castor might have fled to a higher floor or he might have gone down the back stairs and on out. Neither seemed likely, or perhaps he wanted Castor to be in his apartment with no way out. Whatever had happened, he had to check out his apartment.

He stopped before his door and bent his knees so that he could look into the insertion hole. He saw nothing except darkness, which meant that Castor had not used his weapon to drill a hole through the code device inside the door. He straightened up and inserted in the hole that tip of his disc-star which would transmit the entry code. He waited a few seconds, then pushed in on the door. It swung easily and noiselessly, stopping short of the inner wall by a foot. The anteroom and the hall beyond were empty.

After going inside, he used the knob on the inside of the door to shut it quietly. He did not want anyone coming through behind him. During the next four minutes, he passed through every room swiftly but quietly, opened closet doors, and even looked under the bed, though he felt foolish doing so.

Then he walked along the stoner cylinders, pausing at each to look carefully at the faces behind the windows. None was Castor's or Snick's. That left the two empties, his and his wife's. He had not gone close enough to look down to find out if anyone was crouching below the windows. He had, however, kept glancing at the cylinders behind him while checking out the others.

No one was in the rooms or on the balcony. Anybody here had to be in the two Wednesday cylinders. If each was occupied, then one person was probably a corpse.

Crouching down so that he would not be seen if Castor dared a peek through the window, Tingle went to the nearest cylinder. Pointing the gun with one hand, he reached out with the other and swiftly pulled the door open. The cylinder was empty. Which meant that the other stoner should also be empty. Unless there were two persons in there and one was dead.

He repeated the procedure and sighed with a mixture of relief and puzzlement. No one there either. Where were they? He was almost certain that they had not left the building.

Frowning, he went out onto the balcony and scanned the neighbourhood. Snick and Castor were not in sight. For a moment, he thought of telling Paz what had happened, but he rejected that. What good would it do? His chief could not help him, and he might order him out of the building or tell him to stay in the apartment. The only thing for him to do was to search the places available to him.

He walked to the hall and started down it to search the other rooms. At its far end was the entrance door. It was luck that allowed him to escape the beam that evaporated the code-lock device and shot straight down the hall. The glowing white rod-shape almost touched his left shoulder. A second later, the door swung violently inwards.

Tingle did not share all the same reflexes with Caird. He had slowly built up his own characteristics to correspond with his role. Thus, he stood frozen for a second longer than Caird would have done. Caird would have instantly thrown himself down on the floor, his gun held out pointing at the door even while falling. Tingle did recover in time to press the firing button even though he did not know who was coming through the door.

14

Castor screamed, dropped his weapon, clutched his left upper arm, and was gone. Tingle raced after him and into the hall. The odour of burned flesh and plastic wrapped itself around him. Castor's head was just disappearing down the back stairs as Tingle came through the door. Tingle ran after him, but, by the time he got to the porch, he had lost Castor. He was tempted to run out and circle the building. The madman might be hiding around the corner or behind a bush or tree in the yard. It might take just a minute to catch and kill him. But what if someone saw him shooting a man? The organics would be here in sixty seconds. And if he searched the neighbourhood, he might be caught because someone had seen the wounded Castor and called the organics.

Castor was not going to get far before he attracted attention and was caught or pursued. Tingle did not want to be anywhere near Castor when that happened.

It was possible, however, that Castor had a place nearby into which he could dive like a rat into a hole. Such as, for instance, the tall yellow access tube on the corner of the little park near the canal. This was an entrance to the underground goods-transportation system. If he had gotten down there, he was long gone.

He waited until his hard breathing had softened before he spoke Paz's codecall into the watch. Paz answered at once. Tingle told him what had happened; Paz cursed. When he was finished with his blasphemies and invective, which included a dozen Hindustani loanwords, he said, 'My agents are in your area now. I'll tell them about this, and I'll send some more. We have to find Castor *now*!'

'Tell me something I don't know,' Tingle muttered. More loudly, he said, 'I'm going to look for Snick. I have an idea where she might be. Call you later.'

By law, at least one building in every block had to have four extra stoners. These were mostly used for emergencies such as immediately stoning people who had been injured in the neighbourhood streets or for the use of organics who had just made an arrest. Stoning a suspected criminal was a far superior restraining method to handcuffing.

Tingle went to the basement door, nodding at a couple who had just come down the staircase. Fortunately, he had put the gun back under the blouse. Even so, they looked suspiciously at him, though that might be his excited imagination. He walked down the steps into another recreation room. A TV strip was shedding its ghostly light; someone had forgotten to turn it off. Whoever had done it was going to be reprimanded and perhaps fined, if the culprit could be identified. Tingle turned it off.

The emergency cylinders stood in a corner of the utility room. Tingle went by them to a wall panel marked EMER CYL PWR and slid it into the recess. The number-three button was glowing. Tingle punched it, and the light went out. He went to the cylinder marked NO. 3 and opened the door. Snick was slumped down in it, her head against her drawn-up knees. She was grey-blue and hard and cold as metal to the touch. A bruise on her forehead indicated that Castor had knocked her senseless. Or perhaps he had killed her. In any event, he had not had time to mutilate her, if he meant to, as he had Doctor Atlas.

Tingle shut the cylinder door, returned to the control panel, punched the number-three button, and then turned the PWR rheostat to ON. A second later, the rheostat automatically returned to the OFF position. He went to the cylinder, swung the door open, bent down, and put a finger on her jugular. It was pulsing feebly. Good! Or was it good? Alive, she was a danger, though not if she could be hidden away someplace.

After stoning her again, he stood thinking for a moment, then called Paz over his wristwatch. The tiny scrambler in the watch would make the transmission unintelligible to anyone listening in except Paz. The government had the right to tap into any transmission; it had also given its citizens the right to use scramblers, providing them with the illusion of freedom. Put a leash on the dog but make it happy by making the leash a long one.

He told Paz just what had happened.

Paz said, 'I'll send two agents to get her out of the house.'

He said, 'I have to know where she's being taken.'

Paz said sharply, 'Why is that?'

'I have to question her, find out what she's up to. I won't feel safe until I do so. Not about *her*, I mean. Castor's another matter.'

'We'll take care of that.'

'I don't like working in the dark,' Tingle said. 'Anyway, you really need me for the interrogation.'

Paz sighed. After a pause, he said, 'Very well. As soon as the situation's stable, I'll notify you.'

He sounded as if his mouth was full of food. He had probably stuffed it as soon as he realized that Tingle was going to argue about his orders.

After being told to stay in his apartment until he heard from Paz, Tingle went upstairs. He called the Department of Repairs and Plumbing and ordered a new code-lock installed. He was told that that could not be done until tomorrow. That is, next Wednesday. Tingle cancelled the order. He called Paz, who was beginning to sound cross and harassed. Paz said that he would send someone to install a new lock within the hour. It was not wise to bring DORAP in. It might investigate the matter, and how could he explain the damage? The corpspersons would realize that only a charged-particle weapon could have burned through the lock. Tingle said that he knew that, but most corpspeople he had met were not inquisitive about the cause of the damage. They were required by law to record the cause, but that was usually as far as the matter went. Unless some high official got nosey.

'This is getting worse and worse,' Paz said. 'I hope you don't have any more difficulties.'

'I don't make them,' Tingle said, and he cut Paz off. Paz was beginning to sound as if he were at the cracking point or perilously close. Perhaps the immer council should be told to watch Paz closely for signs of emotional instability. The trouble with that was that he would have to send the suggestion through Paz. No. He could do that through his Thursday superior, who would see to it that Thursday's council got word. It would then transmit the suggestion to Wednesday's. But that council would not know about it until it was destoned on Wednesday.

Tingle shrugged. He was not so calm and relaxed and in control of himself. Who was he to throw stones at Paz?

He went into the bathroom and turned up the power on his watch so that he could hear it above the shower water. The bathroom door was locked, and his weapon lay on a rack to one side of the shower. Though he did not think that Castor would return, he was not going to be careless.

Then he heard a shrilling and saw orange flashing. He swore. The sound and light came, not from his watch, but from the strip on the wall opposite the shower cubicle. The soap slipped out of his hands. He started to pick it up, changed his mind, turned the water off, and pulled the shower door back. Who could it be? Nokomis? If she came home early for some reason, he would have a hard time getting away from her to call Paz.

He felt the soap under his foot, and he fell backwards.

When he awoke, he was in a hospital bed. Nokomis' broad but beautiful face hung above him.

'No, I'm not going to be careless,' he muttered.

Nokomis said, 'What did you say, dear?'

His mind felt jellied, though not so much that he could not understand her when she told him what had happened. She had been called from the stage during a crucial point in the rehearsal. But he was not to worry about it. He was far more important to her than her career. The producer and most of the cast were furious with her, but he was not to be disturbed by that. To hell with them. The hospital had called her, and she had rushed down in a taxi. And she was so happy that he had not been killed.

However, she was puzzled because, so the hospital said, it had gotten an anonymous call. The anonym had spoken through a strainer, which removed all possibility of identifying the caller by a voiceprint. After saying that Tingle was unconscious in his shower, the caller gave the address and turned off the strip. When the paramedics got to the apartment, they found the door unlocked – she said nothing about the lock mechanism – and Tingle was lying senseless in the shower. The whole thing was so strange.

By the time she was through, Nokomis looked more suspicious than concerned. Tingle said that all he knew was that he had slipped on a bar of soap.

The attendants brought up a machine and subjected him to various tests. After a while, a doctor came in and read the results. He told Tingle that he had no serious injury and that he could go home as soon as he felt strong enough. However, a few minutes later two organics came to question him. Tingle repeated what he had told Nokomis. They looked grave, and one said that he would see Tingle again next Wednesday.

After they had left, Tingle groaned. When Wednesday rolled around, he would be questioned again. If he did not have an explanation to satisfy the organics, and he probably would not, he would be given the ultimate inquisition. Truth mist would be sprayed at him, and, after he had breathed that, he could not lie. He would tell the organics all that they asked.

And he and the other immers would humpty-dumpty into utter ruin.

'One bad thing after another, each worse than the one before it!' he muttered.

'What, dear?' Nokomis said.

'Nothing important.'

Fortunately, Nokomis had to go to the toilet. While she was gone, he called Paz again, and Paz cursed again.

'Quit it!' Tingle said sharply. 'My wife'll be back in a minute! What happened to me?'

Paz settled down and rapped out an explanation. The agent who had come to repair the doorlock had found him in the shower. He had put the weapon in his own shoulderbag and had then called the hospital. Tingle quickly told Paz about the organics and the inevitable interrogation. Paz said, 'That can be avoided, I think. I'll pass on the message. What a mess!'

He paused, then said, his voice very low and soft, 'Bob, I've got even more bad news.'

Tingle said, 'Wait! I hear my wife!'

He listened for a few seconds, then said, 'Tell it quick. She's stopped in the hall to talk to somebody.'

'I got a recording,' Paz said. 'From yesterday. It said I should tell you that Ozma Wang *is* dead. I don't know what that means, but . . .'

'God!' Tingle said. Then, 'I think my wife's about to come in. I'll talk to you later.'

He cut off the transmission and put his arm down by his side. He felt something quiver inside him, a thing struggling to get loose and ravage him. It was, he knew, grief, but it was deep within him, far away. It had to be Jeff Caird's grief for the death of his wife.

Nokomis entered the room, stopped, and said, 'Were you talking to somebody?'

'No. Why?' he said. The thing that was struggling in

him was quieting down now.

'I saw your watch close to your mouth. You must . . .'

'No, I wasn't talking to anybody. I just happened to be wiping my mouth with the back of my hand. For God's sake, Nokomis! If people were classified grammatically, you'd be in the accusative case!'

She stiffened, glared, and said, 'You needn't be so touchy!'

'I'm sorry, dear. It must be the injury to my head.'

On the way home in a taxi, Nokomis said, 'The whole thing does look peculiar, doesn't it? What could we have that anyone else doesn't have? Is there somebody you haven't told me about, somebody who hates you and is crazy enough to revenge himself? Or . . . herself? You never told me about anyone who might hate you that much, but . . .'

Tingle told her that he needed silence until he felt better. Would she mind not talking? Any noise hurt his head. Nokomis stiffened and moved away from him. He was too upset to worry about offending her. His doubts and anxieties were whirling him around like Dorothy's house in the tornado. He had to talk to Paz again and find out if measures had been taken to deal with his scheduled interrogation on the coming Wednesday.

After a few minutes, he calmed down, and he tried to talk his wife into going back to work. She refused to leave him until she was sure that he was entirely recovered from his fall. She would not listen to his argument that the hospital examination had showed without a doubt that he was not dangerously injured.

He gave up on her and spent a more or less quiet evening (no evening with her was really quiet) until she said that she was going to bed. Knowing that she would not sleep until he was beside her, he said that he did feel tired. He planned to sneak out into another room and call Paz as soon as she started snoring. However, while waiting for her to do so, he fell asleep.

He woke up with the alarm strip whistling. For a moment, he was confused because of the vividness of a dream. Snick had been calling for help from somewhere in a fog, but he could never find her. Though he had several times seen vague dark figures in the mists that might be her, he could not get close to them.

Helpless, he raged inside himself against himself. A man who was a different persona every day should not be married. Though he had known that well, he had allowed his strong need for the domestic life to overcome his reason. Only the Father Tom Zurvan persona had never married, and he had had to be very disciplined and stern with himself when he had built that role.

Just before they went into their cylinders, Nokomis kissed him good night, though not as passionately as she usually did. She had not fully accepted his excuse for not trying to get coercion data on her colleagues. He stepped into the cylinder, turned around, and waved at her. In the dim light through the window he saw her face petrify. He looked at his watch to check that the power had been applied to her cylinder. A delay circuit that he had installed behind the wall gave him enough time to get out of the cylinder and inflate his dummy.

Two minutes later, he ran out of the apartment building. His dash towards the building across the southwest corner of Washington Square was accompanied by the wailing of sirens and the flashing of orange lights from the public strips.

Thursday-World
VARIETY, Second Month of the Year
D5-W1 (Day-Five, Week-One)

15

James Swart Dunski, professional fencing instructor, stepped out of his stoner. At the same time, Rupert von Hentzau, his wife, walked from her stoner. They embraced warmly and said, 'Good morning.' Rupert was nude, golden-coppery, willowy, kinky-haired, and beautiful. The genes of her American mulatto, Afrikaans, and Samoan ancestors had produced a striking woman, one whose body and face made a magnetic field that clamped on to the attention of males wherever she went. Sometimes, she was an artist's model; more often, a fencing instructor.

Having greeted one wife, Dunski embraced the other two, Malia Malietoa Smit and Jannie Simeona White. He also embraced the other husbands and three children, none of whom he was sure was his, though he could have established his fatherhood by genetic-blood tests. All chattering except Dunski, who felt Tingle struggling to keep his persona, they trooped from the basement room to the ground-level community room. Any other day, Dunski would have enjoyed the verbal byplay, the ass-slapping and breast-rubbing. This Thursday, he was being invaded by a partial recall of the last two days. It angered him, though he also admitted to himself that the intrusion was necessary. Jim Dunski could not live for Thursday only. He could be hurt badly at any moment by Tuesday's and Wednesday's bad events.

One benefit from his present situation was that Rupert was an immer. She, however, was a citizen of this day only. He was desperate to tell her their dangerous situation at once, but he had no acceptable excuse to get her aside.

They would have to go through the rituals and conventions all had long ago agreed upon.

First, the sleepy children were put to bed.

Second, they massed in the huge bathroom, brushed their teeth, washed whatever needed washing and urinated, if need be.

Third, they went to the kitchen and drank milk and, if hungry, ate some berries and cereal with milk. By then the joshing, touching, stroking, and rubbing had swelled the penises and nipples and started the natural lubrications.

Fourth, they went into the living room, sat down in chairs arranged in a circle, and spun a milk bottle. This was an antique, which might have been used by children a thousand or more years ago at parties. Its purpose was rather more serious now, a democratic pure-chance procedure designed to avoid jealousy and favouritism.

Dunski hoped that he would get Rupert first so that he could inform her of what she deeply needed to know. However, the bottle he spun pointed at Malia when it stopped. Sighing, though not noticeably, he went with her into a bedroom and did what he would at another time have thoroughly enjoyed, though not as much as if she had been Rupert. Afterwards, Malia said, 'Your heart, not to mention other things, didn't seem to be in it.'

'It's no reflection on my love for you,' he said. He kissed her dusky cheek. 'Every man has his down days and his up days.'

'I'm not complaining, mind you,' Malia said. 'I love you, too. But I think, if you don't mind my saying so, today's one of your down days.'

'You were faking your orgasms?'

'Never! I don't fake!'

'Well, I'm sorry. I must be off my feed or my biorhythm or something.'

'I forgive you, although there's really nothing I have to forgive,' Malia said. 'Don't worry about it.'

They went to the bathroom, Dunski thinking that she should not have complained if she thought it unimportant. They found Jan Markus Wells and Rupert there. While washing, Dunski tried to catch Rupert's eye so that he could sign to her that he wanted to speak privately to her. She was too occupied in douching to see him.

They returned to the living room, where they had to wait four minutes for the other couple. This time, chance did its best for Dunski. When he spun the bottle, it stopped with its opened end pointing at Rupert. Sighing quietly with relief, he went hand in hand with her to another bedroom. It reeked of sexual scents, and the bedclothes were sweat-soaked. He, Dunski, was accustomed to this, but Tingle, looking over his shoulder, and Caird, looking over Tingle's shoulder, might have caused his slight revulsion.

Rupert lay down on the bed and stretched out, her hands behind her head, her back arched, her perfectly conical breasts staring nipplewise at the ceiling. He sat down by her, took her hand, and said, 'Let's skip the lovemaking, Rupert. I . . . we're in trouble. We have to talk about it.'

She sat up and said, 'Deep trouble?'

He nodded and squeezed her hand. After sketching the last two days, he said, 'So, you see, we have to figure out what to do today. We'll have to omit much of what we usually do. But we can't attract attention.'

She shuddered.

'This Castor . . . it seems impossible . . . what a monster!'

'He has to be found and stopped. And I have to find out where Snick is and get the truth out of her.'

'And if she's a danger to us?'

'I don't like it, but she'll have to be stoned and hidden away.'

'Better her than us, right?'

'I suppose so.'

'Won't that make us no better than she?'

'Damn it,' he said. 'I'll wrestle with the ethics when I have to. First, I have to find her. I'll have to go to my contact. He's probably gotten the word by now, though, and he'll probably call me.'

'How are you going to question Snick? You can't let her recognize you. If you do, you have to stone her no matter what she's doing here. She *is* an organic.'

'She'll be in deep chemicogenic hypnosis. She won't remember me when she comes out of it.'

'Poor Ozma,' Rupert said. 'She dies because she was your wife.'

'I'm sorry I had to tell you about her. I've never said anything about the other days unless it was immer business.'

'That's all right,' she said. She released his hand and hugged her knees. 'I've always wondered about your other lives. Especially the women.'

'Those women are not mine, not Jim Dunski's. Dunski isn't a stranger to those other men, but he knows them as slight acquaintances.'

That was not entirely true. He did not wish, however, to talk about them. The less she knew, the better for her and for him.

Rupert got off the bed and hugged him closely. 'I'm scared.'

'So am I. Wary, anyway. Listen. If I tell you at the gym that I have to leave, you'll know that I got word about Castor or Snick. I won't be keying-out because I don't want the Credits Bureau to know that I was even at work. I'll lose today's credits, but it can't be helped. I've got overtime credit anyway. That'll help.'

'Why work at all?'

'Because I want something to do to take my mind off this, keep me from worrying. Also, my superior will expect to contact me there. And I don't want to miss out on any more practice than I have to. Got to keep in shape, you know.'

Rupert asked him to describe Castor so that she would know him if she saw him. Dunski listed in detail Castor's physical characteristics and his clothing. Then he said, 'He thinks he's God. And he thinks I'm Satan. In a way, that's to our advantage. If he was just slightly insane and wanted to destroy us immers, he'd just turn us in to the government. You know what that means.'

She shivered again and said, 'Would you take the cyanide?'

'I hope so. I swore an oath. You did, too. We all did.'

'It's the only thing to do. The only logical and honourable thing, I mean. But . . .'

There was a knock on the door. Malia called, 'You going to stay in there forever?'

Dunski told her that they would be out in a minute. He said to Rupert, 'I'm getting fed up with this group marriage thing. I'm just not the type to integrate well with it. I need more privacy, and I resent all the demands made on me.'

Rupert's eyes widened.

'You really feel that way?'

'Would I say it if I didn't?'

'No. It was just a rhetorical question. To tell the truth, Jim, I'm pretty irked sometimes. And I do get a little jealous, though I know I shouldn't.'

'As soon as this business is cleared up, let's quit. Declare the contract null and void. If we're lucky, we can do it today. This is just not working out for me and, obviously, not for you. I'm basically a monogamist.'

She smiled and said, 'Yes. Only one wife for you. One for each day, that is.'

'When I created the persona of Jim Dunski, I did it with group marriage in mind. Dunski was the type of person who would fit right in with it. But I failed. Or I'm being too much influenced by my other personae. I don't know what in hell's wrong, but I just can't take this anymore.'

'We'll talk about it later,' she said. 'We'd better get going.'

'Meanwhile, no deviation from the routine.'

Which meant that there would be no bottle-spinning the third time because this coupling had been determined by the previous two. Jannie White was Dunski's next. He went with her into the bedroom and did no better than with Malia. *No better* was satisfactory but not a cause for ringing bells, blowing whistles, and setting off firecrackers.

'You'd better get more sleep before tonight,' Jannie said, 'I usually take a nap before supper.'

Dunski grunted and headed for the bathroom. He went to bed by himself, after telling the others that he had had trouble with insomnia and was going to use the deep-sleep-wave machine. He crawled into the wall niche, attached the electrodes to his head, and lay down on his back. Before turning the device on, he thought about Castor. The man had probably long ago made provisions for daybreaking. That required fake ID star-discs and also the knowledge of how to implant false records in the data bank. The latter could be learned, however, it was not a data banker monopoly.

Castor could hide in the ancient subway system, part of which still existed, and he could steal or rob food. But that would bring the organics in. They would be looking for him anyway, and they might figure out that he was the thief. Then they would search the area in depth. He would not have much chance of escaping the odour sniffers and heat and sound detectors.

After trying to think of where Castor could be hiding out, Jim Dunski came to the same conclusion as before. He had no way of finding out. He would find Castor when Castor found him. The madman had attacked him once and would try again.

The alarm woke him. He went through the routine of eating breakfast, always a noisy ritual, of washing, then helping to get the children off to school. He and Rupert walked into the ten o'clock heat and were sweating before they got to the building, which had once housed New York University students. Their pupils were waiting in the air-conditioned gymnasium, their padded sensor-packed uniforms on and holding masks and foils. The two greeted them, and work started. At another time, Dunski would have been eager to instruct, especially one of them, a long-armed lithe youth who had the makings of a champion. Try hard though Dunski did, he could not keep Castor and Snick out of his mind. The youth scored twice on him, the bells clamouring and orange lights flashing on a wall strip as the sensors transmitted the exact point of thrust.

'You're improving enormously,' Dunski said after he took his mask off. 'And I'm off my feed. Not that you wouldn't have gotten me, anyway.'

He was relieved, instead of tensing up, when he saw a man and a woman enter the gymnasium. Though he had never seen them before, he *knew* that they were immers. Their smiles were strained, and their eyes fastened upon him as if they were radar beams. He said, 'Excuse me,' to the youth and walked in what he hoped was a casual manner to the two. One was a gaunt man with a big nose, light skin, and pale-wheat hair. He looked as if he was about forty-five subyears old. The woman was young and pretty and obviously had many Asiatic Indian ancestors.

The man made no effort to introduce himself. 'We're to take you there at once,' he said. The right hands of the two strangers were fisted, the thumb held under the first two fingers. Dunski closed his hand quickly in the identification sign, held it long enough for them to see it, and opened his hand.

'Be with you just as soon as I change,' he said. He

walked towards the locker room, and they followed him. When they were in front of the locker that held Thursday's clothes, he voice-activated the strip on the inside of the door. Channel 52 blared current hit number four of the juvenile 'pizza' music, 'I'm Alone on a Bicycle Built for Two.' The man grimaced and said, 'Is that necessary?'

'To cover up our voices, yes,' Dunski said. While he was removing his fencing clothes, he said, 'Has she been destoned yet?'

'I don't know. Let's wait and see.'

'Silence is the word, then?'

The two nodded. Two minutes later, they left the building. Dunski felt dirty and self-conscious because he had not showered, but he knew that he could not waste the time for that. Nevertheless, he thought that under the circumstances, the couple could have been more polite. They did not have to walk so far away from him. He shrugged and muttered, 'Ah, well.'

Though the air was even hotter, dark clouds were massing in the west. The meteorologist on the public news strip on a street-còrner post foretold a drop in the temperature and a heavy rain by seven that evening. Dunski thought briefly of the melting Arctic icecap and the rising waters along the seawalls surrounding Manhattan Island. Thousands were working on them now in the searing sun, adding another foot to the height so that Manhattan would be safe from inundation for another ten obyears.

The three walked west on Bleecker Street, turned north at the house where – he tried not to think of it – Ozma Wang had been murdered and mutilated, and walked along the side of the canal. At the man's whispered direction, Dunski turned left and crossed the West Fourth Street bridge. He turned left again at Jones Street and stopped midway in front of the block building. The man stepped ahead of him, punched a button by the wide green door, and waited. Whoever was inside, seeing them on the slanting strip above the door, was satisfied that they had business there. The door swung open, and a blonde woman with blue eyes and very dark skin waved them in. She looked as if she was about thirty subyears old. Dunski thought that she had had an optic pigmentation removal, all the rage then and not only in Thursday. The government was trying to make Homo sapiens one brown species, but the people, as usual, had found ways to bypass official policy. 'Pigchange,' as it was called on this day, was not illegal if the government was notified of it.

They went silently down a hall and stopped halfway before a door bearing a plaque with the names of the seven days' occupants. Thursday's were Karl Marx Martin, M.D., Ph.D., and Wilson Tupi Bunblossom, Ph.D. The blonde inserted an ID tip into the hole and pushed the door open. They entered an apartment like most, a hall running the width of the building with rooms on either side and the kitchen at the end. While they were going down the hall, the blonde said, 'This isn't my place. Martin and Bunblossom are on vacation in L.A. They have nothing to do with us. They don't know we're using their apartment.'

'Then you'll have to get Snick out of here before midnight,' Dunski said.

'Of course.'

The apartment looked drab and unused because the decorative wall strips had not been switched on. They passed the stoner room, where Dunski counted nineteen cylinders. Fourteen adults and five children. The faces were those of statues; the eyes did not know that they were staring at criminals.

The blonde opened the door to the personal possessions closet, pushed aside a rack of clothes and said, 'Bring her out.'

The gaunt man and the dark woman pulled out Snick,

huddled in a near foetal position. Dunski bent over to look at her. The bruise where Castor had struck her was a dark red. Her eyes were closed, which, for some reason, made him feel relieved. Their hands around her head, they dragged her to an empty stoner and shoved her inside. The gaunt man closed the cylinder door; the dark woman went to the wall and opened a panel. 'Not yet,' the gaunt man said.

16

The gaunt man bent down to reach into his shoulderbag, which he had put on the floor. He straightened up with a gun in his hand. Holding it out to Dunski, he said, 'Do you want it back?'

Dunski took it and said, 'Thanks. As long as Castor is alive, I want it.'

The man nodded and said, 'We're still looking for him. Now, we've been told about your situation, but I'd like to hear it from you. We don't have all the details, we have to evaluate the situation.'

'It's more than a situation, it's a predicament.'

'How about talking over coffee?' the blonde said. 'Or isn't this going to take that long?'

'Coffee'd be fine,' Dunski said.

They went to the kitchen and all sat down except for the blonde. She inserted her ID tip into the cabinet door marked PP-TH. She swung the door open and said, 'I had the ID made when I found out Martin and Bunblossom were going on vacation. I'm a good friend . . .'

The gaunt man coughed, and he said, 'That's enough. The less Oom Dunski knows about us, the better.'

'Sorry, Oom Gar –'

The blonde clipped off the rest of his name and looked embarrassed.

'You talk too much, Tante,' the gaunt man said.

'I'll watch it,' the blonde said. She was silent as she removed two cubes of stoned coffee, put them in the wall, closed the door, pushed a button, opened the door, and removed the coffee in its paper containers. The gaunt man said, 'I'll tell you what we know, and then you fill in. We got our data from . . . a verbal source. The data lines weren't used, of course, except to transmit to our superior.'

While Dunski was talking, the blonde poured coffee for them and silently indicated the cream and sugar containers. By the time that he had drunk two cups, Dunski had given them all that they should know.

There was a long silence after he quit talking. The gaunt man stroked his chin, then said, 'We'll have to find out what this Snick knows. Afterwards, we decide.'

'Decide what?' Dunski said.

'Whether we kill her before we stone her again or just hide her someplace. If we don't kill her, there's always the chance that she might be found. If she is, then she can talk.'

Dunski grunted as if he had been hit in the ribs, and he said, 'I know it may be necessary, but . . .'

'You knew when you took the immer oath that you might have to kill someday,' the gaunt man said. His dark brown eyes looked steadily into Dunski's. 'You aren't thinking of arguing about this, are you?'

'No, of course not. I don't take the good but dodge the bad. Whatever's in the package, I accept. But killing . . . it should be done only if absolutely necessary.'

'I know that,' the gaunt man said. He tipped his cup, swallowed the last of his coffee, set the cup down, and stood up. He nodded at the blonde. 'Tante, you get Snick ready.'

The blonde told the dark woman to follow her. The gaunt man put the shoulderbag on the table and began removing the interrogation tools. Dunski looked away from them and out through the sheers over the tall and wide window. There were only a few pedestrians and cyclists on the street, none loitering. All were intent on their own affairs or seemed to be. If there were any organics among them, they did not look towards the window. Innocents, Dunski thought, minding their own business, unknowing that something bad was about to take place a few feet from them. Bad. Not evil. The immers were not trying to overthrow the government. They just wanted to live within its forms – more or less – without being disturbed, and they hoped to change it just enough so that all would have true freedom. What harm was there in that?

The gaunt man put some of his tools back into the bag and took the rest into the living room. 'We'll put her there,' he said, indicating a sofa. 'All of you . . . get out of her sight.' He tied a handkerchief over his face and stood by the cylinder with a gas-spraying can in his hand. The blonde woman, at a nod from him, turned the power on. A second later, the power having gone off automatically, she closed the panel.

The gaunt man had the door open and had shot the gas into the cylinder and closed the door again before the blonde had turned away from the panel. Dunski glimpsed Snick's wide open eyes, her agonized face, and her attempt to rise from her womb-crouch. He saw her face at the window and the palms of her hands. Both face and hands slid away. The gaunt man lowered the handkerchief to his neck and counted thirty seconds by his watch before he opened the door. Snick fell as it swung out, her head striking the floor, her legs doubled beneath her, buttocks in the air.

Dunski helped the dark woman carry Snick's limp body to the sofa. 'Gaunt,' as Dunski thought of him, passed a circular device, held in his fingertips, over her upturned face and body. After telling Dunski and 'Dark' to turn her over, he moved the device over her back. As it passed over her left thigh, it shrilled. Gaunt said 'Ah!' and brought the device back to the area that had triggered it. He took a pen from his robe pocket and outlined a two-inch square area in red. Having put the round device in the pocket, he removed a thin cylinder with a bulb at its end. Holding this bulb close to Snick's skin inside the square, he moved it slowly until it shrilled most loudly.

Gaunt took a pair of thick opaque spectacles from his pocket. He put these on and bent over to stare at the area. Then he marked a tiny *X* almost in the centre of the square. He took off the spectacles, folded them, put them in the pocket, and said, 'Transmitter. Homing pigeon. It's not activated, of course.'

'How do you know?' Dunski said.

'If it was, we'd be in custody by now.'

Gaunt placed a reader on her pulse. 'A little fast,' he said, 'but that's normal with the gas.' He turned a dial on the reader and held the machine on her arm. 'Blood pressure normal, considering the circumstances.'

Dunski felt an impulse to close Snick's hanging jaw but repressed it. The others might think that he had some sympathy for her.

'I don't know what the blow on her head did for her,' Gaunt said. 'Let's hope that it hasn't addled her wits. Or that she doesn't die on us from a fractured skull.'

'Not until the questioning is over, anyway,' Dunski said.

Gaunt seemed unaware of the sarcasm. 'Yes.'

Gaunt passed a vein selector over her lower arm and stopped it when an orange light flashed from its end. He moved it slowly back and forth until the light was at its brightest. Then he pressed the point against the skin and lifted it away. A round orange smudge marked where the injector should enter. He rubbed alcohol on the skin; the orange mark was not dissolved. With a throwaway hypodermic air syringe, he injected three cubic centimetres of a dark reddish liquid. Snick's eyelids fluttered.

Gaunt followed the questioning procedure of the Organic Department by the book. For all Dunski knew, Gaunt might be an organic. Though he was asking questions in the manner and form required by law, he departed from the legal procedure in all other respects. There were no judges present, no doctor, no defence lawyer, no camera recording crew, no state prosecutor, no data banker to testify that the one questioned was indeed the one the state had identified as Panthea Pao Snick.

Gaunt must have used her ID star-disc to check out all the data therein, but there were things that he had not been able to find out, otherwise he would not be interrogating her now.

One of the missing items was the reason for her mission.

He went straight to the heart of matters and asked her what that was. He did not do it by putting a single question to her and then letting her pour out all she knew about the mission. The drug did not open the dam. What she knew had to be pulled out item by item through a patient interrogation. But they came out quickly and easily like well-oiled bureau drawers.

When he was done, Gaunt sat down on a chair near her. Sweat was running down his forehead as if the air-conditioning had gone off.

'I'm relieved that Snick wasn't looking for us,' Gaunt said. 'But she would have stumbled on us eventually. In fact, she did, but we were lucky we got her before she could inform the organics.'

Snick's primary mission had been to find and arrest a daybreaker named Morning Rose Doubleday. She was a scientist who had held a high position in Sunday's Department of Genetics. She was suspected of being a member of a secret organization dedicated to the violent overthrow of the government, though, so far, the organization had committed no violent crimes. When Sunday's organics had gone to arrest her, they found that she had gone underground. Someone had warned her, probably someone in the organics force.

Doubleday was so important that Snick had been given a

temporal visa to track her down. While in Monday, Snick had been told about Gril and asked to keep an eye out for him. When she was in Wednesday, Snick had also been told that another dangerous criminal, Doctor Chang Castor, was on the loose. Would she, while searching for Doubleday, report to the organics if she heard anything about him?

The governments of the various days wanted her true mission kept as quiet as possible. Thus, Snick had pretended to be looking for the most innocuous of the criminals, Gril, when she had talked to Tingle. She must have known that this was a flimsy reason. Tingle would wonder why a Sunday organic was looking for a Monday daybreaker. But she was immune from questioning by a civilian, and she must not have cared what he thought.

When Snick had seen Castor in Washington Square Park, she had followed him. She should have summoned organics to help her arrest him, but she had some reasons, all invalid, of course, to suspect that Castor might be a member of the organization to which Doubleday belonged. Unlike her superiors, she thought it likely that Doubleday's organization existed in all the days. Arresting Castor at once would have removed any chance of his leading her to other revolutionaries.

It was true that everything Castor knew about the immers would have been revealed by the organic interrogation. But his comrades might have gotten wind of it and killed themselves or, like the non-immer Doubleday, have become daybreakers. They would eventually be chased down, but by then they might be desperate enough to swallow the poison they carried. Or do what some had done and Doubleday should have done. Speak the codephrase that would explode the tiny bomb implanted in her body.

'She must be a coward!' Blonde said.

'Who?' Gaunt said.

'Doubleday, of course. She should have killed herself!'
'We're supposed to do that, too,' Dunski said.
'I hope none of us will be like Doubleday!' Blonde said.
'I hope none of us have to find out if we are,' Dark said.
Dunski wondered if he would have the guts. Jeff Caird would do it. Tingle might. But would Dunski? And tomorrow, what would Wyatt Repp do? Probably find a perverse exaltation, satisfaction, anyway, in dying like a hero. The others? He did not know about them. At the moment, they were too remote from him, ectoplasm, not flesh.
'We know,' Gaunt said, 'that Snick wanted to question you as Tingle because she wanted to put some of Wednesday's data bankers to work for her. You weren't the only banker she talked to. But she was cagey, she didn't tell you what her mission was because she had to check you out first. For all she knew, you might be a member of the revolutionaries. She didn't get back to you because she thought she had a hot lead on Doubleday and she spent too much time on it. It turned out that the lead wasn't too hot.'
'You talk too much,' Dunski said. 'Blondie here is a deaf-mute compared to you.'
Scowling, Gaunt rose from the chair.
'What do you mean?'
'You haven't told me your names. With good reason. But you just said the name of my Wednesday identity. That's stupid, Oom Gaunt!'
'Gaunt?'
'My nickname for you. You chew out Blonde for running off at the mouth, yet she didn't say anything dangerous to us. But you . . .'
Gaunt tried to smile.
'You're right. That was stupid, a slip of the tongue, anyway. I apologize. I won't do it again. But there's no real harm done. She' – he pointed at Snick –

'can't hear us.'

'Her unconscious can. The organics' scientists are working on ways to get information out of the unconscious. One of these days, they might find out how to do it. If they do, then they could run off the interrogation, our conversation, what she heard when she was unconscious, even what she saw if her eyes were open while she was drugged.'

Gaunt sighed, and he said, 'They won't be able to get anything out of the dead.'

Blonde gasped. Dark stared wide-eyed at him.

Dunski felt sick and a little faint. He broke the silence by saying, 'You meant all along to kill her?'

Gaunt bit his lip and looked at Snick. Her mouth was closed now; she looked as if she were sleeping. And she really looks beautiful, Dunski thought. A study in brown, as soft and innocent as a seal pup. Yet, according to her bio-data, she was a swift and determined and sometimes ingenious tracker of criminals.

'I don't want to,' Gaunt said. 'I've never killed before; I loathe the idea of killing. I will do it only if there is nothing else to do, no other way out. But I can't let somebody else make the decision, dodge the responsibility by letting a superior assume it for me. I . . .'

He was silent for a moment. Dunski had another attack of faintness. It was not caused, however, by reaction to Gaunt's decision. Something flashed. A burst of light and great warmth surrounded him. Though the 'interruption' – how describe it as other than an interruption, something breaking in and then out? – was brief, he felt a great love for Gaunt, who was thinking of murdering, and a great love for Snick, who might be murdered.

The light, warmth, and faintness passed. He shook his head slightly as if he were trying to shake off water. What the hell had happened then?

The thought that perhaps Father Tom Zurvan had

thrust through for a second swelled and faded. He did not want to think about that. That Zurvan could do that was a weakness in his, Dunski's, defence, a fault in mental fencing. It also showed him – again, something he did not wish to dwell upon – that the selves more widely separated by the day of the week were as near as, perhaps nearer than, those closer in terms of days. Travelling through time was not always done chronologically.

Whatever had caused this, the ballooning glow was now a fast-shrinking flicker.

'I don't think that she has to be killed,' Dunski said. 'Look at what she knows. She was trailing Castor, and he knocked her out. She wakes up in a stoner and sees only a masked man who makes her unconscious again. For all she knows, the man who knocked her out again is Castor. She –'

'Is Castor the same height and build as I am?' Gaunt said. 'Was he wearing the same clothes?'

'No,' Dunski said slowly. 'But she only glimpsed you. The door partly hid your body. Anyway, she doesn't have the slightest idea that anybody but Castor is involved. What could she tell the authorities if she was found and destoned?'

He paused to swallow and said, 'Does she even have to be stoned permanently? Wouldn't it work out better – for us – if she's found tomorrow, no, wait a minute, she might not be found until next Thursday.'

He turned to Blonde. 'How long will they – Martin and Bunblossom – be on vacation?'

'They'll be back tomorrow, I mean, their tomorrow, next Thursday.'

'That gives us a week before she's found,' Dunski said, turning to Gaunt.

'Not us, you,' Gaunt said. 'The rest of us get stoned before midnight.'

'By us, I mean immers,' Dunski said. 'We should have

Castor out of the way before then. We'd better, we have to get him today. We're wasting time with Snick. We should all be out looking for Castor.'

Gaunt looked down on the gently breathing woman. He turned towards the others but looked directly at Dunski.

'You haven't really thought this out,' Gaunt said. 'You're letting your humane feelings kill your logic, your sense of duty and of right, what's right for us.

'Castor is our out for this problem. I mean by that, the Snick problem. The organics here know he's killed and mutilated two women. If . . . if Snick is found dead and mutilated, the organics will think that Castor did it. That diverts suspicion from anyone else. And it'll be next Sunday before its government sends out a replacement. If it does.'

Blonde, her hand to her mouth, said softly, 'Oh, God! You're going to butcher her!'

17

'You . . . can't . . . do . . . that,' Dunski said.

Gaunt mocked him. 'And . . . why . . . not?'

'That's not very prosocial behaviour,' Blonde said.

Dunski found himself laughing hysterically at that.

'Oh, my God, prosocial behaviour!' he said, choking. 'We're talking about a human being here.'

'Yes,' Gaunt said. 'But it's for the greater good. All right! No more talk! I've never seen such a gabby bunch, parrots, my God! You're supposed to be immers, but you . . . you . . . !'

Dunski had managed to get hold of himself almost literally. He felt invisible hands, coming from somewhere, placed upon something somewhere within himself. Father Tom?

Gaunt said, 'I've made up my mind, and I'm the leader here. You have to do what I tell you.'

'I haven't been told that you're in command,' Dunski said. 'What's your authority?'

Gaunt's nostrils flared; his face got red.

'Your superior didn't tell you that I'd be in command?'

'My superior tells me as little as possible,' Dunski said coldly. 'Apparently, he told me less than he should. Anyway . . .'

He turned and walked to his shoulderbag, which was on the floor in a corner. He picked it up, opened it, and put the strap over his right shoulder. Though Gaunt was furious, he was cool enough to realize that Dunski had made a threatening, if subtle, move. Gaunt had not forgotten that Dunski had a gun.

Gaunt's voice was firm, though his head shook a little.

'As you said, we don't have time to discuss this. And I *am* in command here. We will dispose of Snick as I said we would because it's the only logical thing to do. And because I said so.'

'Are *you* going to mutilate her or are you going to get someone else to do it?' Dunski said.

'What does it matter who does it!' Gaunt said, his voice louder. 'It'll be done!'

He had looked at his shoulderbag, which was on a small table near the end of the sofa close to Snick's feet. Dunski supposed that Gaunt had a weapon in his bag. He asked himself what he would do if the man went for the gun. Was he really prepared to shoot a fellow immer to stop him from killing an organic? He would not know until the time came, and he did not want that time to come.

Time, however, was creeping or sliding or flowing or proceeding in whatever unknown manner Time used to make Then into Now. During the next few seconds, one of the two alternate futures would be chosen. Or would just happen, choice not being one of the factors in the taking of the road.

Blonde said, her voice thin, 'I can't believe this is happening!'

'Neither can I,' Gaunt said. He moved backwards away from Dunski, coming closer to his shoulderbag. 'I may have to report your emotional instability to the council.'

Dunski lied. 'It isn't so much the killing. It's the butchering. It makes me sick. You should understand that. I was . . . am . . . close to vomiting. But if it has to be done . . .'

Gaunt seemed to loosen a little. 'It does. And I'll do it. I wouldn't ask anyone else to do it.'

He looked down at Snick. 'Believe me, if there was any other way . . .' He spoke to Blonde. 'You and this man,' meaning Dunski, 'put her in the stoner.'

Gaunt was shrewd. If Dunski had his hands full, he

could not go for his weapon.

'You can't kill her here,' Blonde said. 'The organics will investigate everybody in the building. They might stumble across something. I'd be implicated.'

'I know that,' Gaunt said coolly. 'She'll be taken elsewhere. I don't even want you to know where. None of you.'

Dunski lifted Snick by her shoulders. How soft and warm she was. How soon to be hard and cold. And then soft and warm again, and then torn apart. He felt numbed. As if he was sharing a little her death.

Blonde grabbed the legs, and the two carried her to the stoner. They propped her up, pushed her into the cylinder in a sitting position, and pushed again on the torso, which had fallen forward. Dunski lifted her legs and pushed them so that they were against her breasts. He raised himself up and backed away while Blonde shut the door. Gaunt turned the control that applied the power and watched the dial as it spun back to OFF.

'All of you clear out,' Gaunt said. 'Go back to whatever you were doing. We'll get in touch with you when we need you.'

Blonde started weeping. Gaunt looked disgusted. Dunski patted her on the shoulder and said, 'There's a price to pay for immortality.' That made Gaunt look even more disgusted. Dark, her eyes lowered, took Blonde's hand and said, 'Let's go.'

Dunski watched them leave through the door to the hall. When the door had closed behind the two, he looked at the cylinder holding Snick. The window was as empty as her future.

Gaunt said, 'Well?'

He was standing by the shoulderbag, his right hand resting on it. Dunski said, 'Don't worry. I'm going.'

Gaunt looked at him and down at the bag. Smiling slightly, he said, 'You'll see that I'm right. Get a good sleep. You'll wake up a new man tomorrow.'

'I always do,' Dunski said. 'Maybe that's part of the trouble.'

Gaunt frowned. 'What do you mean?'

'Nothing.'

Hc did not care to say good-bye or anything that indicated that he would like to see him again. He started towards the door, conscious that Gaunt was watching him closely. Dunski was not sure that he was not going to make a last appeal for Snick. It would not be with words, it would be with the gun. But that would be stupid, nonsurvival. Even if he could save Snick, what would he do with her? He did not have the means that the immer organization had for spiriting her away. And Gaunt was right, logically right, though he was emotionally wrong. Or was he? What was, in the absolute sense, right?

He had just reached the door when he heard a shrilling. He turned and saw Gaunt walking to an orange-flashing wall strip. Gaunt said something softly, and the strip showed the face of a man. Dunski walked back to where he could see the strip from behind Gaunt. The man saw Dunski and said, 'Is . . . should he hear this?'

Gaunt said, harshly, 'How would I know? I don't know what you're going to say.'

The man said, 'Well, this concerns all of us.'

'What is it?'

'It's Castor. He's killed again!'

Dunski felt as if something inside him had turned over and died. He *knew* what the man was going to tell them.

'The organics have just found a woman's body in an apartment on Bleecker Street. She was mutilated, just like the other women. Her intestines were ripped out, and her breasts were cut off and glued to the wall. Her name was Nokomis Moondaughter, a tante of Wednesday. She was the wife of a Robert Tingle. He's not a suspect because he's still in his cylinder, and it's evident that the woman was killed less than an hour ago. Castor must have gotten into the apartment, destoned her, and killed and butchered her while the tenants were gone. They came back and found her. It's his handiwork, all right.'

Dunski made a strangled noise and turned away. He walked to the sofa, sat down, stared at Gaunt, who was talking and glancing back at him, got up, and walked to the kitchen. He poured out coffee with a shaking hand, sipped it, put the cup down, and walked to the big window. His grief was there but numbed. He was as sluggish as a glacier from toe to scalp.

Staring through the sheers at the street scene, he muttered, 'I can't take much more of this.'

Gaunt coughed behind him. He said, 'The woman . . . she was your wife?'

Dunski kept looking through the windows as he said, 'In a way.'

The bright sunshine was gone. The lighter heralds of the advancing storm had coloured the sky grey.

'I'm very sorry,' Gaunt said. 'But . . .'

'There's always a *but*, isn't there?'

Gaunt coughed again. 'This time, there is. We have to get to Castor fast. The organics may not have been too upset by what Castor did Tuesday, but they know now what he did on Wednesday and will probably do today. They'll launch an all-out search.'

Dunski said, 'Rupert!'

'What?'

'My wife. She's in grave danger.'

'No more than you,' Gaunt said. 'He's tried once to kill you, and he'll keep trying until you're dead or he's dead.'

Dunski turned to face Gaunt. The man looked pale.

'Rupert has to be protected.'

'I've already sent two to guard her,' Gaunt said. 'They'll tell her what's happened.' He shook his head. 'This is getting worse and worse.'

'I don't know what to do. There's no sense in just roaming around hoping I'll see Castor.'

'I know that,' Gaunt said. 'I think you should go home with Rupert and wait there. Castor may try to get to you there. The guards will be out of sight but watching.'

'We'll be decoys?'

'A waiting game. Meanwhile, every immer in Manhattan and many in the neighbouring cities will be here looking for Castor.'

'I doubt that Castor would try to get into my apartment. There are too many other people there.'

Gaunt bit his lip and said, 'Yes, I know.' Evidently, he did not approve of communal marriages.

Gaunt had said nothing about Tingle's dummy being disturbed, and, if he had heard anything, he would not have kept quiet about it. Castor could have removed the dummies of Caird and Tingle and so revealed to the organics that they were daybreakers. He had not done so because he wanted to kill Caird. If the organics got hold of him first, they would prevent Castor from getting his revenge and from ridding the universe of Castor's Satan.

Dunski said, 'I think I'm going into shock.'

'You look like it,' Gaunt said. 'Follow me.' They went into the living room. Dunski sat down. Gaunt took a syringe from his bag and picked up the bottle of alcohol. 'Lift your arm.'

Dunski did so, saying, 'What's that for?'

'It'll make you feel better for a while. The drug doesn't get rid of the shock; it just delays it.'

The syringe shot a bluish liquid into Dunski's arm. He felt a warmth and a rush of blood. His heart pounded; the numbness evaporated. He could almost see it steaming off.

Gaunt said, 'Feel better now?'

'Much better. I'm glad it wasn't a sedative. I need to be on my toes.'

'It perks you up for a while,' Gaunt said. 'But you have

to pay the price later.'

Dunski thought, There's always a price. What's the price for being an immer? Why do I ask that, stupid? I'm paying it now and am a long way off from paying all of the debt.

He rose, started towards the door again, stopped, gestured at the cylinder, and said, 'Does she . . . ?'

'Yes, she does,' Gaunt said. 'I don't know about you, Dunski. You seem to have trouble accepting the inevitable. I can understand how you must feel, I think I can, anyway, but you're not showing immer quality.'

'It just doesn't seem right,' Dunski murmured.

'The right way is the best way. Go on now. Your wife will be waiting for you.'

Dunski opened the door and turned for a last look. Gaunt was staring hard at him. The man's will was as hard as the bodies in the cylinders. He closed the door and went down the hall to the door. Opening it, he was wetted by the rain. He stepped back in and took from the bag a yellow roll no longer or thinner than his index finger. Holding a tab at its one end between two fingers, he snapped it. The roll became a raincoat with attached hood, electric sparks crackling from its hem.

Clad in the raincoat, he stepped out into the fierce downpour. The street was deserted except for a bicyclist pedalling madly, bent over, the wheels splashing water. From far off, thunder rumbled, and lightning coursed through the dark western mass like the shining arteries of a god.

He did not have to go home at once. Rupert should be safe. Gaunt would not like his orders disobeyed, but what could he do? Not much if he, Jim Dunski, did nothing but hang around for a while here and then take his time going home. If he did what was so raging, though so vague, in his mind, he would suffer severe punishment. Perhaps, Gaunt might arrange an *accident* for him and so dispose of him. That, however, would cause a chain of problems for the immers. If Dunski disappeared or was killed, then Caird, Tingle, Repp, Ohm, Zurvan, and Isharashvili would also disappear.

The seven roles had put him in danger. On the other hand, they were insurance of a sort against the immers' turning against him. If the situation became desperate, though, the immers could cancel his policy and take their chances.

18

Jim Dunski stood for a while and wondered what he would do, what he should do, when the second of decision came. He could walk away and leave Snick to die. Or he could try to rescue her. Logic, self-survival, and common sense urged him to leave here as quickly as possible. His horror at the concept of murder and his vision of Snick being murdered – no concept, this, but a vividly red image – rooted him.

Do the ends justify the means? That was an ancient question that had only one answer if you had a heart.

But if he did what was right, then he was wrong.

'I should have thought of this when I swore utter loyalty forever,' he muttered. A little later, he said, 'But it's not like I'm turning them in, exposing them. If I just get her away, somehow, and hide her, all of us immers will still be safe.'

At that moment, he knew that he was not going to let Gaunt kill her. Not if he could help it. He did have a plan to do this, though it was wild and could easily go awry. Read for *awry*, his death.

He looked up and down the street. The two whom Gaunt had said would be watching him were not in sight. No doubt, they could see him. If Castor appeared, they would close in and kill him, though they might be too late to save their fellow immer, himself. For all he knew, Gaunt had decided that he should be the sacrificial victim, the throwaway decoy.

No. Gaunt would not wish Dunski to die in these circumstances. He would want a well-planned cover-up before that happened.

The rain fell heavily as he walked. Behind him, thunder and lightning came nearer as if they were stalking him. He stopped at the corner of Jones and Seventh and looked up and down the broad avenue. There were no pedestrians or bicyclers, and the car traffic was much lighter than usual. Two taxis, a government limousine, and an organic patrol car. The latter was cruising at five miles an hour, its headlights on, its two occupants rain-blurry behind the windscreen. They did not seem to have looked at the lone man in the yellow hood and coat.

The storm was what Gaunt should have asked for. It was blocking the sky-eyes and removing possible witnesses from the streets. Even people looking out their windows would be half-blinded.

Presently, a white van with black zebra stripes appeared north on Seventh, two blocks away. There were three thousand such in Manhattan, all vehicles of the State Cleaning Corps of all days. It slowed at the light and eased through on the yellow. Dunski was not surprised when it turned onto Jones Street. The SCC van could stop at the apartment, its corpspersons could enter the building and come out with a large package or a cart filled with something concealed by a tarpaulin, and no one would be suspicious. Any watcher might commend the Corps for doing its duty in such bad weather.

He turned to watch the van do just what he thought it would. Two men in the uniform of Thursday's SCC, green trousers with bellbottom cuffs and loose scarlet coats, got out of the van. One opened the rear doors; the other reached in and pulled out a folding cart. They stood before the door a few seconds, waiting for Gaunt to identify them on the strip. As soon as they had disappeared into the building, Dunski walked slowly down the long block towards the van. He looked across the street at the building opposite. It was one of the modern boat-shaped structures with a large yard with many trees and bushes. He spotted a dark figure standing in a doorway under the overhang of the building. That must be one of his guards.

The watcher was probably wondering why he had not started for home. He might be asking questions of Gaunt now via radio. And where was the other guard? If he was in the bushes or behind a tree, he was well hidden.

Other than the man in the doorway, the only person visible was a bicyclist who had just turned off West Fourth onto Jones Street. Through the driving rain, Dunski could see a figure in a dark raincoat and wide-brimmed rainhat, bent over, his face hidden, his legs moving hard as he drove the bicycle through the now inch-deep water. Dunski slowed even more. He should have waited a little longer. The two pseudo-SCC-men would take about three minutes to go inside, load Snick into the unfolded cart, get back to the van, and load her in. Unless Gaunt delayed them with more instructions.

Dunski did not want to arrive too soon. He should get to the van just after the two had stored their hard burden inside it. Before they closed and locked the door.

'I'm doing it,' he thought. 'I'm crazy, but I'm doing it.'

He stopped and waited. He cursed. It wouldn't work. The man in the doorway of the building across the street would radio Gaunt, and Gaunt would come out with the two men to find out what was happening. Or he might have them stay inside until he found out why Dunski was loitering there. Or he might send one man out to do that.

'I'll improvise,' he muttered.

The door to the building swung open. One of the men backed out, pulling on the now-unfolded cart. Dunski waited until both were out, the cart between them. He started walking. The man in the doorway of the building across the street had stepped out into driving rain. He hesitated as if he were wondering what he should do. Then he broke into a run on the sidewalk through the yard, and he began shouting.

At the same time, another man lunged out from a cluster of bushes. He was carrying something dark in his right hand. A gun. By then the other immer had his gun out. Dunski swore again. He did not want to murder while trying to prevent a murder.

The two SCC-men did not seem to hear the shouts. They had retracted the cart wheels and lifted it between them and were shoving it into the van. Dunski started running towards them. He reached into the shoulderbag, gripped the butt of the gun, and snatched it out. He would hold the two SCC-men with the gun. He would threaten to shoot them if the two guards did not throw down their weapons and walk off. He hoped that his bluff would not be called. Or was it a bluff? Not until the moment of action came would he know.

By then, the shouting man was near enough so that the SCCs could hear him against the west wind and the quickly descending thunder and lightning. They turned towards him. At the same time, the bicyclist straightened up, and white teeth flashed in a grin or a snarl. His right hand came up from his belt holding a gun. It rose swiftly, steadied, and man-made lightning spat whitely from him to the nearest armed man. The distance was about sixty feet, which meant that the ray had lost much of its deadliness. The charging man, however, fell on his face and slid on the rain-slicked pavement for a few feet. His weapon rang as it struck and bounced away from him. He did not try to get up; he lay quivering on the street.

The other armed immer shot once and missed, the white beam passing just behind the bicyclist's back. Laughing so loudly that he could be heard above the crashing of the storm, the bicyclist shot again. The beam half-cut the leg off the immer just above the knee.

Dunski screamed, 'Castor!'

The two SCCs ran to the front of the van, leaving the back doors open. Gaunt stepped out of the building door, his weapon in his hand. He was shielded from Castor's view, but he also could not see Castor. Then Castor had sped beyond the van. Dunski, Gaunt, and Castor shot simultaneously. Because Castor had braked his vehicle somewhat, the beams aimed at him crossed and neutralized each other. The slowing down and slight skidding spoiled Castor's aim. Dunski threw himself to one side, pressing the firing button again as he fell. The beam struck the sidewalk, hissing.

Castor was crazy, but he was cool. Seeing Dunski fall and thus knowing that he would be out of action for several seconds, he aimed at Gaunt. Their beams struck and cancelled each other. Castor did not make the mistake of Gaunt, who had released his button, and then pressed it again. Castor kept the beam on, though that drained the weapon's powerpack quickly. His beam, unhindered, burned through Gaunt's belly. Gaunt dropped his gun, clutched his belly and fell backwards, his head striking the side of the building.

By then Dunski had rolled twice and come up on his stomach, elbows on the pavement, both hands clutching the gun. He fired. Lightning, Nature's, not man's, smashed into the street near the yard of the building across the street. Another bolt split an oak tree in half.

Both SCC-men had jumped out of the van with guns. Dunski saw all this just before the flash that dazzled him and the explosion of electricity deafened him. For a moment, he thought that he was struck. The weapon play had not scared him because it had taken place so swiftly. The lightning stroke terrified him, boiling out in him all the fear and helplessness that human beings have felt since they were cavemen and the wrath of the gods was loosed in the skies.

During Dunski's brief paralysis, Castor scrambled up from the pavement where he had fallen off his bicycle. He got down on his hands and knees again and groped for his gun. The SCC-man nearest him seemed to be stunned. He did not shoot while Castor was a helpless target. The other man ran around the van after crouching for a moment after the bolt had slammed into the street. Castor found the gun and rolled away as the beams from the two men steamed the water near him. Dunski got to his feet and ran towards the van. Castor, rolling, managed to beam steadily towards the SCC-men. It cut through the plastic of the van body at the right rear corner and across the man closest to him. The man cried out and fell.

The other man also held his firing button, but, a third time, the two beams crossed. Now Castor had stopped rolling, and his beam slid to one side, jerked back and caught his enemy in the eyes. Screaming, the man dropped his weapon, clutched his eyes and staggered off.

Yelling exultantly, Castor, still on the ground, aimed his weapon at the running Dunski. Dunski shot; his beam struck close to Castor's shoulder. Castor screamed with fury because the powerpack in his weapon was empty. He bounded upwards as if off a trampoline, came down running, and headed for the van. Dunski passed the stumbling blind man between him and the building. He snapped a shot over the man's shoulder but only cut off the lower corner of the right back door of the van. By then, Castor was hidden behind the van.

His breath grating, Dunski ran at an angle, knowing that he would have to get into the street before Castor picked up the weapon dropped by the first SCC-man he had shot. He got to the corner of the van just as Castor was rising after reaching out from the protection of the rear wheel to grab the gun. Dunski smashed into him and knocked him backwards, though he fell on top of him.

Castor's breath went out of him in a big oof. Lightning struck somewhere down the street. Castor grabbed Dunski's wrist and turned it savagely. The gun fell from Dunski's hand, but he did not try to regain it. Shouting, he grabbed Castor's throat. Castor screamed, 'Now I have you in my power! God will not be denied!'

Though he was choking, Castor's hands closed around Dunski's throat. Dunski let Castor loose and tore himself away. He got to his feet before Castor did, and he charged, knocking him down again. He picked Castor up by the neck and shook him, then ran him against the side of the van. Castor slumped. Dunski held him up with one hand and slammed the base of the palm of his left hand again and again on Castor's chin. He kept driving the back of Castor's head against the van until his arm was too weary to lift.

Finally, gasping as if all air had suddenly been taken from the face of Earth, he dropped Castor onto the pavement.

God was dead.

Dunski shook uncontrollably. He would have liked to lie down on the street and let the rain and lightning do what they would with him. It seemed to be the best bed in the world, the most desirable of all desires and an utter necessity. But . . . there was always a but . . . he could not do what he most wanted to do.

People were coming from the building near him and from across the street, despite the almost solid rain and the lightning still smashing nearby. Some would have called the organics. He had to get away. Now.

He staggered around the van, stopped halfway to the driver's seat, turned, staggered back to his gun, picked it up, started away, turned again, and picked up his shoulderbag, which had dropped off just before he had charged around the corner of the van into Castor. After picking up the gun dropped by the SCC-man, he set its charge to BURN and fried the skin bearing his finger-marks on Castor's neck. He closed the back doors of the van, got wearily into the front seat, breathing as if a knife were cutting his throat, and drove off.

No one tried to stop him.

Though he wanted to turn left onto West Fourth so that the witnesses would tell the organics that he had gone that way, he did not. Sheridan Square was too close in that direction. There were usually some organics there. He drove to the right from Jones Street, passed Cornelia, and went over the bridge above the Kropotkin Canal. He had to get out of the van very quickly, but he also had to hide Snick someplace. If he did one, he could not do the other.

19

Just as he passed the little park on West Fourth east of the canal, he saw headlights behind him. He was too tired to swear. A patrol car? Probably. He could not even get out of the van and run. An eighty-year-old could catch him on foot now. The car swung out to pass him, then slowed to match the pace of his van. A window went down, and the man behind the wheel shouted at him. What he said was drowned in thunder, though the window on Dunski's right was up and so would have muted the man's voice. Dunski put that window down and shouted a question at him. The driver was not in uniform, and the car was unmarked. That did not mean the two in the car were not organics. However, if they were, why had they not slapped the orange flasher on top of their car? Perhaps they were immers sent to aid him.

He stopped the van and waited for the two to come to him. They were organics. But they were also immers, and they had been dispatched to see that he got a ride. Gaunt had been warned by one of the guards across the street that Dunski was not leaving at once as ordered. They were on their way to pick him up when Headquarters had ordered them to Jones Street. Someone had called in about the shooting.

'I'll tell you later what happened,' Dunski said. 'Just now, get the stoned woman into your trunk. I'll leave the van here.'

The man's partner, a woman, said, 'We have orders to take you to our superior.' Dunski turned the motor and lights off and got out. The woman hurried to help unload Snick. Dunski said, 'Oh, I forgot!' and he wiped the wheel and the door handle of the van with his handkerchief. Then he crawled into the back seat of the car and lay down. The trunk lid slammed, and the two got into the front seat. 'Maybe he should have gone into the trunk, too,' the woman said.

The man did not reply. The woman spoke into a wristwatch in a voice too low for Dunski to distinguish the words. Not the organic frequency, Dunski thought. The man drove to Womanway, two patrol cars, sirens wailing, passing him towards the west. The car turned left to go north on Womanway, turned right on East Fourteenth Street, and then left onto Second Avenue. Just past Stuyvesant Square, the car stopped before a block building. Dunski had seen this before, a structure resembling the Taj Mahal, though smaller. It housed high government officials and also contained the offices of many residents, stores, an empathorium, a restaurant, and a gymnasium. The situation must be bad indeed. Only if the council had no other way out would he have been brought here.

The man stayed in the car to listen to the organic channels. The woman conducted him into a large marble corridor lined by the stoned bodies of elegantly clothed officials who had once trod these halls of power. Some of them needed dusting. They stopped at one of the elevator doors, where the woman said, 'He's here' to a wall strip.

'He'll come up alone,' a deep male voice said. 'You get back to your post. After the disposal.'

'Yes, Oom,' the woman said. She did not leave, however, until Dunski had gotten on the elevator and the doors were closing. He rose to a floor in the dome, got out into a luxuriously carpeted and decorated hall, and said to the man waiting there, 'Dunski.' The man nodded and escorted him down the hall to a door. Its plaque bore two names, Piet Essex Vermeulen and Mia Owen Baruch. He knew the names, though he had never met their owners.

They were his second cousins, once removed. Vermeulen on the paternal side and Baruch on the maternal. Since they were related to him, he had surmised that they were immers. Until now, he had had no proof of that.

That they were among the loftiest officials was evident by their single occupancy of the apartment. They had antiques and knickknacks and wallpaper, numerous items that did not have to be stored six days out of the week. Their situation was even superior to that of his friend of Tuesday, Commissioner-General Horn, who shared her apartment with one other, a woman of Thursday.

Vermeulen, a tall thin man, took Dunski's rain apparel and hung it up. His short and thin wife asked Dunski if he wanted anything to drink or eat. He spoke hoarsely and slowly. 'A bourbon and a sandwich, thank you. I'd also like to use your toilet.'

When he returned to the living room, he sat down on a huge stuffed couch covered with factory-grown fur. His pants and shoes were wetting the sofa and the carpet, but he did not care.

Mia Baruch brought him the drink and then sat down by him. He swallowed a fourth of it and sighed.

Vermeulen sat down but said nothing until Dunski had eaten his sandwich. 'Now,' he said, hitching forward in his chair, 'you report everything. My people gave me some details on radio, and I've had reports from other days and from your immediate superior. But I want the whole story, all that's relevant, that is.'

Dunski gave it to him, stopped now and then by questions from Vermeulen and Baruch. When Vermeulen was satisfied that he had heard all, he sat back, his fingers church-steepled.

'It's a mess, but it can be cleaned up. The organics won't be looking for Castor now, but there's all those dead men. The authorities will be wondering what they had to do with him. They'll research the dead, study their bio-data, review every recorded minute of their lives, seek out and interview people who knew them. They'll try to connect all of them. I don't think they'll solve the mystery. Let's hope they don't. We've covered our tracks very thoroughly. But you never know what little meaningful item they might find.'

'What about next Wednesday?' Dunski said. 'The organics will be questioning me. As Bob Tingle, I mean. If they get suspicious, they'll use truth mist. You know what that means.'

Vermeulen dismissed the possibility with a wave of his hand. 'What do they have? The lock that Castor ruined was replaced before the paramedicals got there. Your weapon was taken away. You had an accident, slipped on a piece of soap and struck your head, that's all. Our people in Wednesday, some very high-placed officials, will take care of all that.'

He was probably right, Dunski thought. But too many immers had become involved in getting him out of this mess, and too many knew one or more of his identities.

Vermeulen said, 'You've covered your tracks well. However, there may be witnesses, people who looked out from the nearby buildings and saw you.'

'It was raining hard, it was dark, and I was wearing a coat and hood,' Dunski said. 'Could I have another drink? Thank you. Some people did come out just as I was getting into the van, but they didn't get close. And the clouds stopped the sky-eyes from following me.'

'I know that,' Vermeulen said. 'The organics will work on this until close to midnight, then they'll close shop. They'll leave messages for Tuesday's and Wednesday's authorities. But those will consider the matter closed. Castor, an obvious psychopath, has been killed. End of the trail. Today, though . . . there's all those corpses. That's Thursday's business only, but the immers in other days will be notified of this so that they can come up with something to erase all tracks. A false explanation, maybe. That might be best.' His face lit up. 'Any explanation, if it seems to fit, will be better than none. They'll keep an unsolved case in the bank, theoretically always active. Solved, it'll be in the history section.'

Dunski fought to keep his eyes open.

'That's probably the best plan. Only . . .'

'Only what?'

'What about Snick?'

Vermeulen shook his head and said, 'Garchar went too far.' (Garchar must be the man I called 'Gaunt,' Dunski thought.) 'I wouldn't have condoned killing her, though the mutilation would have been blamed on Castor, a very good idea. But I don't think I could have done it. I can't fault Garchar. He was in command and had no time to check with us. Still . . . anyway, that's past. Snick will stay stoned and will be put in a safe place.'

Vermeulen church-steepled his fingers again.

'Today won't miss her. They'll think she's off on her own chase, if they'll think about her at all. Castor's kept them pretty busy. And what happens tomorrow? Will Snick appear at organics HQ with her visa and her orders from Sunday? No, she won't. So how will Friday know that she's supposed to appear? It won't, and the following days won't know about her, either. Nobody will know that she's missing until Sunday comes and she doesn't report to her superiors. Sunday can do nothing about it except to leave inquiries for the following days. When Sunday comes again, it will get the news that Snick disappeared on Thursday. We'll have plenty of time to get ready for then, and we might not have to do anything at all.'

'I hope so,' Dunski said. He thought about Panthea Snick, cold and hard, stuck somewhere, perhaps for centuries, until she was found, if she was ever found.

'Poor man,' Mia Baruch said, patting his hand.

Dunski looked at her, and she said, 'Your wives . . .

murdered, so ghastly.'

'He got his revenge, anyway,' Vermeulen said.

She snatched her hand away and moved away from him. Of course. He had killed a man. It did not matter that he had done so in self-defence or that Castor should have been killed. She was repulsed by the idea of sitting so close to such a violent man.

'I know that revenge doesn't bring back the dead,' Dunski said. 'It's an old cliché. But revenge does have a certain satisfaction.'

Baruch sniffed and moved further away. Dunski managed a tired grin and said, 'What about Rupert von Hentzau, my wife?'

'She's been notified,' Vermeulen said. 'She'll set up your dummy for you in your cylinder. Or, as I suggested, she should leave the commune tonight, tell them that you and she are divorcing them. Some excuse. If she does leave, she'll go to an emergency stoner. She'll take your tomorrow's bag with her. Whether she leaves or not, she's made arrangements to get your bag to you. She sent her love to you and said she'll see you tomorrow. That is, next Thursday.'

Dunski saw no reason to tell him that he had planted duplicate bags around the city.

Vermeulen paused, then said. 'As for you, you'll stay here. There's no problem with that, is there?'

'You know that my wife, Friday's, is in South America on an archaeological dig?'

'Of course. I had to inquire about her because I had to make sure about your situation.'

The man knew too much about him, but it could not be helped.

'I'm very tired,' Dunski said. 'I'd like to shower and then get to bed. It's been an ordeal.'

Vermeulen stood up and said, 'I'll show you to your room. When you wake up, we'll probably be gone. You can get yourself breakfast and let yourself out. I've left a message for your superior, tomorrow's, that is. I just told him that you'd transmit the relevant data. I suppose your superior will get in touch with you as quickly as possible.'

'It depends on whether he thinks it's necessary.'

The bedroom was luxurious and had a king-sized bed that could be let down by chains from the ceiling. Vermeulen pushed a button on a wall panel, and the bed lowered slowly, then settled on its legs, which had extended from the posts during its descent.

'If anything happens before Mia and I stone, I'll leave a message. That strip there,' he pointed, 'will be flashing. You can get a night robe from that closet.'

'Very posh,' Dunski said. 'I'm not used to such high class.'

'We have greater responsibilities, so we deserve more,' Vermeulen said.

Dunski bade him good night. After Vermeulen had closed the door, Dunski tried the door. It was locked. He brushed his teeth with a disposable brush he found in the bathroom cabinet, showered, and got into bed. The sleep he had expected to come so quickly was not on schedule. Derailed somewhere. Images of Ozma, Nokomis, and Castor tramped through the hall of his mind. He began trembling. Tears flowed, though they did not last long. He got up and went to a small bar in a corner, another luxury, and poured four ounces of Social Delight No. 1, another luxury, into a glass. Fifteen minutes passed while he walked back and forth, his legs drained of strength but unable to stop moving, the drink in his hand. Just as he was downing the last of it, he saw Wyatt Repp, grinning under his white ten-gallon hat.

Wyatt said, 'I should have been in that glorious gunfight, Shoot-out on Jones Street, not you! I would've loved it!'

'It isn't midnight yet,' Dunski muttered as Wyatt faded away.

After he got into bed, he began weeping. Images of Snick cold and hard as a diamond were reflected on all sides in the crazyhouse mirrors of his mind. As he floated into a gusty sleep, he thought, I shouldn't be grieving more for her than for the others. It isn't right.

Friday-World
VARIETY, Second Month of the Year
D5-W1 (Day-Five, Week-One)

20

Wyatt Bumppo Repp strode from his apartment, went down the hall, and stopped before the elevator. His white ten-gallon hat, scarlet neckerchief, ruffle-necked and balloon-sleeved purple shirt, factory-grown black leather vest, huge belt with a massive buckle embossed with a cowboy on a bucking-bronco, tight sky-blue jeans fringed with leather at the seams, and high-heeled white tooled leather boots bearing decals of crossed six-shooters were worn by only one man in Friday. Wyatt Repp, the great TV writer-director-producer of Westerns and historical dramas. The only item lacking – he was irked by this – were elegantly tooled holsters and elegantly embossed toy pistols. The government said no to that. If little boys could not play with toy weapons, why should this big boy? He would set a bad example.

Never mind that the government did not restrict the showing of weapons or violence on strips and in empathoria. This government, like all since the founding of Sumer, was split-brained.

Though the tenants waiting for the elevator had seen him often, they stared at him admiringly and greeted him enthusiastically. Repp basked in the sun of their regard. At the same time, he felt a smidgen of shame because he was taking advantage of their ignorance and was, in a sense, a sham. No real cowboy ever dressed like this, and real cowboys had never carried a shoulderbag. However, they should have known this, since his TV shows portrayed cowboys as realistically as research allowed.

The tenants greeted him loudly and exuberantly. Repp replied softly, true to the tradition of the low-voiced and gentle hero who was, nevertheless, as tough as they come. 'Smile when you call me that, stranger.'

On the way down in the elevator, he answered as best he could the questions of the passengers about his forthcoming drama. When they got to the lobby, all scattered and went their own ways. His heels clicking on the marble floor of the lobby, he strode out into the bright sun and cool air. He got into the waiting taxi, and replied softly to the driver's greeting. The driver, having been told via strip of Repp's destination, drove from the corner of East Twenty-third Street and Park Avenue to Second Avenue. He turned the taxi right and drove to the rear of the block building that had once been the site of the Beth Israel Medical Centre. The Manhattan State Institute of Visual Arts was a six-storey building looking more like a corkscrew than anything. This had, of course, given rise to jokes about what the institute was doing to the public.

The driver opened the door and said, 'The storm sure cleared the air and cooled things off, Ras Repp.'

'It cleared up and cooled off a lot of things,' Repp said. 'You have no idea, pardner.'

Events were back in a steady and normal course. Castor was dead. Snick was hidden. The immers were covering up and straightening out the trail. Today could go as the days past had. He would have problems, but they would stem from his profession, not from the acts of criminals and organics pursuing those criminals. Although – he grinned – there were some who said that his dramas were crimes.

He felt elated, and his walk was springy as he strode across the sidewalk and entered the walk leading to the building. The passers-by stared at him, some calling to him though he did not know them. The great fountain midway between the sidewalk and the building shot water from the tops of the heads of the group on the pedestal in its centre. There were twelve men and women there, stone, not stoned, statues of great visual artists of the recent past. Perhaps his statue would be among them someday. The spray fell upon his face and cooled it. He saluted the twelve as he passed them, and he walked between the rows of giant oaks and entered the nine-sided door. An elevator took him to the top floor, where he greeted the receptionist. The room beyond was large and dome-shaped with a huge round table in the centre. Men and women rose from the chairs around it as he came in. He answered their good-mornings, threw his hat on the table, put his bag on the floor, and sat down. His girl Friday, a man, brought him coffee. Repp looked at the time strip on the wall. 'Ten o'clock,' he said. 'Exactly on time.'

Another wall strip was recording his actions and speech. It would tell the government work-monitors that he had not delayed between inserting his ID disc-tip into the office door and his entry into the room. Visual artists were not given credit by the hour; they were paid as specified in their contracts with the Department of Arts. This gave them a weekly credit, the amount varying according to the government-decreed stature of the artist. If the project was finished on schedule, the artist concerned did not have to refund a certain amount of credit. If the project was under schedule, the artist was given a bonus. And if the government visual arts committee decided that the quality of the project was high enough, it awarded the artist another bonus.

The artists, however, could put in as many hours as they wished to make sure that the project was done in time or to raise the quality.

The arrangement was not one that most artists liked. In fact, most of them, including Repp, detested it. They could do nothing about it except to make a formal organized protest. This they had done several times. So far, without success.

Nevertheless, although the schedule was the only really

important item for the government, aside from the budget, of course, the monitors kept a close watch on the time put in by the artists.

Some things had not changed since the ancient days of Hollywood. Repp, for instance, was getting triple credits because he was the chief scriptwriter, the chief director and a lead actor. He had used his own influence and that of an immer on the visual arts committee to secure three simultaneous positions. The political jockeying and jousting had cost Repp many evenings, not to mention many credits for giving parties, but the effort had been worth it. If he could keep the triple positions for his next show, he could get a bigger apartment. If one was available.

Work moved along smoothly if the squabbles and arguments and subtle insults were not considered. These, however, were a part of TV and empathorium-making and to be taken in stride. The first two scenes scheduled for the morning were graphed and regraphed until perfect. Repp had a short but hot dispute with Bakaffa, the government censor, over the use of holographed subtitles. Repp claimed that they distracted the viewer and were not necessary because they had been in so many shows that the audience knew what the archaic words were. Bakaffa insisted that 'nigger' and 'wop' and 'sawbones' and 'accumulation of interest' and 'gat' and 'rod' and 'pansy' and 'morphadite' would not be understood by at least half the audience. Whether they did or did not understand these ancient words made no difference. The government required that all such be explained in subtitles.

Repp lost, but he had the satisfaction of driving Bakaffa close to tears. He was not sadistic. He just wanted to make Bakaffa earn his extra pay as a government informer.

At ten minutes after one, during the third scene, the main character's left leg suddenly shrank to half its length. The technicians tried to locate the malfunction in the holograph-projector, but they failed because the troubleshooting equipment had also malfunctioned.

'OK,' Repp said. 'It's twenty minutes to lunchtime, anyway. We'll eat now. Maybe the trouble'll be fixed by the time we get back.'

After he had eaten, he strode down the wide corridor of the first floor from the sandwich shop. The sun coming through the storey-high windows shone whitely on his Western outfit, and his high heels clickety-clicked loudly. Many recognized him, and some stopped him to get his autograph. He spoke his name and ID number into their recorders, said he was sure glad to meet them, and strode on. There was one embarrassing though not entirely unpleasing incident. A beautiful young woman begged him to take her to his or her apartment and do what he would. He turned her down graciously, but when she got on her knees and put both arms around his legs, he had to call to two organics to pry her loose.

'No charges,' he told them. 'Just see that she doesn't impede this pilgrim's progress.'

'I love you, Wyatt!' the woman cried out after him. 'Ride me like a pony! Fire me like a six-shooter!'

Red-faced but grinning as he got on the elevator, Repp muttered, 'Jesus Christ!'

Since he and his wife had agreed to be chaste while they were separated by her Chilean expedition, he had not bedded a woman. He was honest enough to admit to himself that his celibacy had not been based solidly on morality or lack of desire for any but his wife. He needed a rest from sex; he had to recharge his battery, as it were. Though he had a wife on every day but Sunday, more than one on Thursday, and thus each day should have been stimulated afresh, much like a rooster in a barnyard, he was sometimes not up to the freshness and the challenge. His gonads did not use the same system or arithmetic as his mind.

Feeling good because he was wanted but did not want,

he walked into his office and sat down at his desk. Strips displayed messages for him, number-one priority being from his wife, Jane-John. She looked happy because she was coming home next Friday. Stoned, she would be loaded into a plane on Saturday, tomorrow, and delivered to the airport the same day. From there, she would be cargoed via dirigible to the Thirteen-Principles Towers. He was to pick her up next Friday at one in the morning. Or, if he could not make it, she would take a taxi.

Jane-John Wilford Denpasat was a beautiful dark-skinned woman with depigged blonde hair and depigged blue eyes.

'I love my work, Wyatt, but it's getting to be a drag because we have to be transported two hundred miles every day from the digs to the nearest stoning station. And I miss you terribly. See you soon, bucko. I can hardly wait.'

Waiting was easy for her despite what she had said. Unconscious people did not fret and fume or get nervous. And, though he would not be stoned every day until next Friday, he would be someone else and so not thinking about her. New Era society did have its disadvantages, but it also had many benefits. Check and balance; tit for tat; give and take; loss and profit.

Though the strips had not shown a chess move since Tuesday, Repp still felt disappointed that there was none today. He thought of Yankev Gril – Jimmy Cricket – and felt keen regret that their game had had to be dropped. Where was Gril now? Still playing in Washington Square Park? In jail? Stoned and awaiting trial? Or convicted and permanently stoned?

His other messages concerned business. The most important was a reminder that he was a guest on the *ILL Show*. He should be in the studio at 7:30, and he would be on at 8:00 sharp.

No immer had tried to get into contact with him via

strip or in person. That omission was, he supposed, good news.

21

At the end of the workday, Repp taxied home. After working out on a gym set, he showered and then ate a light supper. He arrived at the Thirteen-Principles Towers Building at exactly 7:25 PM and was in the studio at 7:30. Here he was made comfortable by the secretary of the host of the *ILL Show*, Ras Irving Lenin Lundquist. During coffee, he read the strip display that described the guest list and the topics and suggested a few witty remarks he might like to make.

At 8:40, Repp left the studio. He was satisfied with his performance, though several of Lundquist's remarks had stung him. It was good publicity to be seen on the *ILL Show*, hosted by the self-styled Grey Monk of the Mind. Lundquist avoided the showy and flamboyant and went for the serious and the intellectual. Instead of dazzling stage scenes and a startling and flashy costume, the studio room was modelled like the host's idea of a medieval monk's cell. Clad in a grey robe, he sat on a chair behind a desk on a platform that was a foot higher than the guests' chairs. Lundquist was thus able to give the impression that he was the inquisitor-general of Spain and that his guests were on trial. During the nasty questions and comments he hurled at Repp, Repp made the studio audience laugh. He asked Lundquist when he was bringing in the rack and the iron maiden. Because the *ILL Show* audience was composed mostly of the better-educated or those who thought they were, Repp could be assured that it understood the references. That was one of the reasons Repp had exposed himself to the barbs and insults. Another was that he hoped to give as good as or better than he got. Also, it was well known that Lundquist, no matter how he seemed to despise his guests, invited only those he thought had somehow managed to get at least in the neighbourhood of his intellectual eminence.

Lundquist attacked Repp on the premise that his character was insecure and shaky.

'You seem to be hung up on role-changing and shape-shifting, Ras Repp. I need enumerate only a few of your movies, which reflect this obsession, this compulsion, which, in turn, reflects the basic core of your being. Or perhaps I should say, reflects the *lack* of stable identity. There are, for instance, *The Count of Monte Cristo*, *The Odyssey*, *Proteus at Miami*, *Helen of Troy*, and *Custer and Crazy Horse: Two Parallels That Met*.

'All these have to do with disguises, hallucinations, or illusions about identity, or changing of shapes and, hence, change of identity or a seeming change. Curiously enough, you are best known as the man who writes the best Westerns. In fact, as the man who resurrected the Western drama, which had been dead for a thousand years. Some say, better dead.

'Yet those works which have attracted the attention and even the blessing of *some* art critics have not been Westerns. Except, of course, for your *Custer and Crazy Horse*. And that is a most curious Western. Custer and Crazy Horse both get the idea that they'll go to a medicine man, get shape-changing powers from the medicine man, adopt each other's shapes, and lead their enemies to their deaths. Of course, neither knows that the other is doing this. Thus, Custer-as-Crazy Horse kills Crazy Horse-as-Custer, and then, unable to change his shape, is killed by whites.'

Lundquist smiled his infamous smile, which had been likened to, among other things, a vagina with teeth.

'I have it from a reliable source that your current work-in-progress, *Dillinger Didn't Die*, is based on a remarkably similar idea. In fact, your protagonist, the ancient bank robber, escapes from the FBI, the organics of the twentieth century, by magically turning into a woman. He does this by getting his moll, I mean, his woman lover, Billie Frechette, an Indian of the Wisconsin Menominee tribe, to take him to the tabu abode of Wabosso, the Great White Hare, the Menominee Trickster. This creature of ancient Indian legend and folk tale gives Dillinger the power to turn into a woman at an appropriate time.

'And so, when the FBI starts closing in, Dillinger gets Jimmy Lawrence, a petty crook whose days are numbered because of his heart trouble, to pose as him. Then Dillinger becomes Ann Sage, a Chicago madam of a Chicago whorehouse, and has the real Ann Sage kidnapped by friends and taken to Canada. Then, if my informant is correct, Dillinger-as-Ann-Sage goes to the Biograph Theatre with Lawrence-as-Dillinger after telling the FBI that they'll be there. The pseudo-Dillinger is shot and killed by the FBI. Dillinger-as-Ann-Sage walks away from the execution.'

Lundquist sneered, and the studio audience laughed loudly.

'In other words, your protagonist takes the identity of a woman, *becomes* a woman. I understand that you are planning a sequel, *Guns and Gonads* . . .'

Lundquist sneered again, and the audience laughed even more loudly.

'. . . in which Dillinger has great difficulty with the social, economic, and emotional identity of a woman. Eventually, he adapts, and he even comes to like being a woman. He, she, rather, marries, has children, and then goes back to a life of crime as a female whose gang is composed of her sons and their gunmolls. She has quite a colourful, if violent, career under the name of Ma Barker but is finally killed, her guns blazing in a final but futile gesture of defiance, by the organics.

'However, my data banker tells me that Ann Sage lived to a ripe old age and certainly did not suffer a rich sea-change of sex or identity. Ma Barker was born in AD 1872, whereas Dillinger was born in AD 1903. By no stretch of anyone's imagination, except yours, could the two be identical. There is such a thing as carrying artistic licence too far, Ras Repp. I suggest that you have carried it off into Cloud-Cuckoo-Land, emphasis on the Cuckoo.

'Still, these two lived so long ago that historical anachronism is of little importance. In which case, why didn't you drag Robin Hood in? Though I suppose that he would have turned out to be Maid Marian!'

The audience hooted and roared.

'Do not all these repetitions of a theme, your inability to use a different idea, your constant hammering at the problem of identity, betray your insecurity and doubts about your own identity? Doesn't that undoubted mental instability require examination by the government psychicists?'

The audience was in an uproar. Repp was taken aback by this unexpected disclosure about his drama. While he should have been thinking about his reply, he was wondering which of his colleagues had leaked the information about the movie.

As the cries and boos trailed away, he decided that he would have to start his own inquisition next Friday. After work hours, of course. Meanwhile, he had better take care of Lundquist.

He rose from the chair, stuck his thumbs in his big belt, and swaggered across the platform to the 'pulpit.' Standing, he was able to stare down at Lundquist despite the host's elevated chair. Lundquist was still smiling, but he blinked furiously. He did not like having to look up at his guest.

'Pilgrim, those are hard words, and I'm glad you smiled when you said them. Now, if these were the old days, I'd punch you in the nose.'

Lundquist and the audience gasped.

'But these are nonviolent and civilized times. I've contracted not to sue you for anything you say about me. And you can't sue me, either. It's a no-holds-barred, kick-in-the-nuts-or-what-have-you, gouge-eyes-out, half-alligator, half-bear-wrestling-and-ear-chewing-show. Verbally, that is.

'So, I say you're a liar, and a word-twister and a fact-bender. Out of sixty movies I've made, only nine have been about shape-changing and role-exchanging. Any fool can see that I'm not hung up or obsessed with the problem of identity. Any fool but you, I reckon. As for your careless and malicious remark about my mental instability, if I did have a screw loose, I would've popped you one. See how calm I am? See this hand? Is it shaking? It's not, but if it did, who'd blame me?

'What I am, Ras Lundquist, is the Bach of the drama. I play infinite variations on a single theme.'

'Bach is turgid,' Lundquist said, sneering.

All in all, it was a good show. The viewers were delighted with the violence of the dialogue and enchanted by the threat of physical violence. According to the monitor, exactly 200,300,181 were watching the show. It would be rerun next Friday so that those who were now sleeping could get a chance to view it.

Repp walked out jauntily into the corridor, stopped for a while to say his name into the recorders thrust at him by fans, and then swaggered to the elevator. He taxied to his apartment, drank a bourbon, and went to bed. At 11:02, he was awakened by the alarm strip. After setting up his dummy and changing clothes, he put his bag over his shoulder and went down to the basement to get a bike from the vehicle-pool. The air was warmer than it had been the previous evening; another heat wave was heading towards Manhattan. A few light clouds were moving slowly eastwards. The streets were almost empty. Several organic cars passed him. The occupants looked at him but went on. On the sidewalks were stacks of one-foot cubes, the compacted and stoned garbage-trash put out by Friday's State Cleaning Corps. Saturday's would pick it up. Aside from infrequent data, the only thing passed on from one day to the next was garbage-trash. The cubes had several uses, one of which was as building blocks. It was said, with only some exaggeration, that half of the housing in Manhattan was garbage. 'So, what's changed?' was the usual retort.

At 11:20 PM Repp stopped in front of an apartment building on Shinbone Alley. He looked around the brightly illuminated area before going down the ramp leading to the basement. He did not want to be seen entering the building by organics. They might think that he was just a late-coming tenant, but they also stopped every seventh person they saw out this late for a quick checkup.

No vehicle was in sight, and he could not hear the singing of tyres on pavement. He turned and rode down the well-lighted ramp to its end and into the bicycle garage. After putting the bicycle in a rack, he walked toward the elevator door, twice kicking trash on the floor. 'Damn weedies!' he muttered. He stopped and took from the bag his Saturday's star-disc. It was not supposed to open the elevator door until after midnight, but he had made alterations to admit him. Though not a professional electronics technician, he had taken enough courses to be one.

Just as he inserted the tip into the hole, he heard a low voice behind him. He jumped, pulling the tip from the hole, and whirled. 'Jesus, you scared me!' he shouted. 'Where'd you come from? Why'd you sneak up on me like that?'

The man gestured with a thumb at the four empty

emergency cylinders at the far end of the garage. 'Sorry,' he said in a low gravelly voice. 'I had to get near enough to make sure who you were.'

He wore an orange tricorn hat and light-purple robe decorated with black cloverleaf figures, the uniform of Friday's organic patrollers. For a second, Repp had thought that he was done for. All was lost unless he could get the gun in his bag out in time to use it. The intruder was too big for Repp to tackle with only his hands. And he would have shot the man. He had not had time to think about the consequences of the act. His desperation would have taken over him as if he were a robot.

What had kept him from going for his weapon was that the man was alone. Organics always travelled by twos. So this one must be an immer.

'As soon as you get your colour back, I'll give you the message,' the man said. 'By the way, that was a good show you gave tonight. You really told that snobbish bastard.'

Repp's heart was slowing down, and he could breathe almost normally. He said, 'If you know me, why'd you come up so quietly?'

'I told you I had to make sure. You aren't in your Western outfit.'

'What's the message?'

'This evening, at 10:02 PM, the organics observed and pursued a wanted daybreaker, Morning Rose Doubleday. I was told that you will know of her. Ras Doubleday fled and took refuge in a house that, unfortunately, was next to the house where a woman named Snick, Panthea Snick, had been hidden after she had been stoned.

'When the woman, Doubleday, was cornered in this house, she refused to surrender. She committed suicide by detonating a minibomb implanted in her body. The resulting explosion not only killed the organics pursuing her and the family then occupying the house, but also destroyed the buildings on both sides.'

'Why didn't I hear it?' Repp said. 'Where did this take place?'

'That's not relevant,' the man said, 'but it was on West Thirty-fifth Street. Message continued.

'During the search of the wrecked buildings, the organics found the stoned body of Snick. They destoned her, and she told her story.'

The man paused and looked at Repp as if he expected him to say something. When Repp shook his head, the man said, 'I guess you know what that means. I don't. Message continued. All immers will be or have been notified that Snick is again a grave danger to us. Her description is being passed on. I was told that I didn't have to give it to you.

'All immers are to keep a lookout for Panthea Snick. If she can be killed without attracting attention, she is to be killed at once and the body disposed of. The council suggests putting it in a G-T compacter.

'If the situation is such that she can't be killed on the spot, whoever sees her will notify his contacts, and they will go after her. You will pass on this message to all your contacts, and you will describe her. You will do this every day until you are told to stop.'

The man paused again and said, 'It was assumed that her mission was the search for and arrest of Morning Rose Doubleday. But since she is still conducting a search, that assumption may not be correct. It is possible that she had a multipurpose mission and that Doubleday was only one mission. Or it may be that she is looking for other members of Doubleday's organization, though the organics have received no such report from Snick. That is, the lower echelons of the organics have received no such report or data. She must have transmitted data to today's higher officials that has resulted in permission to continue her mission, whatever that is. And she will transmit this to tomorrow's officials.

'If tomorrow's council hears anything that may immediately affect you re Snick, you will be notified as soon as possible.'

The man spoke as if he were a receiver-transmitter spewing forth organic officialese.

'One more item before message is finished,' the man said. 'We do have a highly placed official in Saturday. That official will endeavour to find out exactly what Snick's mission is. Meanwhile, keep a low profile. Snick will be living in this area. She will move into an apartment in Washington Mews Block Building.'

'Got you,' Repp said. 'She's taken an apartment in this area because whoever she's looking for is in this area. At least, she thinks so.'

'Good luck,' the man said. He looked around at the trash. 'How do you stand this?' He turned and walked towards the ramp before Repp could reply.

'Thanks, I'll need it,' Repp called softly after him. He turned. The elevator door was still open, waiting for him. He entered the cage and punched the button for his floor. Though he was rising physically, he was sinking emotionally. Wyatt Repp, he was thinking, had ridden high all day. And now, shortly before midnight, he had tumbled hard. Very hard.

As he reached his floor, his spirits surged upwards, though briefly. Snick's face had flashed like a mental meteorite through his dark thoughts. Why should he feel joy? Because she was alive. That was very strange and needed looking into. Especially since he was supposed to kill her if he got the chance.

Saturday-World
VARIETY, Second Month of the Year
D5-W1 (Day-Five, Week-One)

22

'Ohm-mani-padme-hum!'

The deep male voice droned the chant. Charles Arpad Ohm batted at it as if it were a gnat flying around his ear.

'Ohm-mani-padme-hum!'

'Go away!' Charlie said. 'I've got a hell of a hangover!'

'Ohm-mani-padme-hum!'

'Shut up!' Charlie said, and he put the pillow over his head. The voice came through the pillow faintly but insistently. It was as if a Tibetan monk was speaking a ritual to awaken the dead, as if he, Charlie Ohm, was buried but not beyond resurrection.

The voice stopped. Charlie, knowing what was coming, cursed. The female voice that succeeded the male was very loud and shrill, the essence of shrew, termagant, and nag. It was his ex-wife's, programmed into the alarm strip by Charlie because it was the only voice that could get him out of bed. It made him angry, raised his blood pressure, and brought him up and out of desirable sloth. Not so desirable if he was to get to work on time.

'You lazy slob! Bum! Drunk! Lech! Sickening weedie! Get your goldbricking ass into gear! Malingering mutt! Pig! Parasite! Dirt balls! There's only one thing you can get up in the morning, and I want none of that! See if you can't hoist the rest of you, your alcohol-soaked carcass, the desecrated and ruined temple you call your body, out of your trough-bed! Get up *now* or I'll pour cold water on you. God knows you need a bath, crud faucet!'

'That does it!' Charlie cried, and he rolled over, lifted the pillow, and tossed it at the alarm strip. His ex-wife's snarling face was displayed on it. She yelled, 'That's right!

Throw things at me, you unreasonable facsimile of a facsimile! You couldn't hit an elephant's rear!'

Charlie had recorded some of his wife's rantings and had excised various bits and put them together in an unharmonious whole. Some irrational wish to be punished – after all, the divorce had been partly his fault – had made him submit himself in early mornings to her decibelish devilings.

Charlie rolled groaning out of bed, stood up somewhat shakily, and shambled to the bathroom. On the way, he kicked aside a crumpled candy-bar wrapper. He swore at the occupant who had failed to drop it in the disposer. Passing the row of cylinders, he shook his fist at the face in the window of Friday's stoner.

'Slob!'

At least Friday had changed the bedclothes. This time. More than once, Charlie had fallen into a bed smelling of sweat, and, once, of vomit. Despite this, he had not complained to the authorities. That was against the unwritten code of the weedies. But he would leave a nasty message for Robert Chang Selassie.

When he was finished in the bathroom, he went through the door that led into the living room. Beyond the pool table, standing against the eastern wall, was the row of seven cylinders. The only one who inspired a thought in Charlie was Sunday's occupant, Tom Zurvan, who stared through the window. His fierce expression, long hair, and long and thick beard made him look like an Old Testament prophet, a Jeremiah of the fourteenth-century New Era. Charlie blessed him ironically, sure that Zurvan never left anything for others to clean up. Charlie also felt sure that Zurvan would not have approved of him.

His ex-wife's voice had stopped, but it would screech out again if he went back to bed or lay down on the sofa or the floor. It was programmed to pounce upon him, if necessary, until he had had his first cup of coffee.

He walked down the hall, passing by strips that had been automatically activated. Their voices were a medley and a babel.

'. . . learned today that ten thousand more square miles have been reclaimed from the Amazon Basin Desert . . .'

'. . . the bad news is that London, despite enormous efforts, is sinking again at the rate of two inches an obyear . . .'

'. . . answer the Number Seven question, and you will win forty more credits, fully government-authorized. What year, in both pre-New Era and New Era dates, did the Battle of Dallas take place?'

'. . . the ancient philosopher, Woody Allen, said that we are all monads without windows. There is some dispute among the historians about the exactness of the reading of the ancient records. Some claim that Allen said nomads, not monads. In which case . . .'

'. . . a vote for Nuchal Kelly Wang is a vote against the continued use of contraceptive chemicals in our drinking water. Stop this obsolete and unwarranted method of birth control! We have room on this great planet for more people! A vote for Wang is a vote for the future! People are crying for children, yet . . .'

A reminder strip, one of several, displayed that Charlie was scheduled to take a voter-qualification test next Saturday.

STUDY HARD, YOU DUMMY. REMEMBER THAT YOU FAILED THE TEST LAST TIME.

'What's the difference?' Charlie growled. 'Wang is the only one I'd vote for, and he doesn't have a chance.'

A news strip in the kitchen greeted him with a view of Pope Sixtus the Eleventh on the porch of his bungalow in Rome. This had been recorded last Saturday during the installation of Ivan Phumiphon Yeti as today's head of the Roman Catholic Church. The camera swept over the fifty or so of the faithful on the small lawn and passed into the house. Ohm paused to watch while getting a stoned four-cup cube of coffee from his PP cabinet. The strip showed the faces of the other six vicars of Christ in their cylinders in a tiny room. They were the faces of old men who looked as if they had suffered much.

'Suffering is good for the character,' Ohm said, and he told the strip to switch to another channel. He was not uncaring; he was stirred by feelings that he could not handle at the moment. But the sight of the Manhattan Manglers being beaten 5-4 by the Rhode Island Roosters did not quiet him. There had been a riot after that soccer match, one that Charlie might have joined if he had been in the stadium. Though the strips had not shown the melee (ten badly injured), Charlie had heard about it via the grapevine.

The sky-eye recordings would be magnified and studied by the organics. After which, those responsible for the injuries would be tracked down to their homes and arrested. The leaders of the infuriated mob and the injured would also be arrested.

Charlie shut the strip off, put the cube in a deep dish and the dish in the destoner, and turned a switch. After opening the door, he took the dish out, poured the ground coffee into a filter, and turned on the coffee-maker. While waiting, he went to the curved window and looked out at Womanway. The sky was clear. Another hot day. The street was filled with men and women in brightly coloured kilts, floppy shirts with wide thick neck-ruffs, and wide-brimmed hats bearing plastic or real flowers. There were many pedestrians, most trying to walk under the shade of the huge oaks or palm trees lining both sides of the street. Many of the cyclists had big teddy bears in their baskets, and many walkers were carrying teddy bears. The faces of these had been modified to look half-ursine, half like those of beloved relatives, spouses, lovers, or, for the more narcissistic, like their owners.

Charlie shook his head – he had resisted the fad – and poured out a large mugful of coffee. Slouching to the table, he dropped into a chair, spilling some of the liquid on the table. Staring moodily at the coffee, the only decent way to stare early in the morning (almost 10:00 AM), he tried to remember the shank of yesterday evening. He had come home quite late, had trouble inserting the disc tip into the hole, had voided much beer, and then had fallen into bed.

Here he was now, unshowered, unshaven, and hung over. His head felt as if it had been cut off and was being used for a bowling ball. Every other beat of blood through his brain was a strike, and the pins flew through in all directions, slamming into the walls of his brain. How had he gotten that headache which no one, not even the sinfullest of sinners, deserved? Oh . . . yes . . . After tending bar, he had not gone home, which he should have done, but had swilled all evening with his cronies at the tavern.

Never again! The wailing cry of the repentant rose from his lips. Never again! And he sat back, startled at the violence of his vow. He had actually spoken aloud.

He got more coffee. What was that dream that had upset him so much? He could not remember it any more than he could remember the specifics of last night's revel. Wait. Out of the dark fog some dim figures were emerging. He tried to grasp them, only to see them slink back into the fog.

It did not matter. He would drink some more coffee, eat a very light breakfast, and exercise on the gym set in the living room. Then, after shaving and showering, he would take his fencing foil and equipment down to the block gymnasium. After a vigorous hour, he would come back to the apartment, shower again, and then dress for work.

Thinking of dress, what was he doing sitting here naked? He thought that he had not taken his clothes off after he had stumbled into the apartment. He must have, though it was strange that he had not seen them on the floor. Surely, he had just dropped them before falling into bed. Perhaps, some time in the night, he had gone to the bathroom. Coming out, he had picked them up and put them in the PP closet. Even weedies, dirty and unresponsible, antisocial, and slobbish, were so conditioned that they automatically did certain things that went against their nature.

'I really must cut down on the booze,' Charlie muttered. He rose to get more coffee but stopped, cup in hand. The strip on the wall behind him had buzzed loudly. He turned and saw it flashing orange. When he had spoken the words to clear it, he saw the man standing before the apartment door. The strip showed a tall and well-muscled man of about thirty subyears. He wore a mauve hat with yellow roses, a yellow loose blouse with lace cuffs and a green neck-ruff, and a black-and-yellow-checked kilt. His shoulderbag was made of alligator leather, the skin for which was grown in a factory in Brooklyn. The teddy bear held under one arm was mauve. Its face vaguely resembled its owner.

Charlie Ohm said, 'What the . . . ?' He suddenly recognized the man with the narrow foxlike face. During the past few subyears, Charlie had served him drinks, which the man nursed as if they were dying birds. Three drinks of bourbon, and the evening was spent for Hetman Janos Ananda Mudge.

'. . . hell is he doing here?'

He told the audio of the entrance-door monitor strip to turn on and said, more loudly than was necessary, 'Just a minute!'

He hurried from the kitchen, groaning as each step jarred loose pain in his head. He went down the narrow hall, the light coming on as he entered, and inserted the tip of his disc-star into the hole below the SATURDAY plaque. A few seconds later, clad only in a kilt, he walked quickly, wincing, to the front door. He paused. What was Janos Mudge doing here? Had he, Charlie Ohm, insulted Mudge sometime last night and was Mudge here to demand an apology? Or was Mudge an organic and here to arrest him for something that he had done last night? Something antisocial? That last speculation did not seem likely, since the hall monitor strip showed that Mudge was the only one in the hall.

'What do you want?' Charlie said.

The strip showed . . . exasperation? . . . flitting over Mudge's face.

'I want to talk to you, Ohm.'

'What about?'

Mudge glanced down both sides of the hall. That there was no one else there did not mean that he was not being monitored. Some weedie might be watching him on his hall strip.

Mudge reached into a pocket on the side of his kilt and pulled out a thin square black plate. Holding it with two fingers, he spoke into it so softly that Ohm could not hear him. Then he held it up cupped in one hand. The strip showed one word flashing orange against the black.

IMMER.

After three flashes, the word disappeared.

'Oh, Lord!' Charlie said.

23

Between seeing the calling card and opening the door, Ohm's hangover vanished. It did not explode. It imploded, burst inwards. The hangover fragments, like shrapnel, tore holes in the persona of Charlie Ohm, and what had been shut out stormed into the breaches. He had been 'remembering' the events of last Saturday night, though they had been vague. And the hangover he had been suffering this morning was, in a sense, the hangover of a hangover. The original had been endured and finally gotten rid of on last Sunday, when he had been Father Tom Zurvan. Father Tom, who never drank alcohol but nevertheless had to suffer from Charlie Ohm's roisterings. Father Tom, who accepted the head pain as part of the bad karma from his previous life.

The hangover had passed five days ago. Yet, when he, as Charlie Ohm, had awakened this morning, he had cocooned himself. All the events and dangers gone through by the four predecessors had been arrested, as it were, and put in a dungeon. Or stoned and put in the psychic cylinders somewhere within him. He, stoned in more than one sense, stoned Charlie Ohm, had remembered nothing. He had been no one but Ohm, the part-time bartender, the lush, the weedie. The days between last Saturday and this had bounced off him as if he were a non-immer, a phemer. Even the hangover that no longer existed had come back to life. It was last Saturday's hand squeezing him to get all the juice of the other days out.

That sudden revelation had been the first shock. The second was that, if an immer was here, he was bringing very bad news. Nothing else would have made the councillors send a messenger.

Mudge entered, looked around as if he expected to be in a pig sty and then looked surprised that he was not. He said, 'Get dressed, and be quick about it. We have to get out of here in five minutes. Sooner if possible.'

'The organics . . . they're coming?' Ohm said. He swallowed audibly.

'Yes,' Mudge said, 'but not for you. Not specifically, that is. It's a sanitary check raid.'

Ohm felt relieved. 'Oh,' he said, 'then . . . ?'

'I'm to conduct you to . . . someone,' Mudge said. 'Get going, man!'

The urgency and authority of Mudge's voice spun Ohm around and sent him running for the PP closet. When he came out, he found Mudge standing in front of Zurvan's stoner. The man turned on hearing him and ran his eyes up and down Ohm. 'OK.' But he turned again and pointed at Zurvan's face. 'This is really a dummy?'

'Yes,' Ohm said. Then, 'How do you know that?'

'I had orders to get rid of it if it didn't look realistic.'

'Why? Is the situation that bad?'

'Bad enough, I guess. I don't know the details, of course. Don't want to know.'

Mudge glanced at the clock strip. 'Good. Two minutes ahead of schedule. You don't have any recordings that should be erased? Or anything you wouldn't want the organics to find?'

'Damn it, no!' Ohm said. 'I may be a weedie, but I'm not sloppy.'

Mudge had turned both his kilt and his hat inside out. He was now wearing a brown hat with a long orange feather and a cerise kilt. Mudge was reaching inside his handbag, which he had put into a brown shopping bag. For a second, Ohm thought that Mudge would bring out a gun. He could feel the blood draining from his head. At the same time, he crouched, ready to spring. But Mudge removed a hat, a wide-brimmed, high-crowned brown hat with an orange feather.

He held it out to Ohm. 'This is reversible, too. Put it on.'

Ohm took his hat off and tossed it on the floor. Mudge raised his eyebrows and looked sternly at Ohm.

'I'll put it away later,' Ohm said. 'You said we don't have much time. Besides, if the organics come in, they have to find some untidiness. They might get suspicious if they don't.'

They started towards the door. Ohm, a step behind Mudge, said, 'Can't you tell me anything about this?'

'Yes.' Mudge opened the door and went into the hall. When Ohm had joined him, Mudge said, softly, 'I was to tell you this only if you asked. The Repp dummy has been discovered. It was found at ten to midnight yesterday. Friday, I suppose.'

'My God! It's all over!'

Mudge said, 'Keep your voice down. And act natural, whatever that is. No more questions.'

'Was Snick behind this?'

'I said . . . no more questions.'

They started down the hall as a door three apartments away from his opened and a loud drunken couple, a man and a woman, staggered out. Mudge steered away from them as if he might get dirty if he got too near. 'Hey, Charlie,' the man said. 'We'll see you at The Isobar.'

'Maybe,' Ohm said. 'I got urgent personal business to attend to. I don't know if I'll make it to work on time.'

'We'll drink to your happiness and success,' the woman said.

'Do that.'

When they got into the elevator cage, Charlie said, 'I know you don't want me to ask questions. But am I going to get to work? If I don't, what excuse do I use?'

'That'll be taken care of, I suppose.'

'Well, maybe it won't be important by then.'

Mudge stared at him and said, 'You'd better get hold of yourself, fellow. Jesus, you don't act like an immer.'

Just before the elevator stopped, Mudge, unable to control his curiosity and ignoring his own command, said, 'Why in hell would an immer live here?'

'No questions, remember.'

How could he tell him that he had built, no, grown, a persona for each day? And that each was based on certain character elements that had coexisted, though not harmoniously, when he had been only Jeff Caird? He had been a conservative and a liberal, a puritan and a flesh-potter, a nonreligionist and a longer for faith, an authoritarian and a rebel, a priss and a slob. Out of the many conflicting elements of character, he had grown seven different ones. He had been able to do many things that would have been denied him if he had lived on only one day. He had contained many in one body, and each man had been given a chance to be what he wanted to be. Charlie Ohm, though, might have been, surely was, the case of going too far.

Just as they stepped out into the underground garage, he flashed the dream that he had tried to recall. He had seen all seven of him in Central Park, riding horses in a fog. They came in from the dimness from different directions and reined in their horses so that the hindquarters formed a seven-pointed star. Or a bouquet of horseflesh.

Jeff Caird had said, 'What're we doing on this bridal path?'

Father Tom Zurvan had said, 'Getting married, of course.'

Charlie Ohm had laughed hollowly and said, 'We act more like we've been divorced. First the divorce, then the marriage. Sure!'

Jim Dunski had pulled a sword from somewhere, held it aloft, and had shouted, 'All for one and one for all!'

'The seven musketeers!' Bob Tingle had yelled.

'May the best man win!' Will Isharashvili had said.

'And the devil take the hindmost!' Charlie Ohm had chortled.

They had fallen silent because they heard the clip-clop of a horse's hooves approaching in the fog. They waited for they knew not what, and presently the figure of a giant man on a giant horselike figure loomed in the fog. Then the dream had ended.

Ohm did not have time to try to plumb its meaning. He was hustled by Mudge out of the building onto the sidewalk. They walked swiftly down the sidewalk past a yardful of screaming children at play and some adults. Ohm had no doubt that some of the infants had no IDs and that they had not been registered in the data bank. Mudge glanced at his wristwatch and muttered, 'One minute to go.' Ohm, looking around, could see no sign of the organics. But when they got to Womanway Boulevard, he saw thirty men and women, all in civilian clothing, standing by several cars. That they were unmarked meant that they were organic. When would the organics learn that everybody knew that?

There would be other raiders collected at other points near the building.

I need a drink, he thought.

But that's the last thing you need just now, someone said.

Nevertheless, as they walked north on Womanway and passed the big dark window of The Isobar, he felt as if some gyroscope inside him was leaning towards the entrance. Leaning also towards the path of least resistance and of hard-to-change habit.

He was sweating, though that was easily accounted for by the heat. That did not account for all the dryness of his mouth. What were today's organics doing about the discovery of Repp's dummy? The first shift would have read the recording left by Friday's last shift. The organics would have taken action on such a serious matter. What action? He was not going to know until he reached his unknown destination.

He felt the weight of the gun in his handbag. Though he had fallen so completely into today's persona, he had automatically transferred the weapon to Ohm's bag. Its presence reassured him, though not much. If Mudge had something bad in mind for him, he would have taken the gun from the bag. But then Mudge did not know much about him, and whoever had sent Mudge would not have told him to disarm Ohm. That would have warned Ohm that the councillors did not want him just to talk to.

I'm really getting suspicious, he told himself. However, I have good reason to be so. I may be a very grave danger to the family.

'Don't get out from under the tree,' Mudge said. 'Stay out of the clear area.'

Charlie had been about to step into the sunshine between the oak trees along the curb and the buildings on the east side of the sidewalk. He said, 'Sorry.'

Eventually, though, they would have to leave the leafy roof and venture out where the sky-eyes could see them. These would record that two men in such-and-such colours and shapes of hats and of kilts had gone under the shield of the trees at such-and-such a point and had emerged at such-and-such a point. This would mean nothing, of course, unless the organics had a reason to track the two men.

Mudge halted when they got to the corner of Womanway and Waverly Place. He looked around – for what, Ohm did not know – and then said, 'Wait a minute, then follow me.' Ohm watched him pull a short plastic-wrapped stick from his bag. He pressed on its butt, and a parasol expanded. Holding it above his head, Mudge walked across the sidewalk and into the GI food store at the corner. Mudge should have brought along a parasol large enough to shield both of them. Then, if they escaped the side-angle sky-eye, the vertical one would have recorded only a parasol under which walked one or two men or women or a mixed couple.

Of course, if the organics were to study the recording, they would observe that a parasol had emerged from under cover where no parasol had entered. No, they could not be sure. At least a dozen parasol bearers had gone under the branches or were standing around. Four of these parasols were the same yellow as Mudge's. And so was the folded parasol slapped into Ohm's hand by a woman who walked on casually as if she were not part of some relay. She, too, held a yellow parasol over her head.

Charlie unfolded the parasol and started towards the store but had to stop when a man stepped in front of him. The man thrust his teddy bear at Ohm, said, 'Take it!' and strolled on. He stopped, however, a few paces away and leaned against a news-strip post. Charlie noted that the man had the same shape and colour of hat and colour of kilt as his. A man his build and with similar clothes and minus a teddy bear would walk out from under the cover of the leaves. Unless the organics computer-analyzed the man's gait, they would think that he was the same as the teddy-bearless man who had gone under the trees.

In two minutes, he had seen more immers than at any one time previously.

Charlie Ohm went into the store and folded the parasol. Mudge, standing near the rear of the store, turned and went into the P & S. Besides Mudge and himself, there were five men and two women there. A medium-sized man with very broad shoulders handed Mudge and Ohm a ball of plastic clothing. He hurried out. Mudge said, softly, 'Go into a stall and change.'

A few minutes later, Mudge and Ohm strolled out of the store. Mudge wore a big-brimmed scarlet hat and a green kilt. Ohm, a few paces behind Mudge, wore a black sombrero with crimson feathers and a green kilt. He followed Mudge up the escalator to the pedestrian bridge across Womanway, went across the bridge, and down the escalator to Waverly Place. They walked west until they came to Fifth Avenue, where they turned north. Ohm scanned Washington Square, which was to his left, but he did not see Yankev Gril. The man could be playing chess somewhere deeper in the square. He could have stayed home because of the heat. Most probably, he had been picked up by the organics. Ohm was curious about the man's motives for daybreaking, though not as curious as Jeff Caird would have been.

Mudge crossed the bridge in front of the square building called the Washington Mews (the Mews had long been gone). Ohm followed him to the west side of Fifth. As he did so, he recalled that Panthea Snick now had an apartment in the Mews building. She must be out in this area now, looking for him. Perhaps. The Friday organics might have had time to run Repp's ID through the data bank and then have passed on the findings to Saturday. If Friday had not done this, Saturday would have.

Which meant one of two actions. One, the Saturday organics would be looking for a daybreaker resembling him, an ordinary, run-of-the-assembly-line breaker. Or, two, they might have tried to match Repp's ID with similar IDs from all of the days. There would have been some delay before the organics could get permission from the North American Superorganic Council for Saturday. But there had been enough time for that. The hounds could know all and be on his scent.

If the latter had happened, what could he do? What had the immer council planned for him?

Mudge walked north on Fifth under the trees. Ohm followed him for a few paces, then stopped. The building on his left was one of the older ones, built before the ship-shape craze. It housed, on Saturday, anyway, Orthodox Jews who used the building gymnasium as a synagogue, worshipping their god amid the odour of sweat socks and sweat shirts. A man was looking out of a second-storey window. Yankev Gril.

The strong handsome face appeared only for a minute. Its expression changed subtly, but Ohm could not read it. Was it a sudden but suppressed recognition of him? Not of Charlie Ohm but of Jim Dunski, who had stood for a while by the table in Washington Square and watched Gril play chess? Or was it just suspicion that Ohm might be an organic looking for him?

Whatever it was, Gril was certainly taking chances by being in that building. It would be one of the first places the organics would search. However, Gril might have moved into it after the search. Or he might just be visiting, perhaps to take part in a religious ceremony.

Bob Tingle, the data banker, had ascertained that there were only approximately half a million Orthodox Jews and two million of the Reformed in all of the seven days. The rest had been absorbed, their identity diffused in the Gentile society. Ohm himself had a Jewish great-grandmother, though she was Jewish by courtesy only. She had not practised the religion.

The government had no public official policy against Jews. It professed toleration of all religions, but it did push a subtle form of persecution of Jews. It was unlawful for parents to arrange marriages of their children or to use any form of coercion to ensure that the children married within the faith. Since it was also forbidden for any group to claim superiority to any other group for religious reasons, the Jews were not allowed to state in words or in writing that they were 'the chosen of God.' That would be antisocial and nonegalitarian. Orthodox males also had to delete from their morning prayer their thanks to God that they were not born as women. That attitude was even more antisocial and nonegalitarian.

All of the sacred or revered writings of the Jews were legally available only in recordings. These had been censored, though not heavily, and interspersed frequently with comments by the officials of the Bureau of Religious Freedom.

For the same reasons, Christians were forbidden to claim that Jesus was the Son of God except in the sense that all Homo sapiens were the children of God. Who, the government said, did not exist. The New Testament was also lightly censored but heavily annotated by the bureau.

24

The thirteen-storey Tower of Evolution looked like a corkscrew. The bright green threadings of its exterior were supposed to suggest the spiralling of life towards higher evolution. Atop the point were the statues of a man and of a woman holding a baby above her head. The baby had its hands raised as if it was trying to grasp something in the sky.

Charlie Ohm followed Mudge into the vast well-lighted lobby and got in line a few people behind him. While waiting, he looked at the outer edge of the circular lobby. Through the plastic walls, he could see the boiling thick-looking liquid and the holograph images of thunder clouds and lightning striking the waters. This was a representation of the primal soup, Earth's oceans, billions of years ago. Here, the numerous strips said, was where life had begun, conceived in violent intercourse by the lightning and out of carbon compounds floating in the thick 'soup.' The first life forms, very basic indeed, had begun in this simple though splendid rape.

Charlie had no idea why Mudge had gotten into the line of sightseers, but he assumed that Mudge knew what he was doing. He moved forward swiftly, though, and was glad of it. Tourists from all over the world jammed the lobby, and the chatter was, if not deafening, annoying.

Charlie finally got to the credit machine standing on a pole at the entrance to an aisle made by posts connected to chains. He inserted the tip of his ID disc-star into the hole. saw the display, ACCEPTED, and passed on into the aisle. He saw Mudge go by the elevator and step onto the stairway to the second floor. Pressed by a man ahead and a woman behind, a close contact Charlie had to endure, he moved slowly up the steps. At the top, he found Mudge waiting for him.

Charlie glanced at the vast and mostly hollow interior rising twelve storeys to the top. He had seen this before at least a dozen times, yet he still felt somewhat awed. The exhibits were in tall and wide recesses in the wall in a staggered ascending arrangement. The visitors travelled on winding escalators that went slanting upwards around and around the walls past the sea- and landscapes with the figures of fish, birds, insects, animals, and plants appropriate to the particular geological time. Standing on the escalator, their altitude ever increasing, the visitors would travel from Pre-Cambrian time (plants and animals with soft tissues) to the Cambrian (the backboneless ocean creatures of the first stage of the Paleozoic Era). Then, moving upwards diagonally, they would go past the Ordovician (the first primitive fishes). They would continue through the Mesozoic and Cenozoic eras, oohing and aahing at the life-sized animated dinosaur robots, and they would end up near the top where Homo sapiens of the New Era was the prime exhibit. They would get off into a recess there and take elevators down to the lobby. Along the corkscrew way, they could step off for a while into recesses to one side of the exhibits to view the curiosities.

Mudge did not get onto the escalator. He turned and went into a doorway to a hall. Passing the two men stationed there, Mudge nodded his head at them. This must have been a signal to let Ohm also pass into the hall. It was not more than ten feet long, ending in a wide strip displaying a montage of some of the life forms on the upper levels. Mudge said something before Ohm got near enough to hear him. Ohm started slightly as the strip before him slid up into a slot in the ceiling and a hall-wide strip slid down behind him from a ceiling slot. For a moment, the two were in a box three feet wide.

Mudge stepped through the entrance, which had been hidden by the wall strip, into an elevator cage. He turned and beckoned Ohm to follow him. Ohm got into it. Mudge said, 'Up.' The doors closed, and the cage rose swiftly. Evidently, since there was no display of floor numbers, the elevator went to one floor only. When it stopped, Mudge got behind Ohm and gently nudged him out. Charlie did not like it that Mudge, who had been in front of him almost all the way, now was behind him. He could do nothing about it and was not sure that he had any reason to try to do something.

They stepped out, facing south, into a large but low-ceilinged room with unactivated wall strips and a thick expensive-looking green carpet. Mudge told him to move on. Charlie went to the only door, which led west. Here was a curving hallway about ten feet wide with another thick carpet and dead-screen strips. As they walked along it, Charlie Ohm saw doors closed on his right. He doubted that these were tenanted. Whoever lived here had plenty of extra rooms and must, therefore, be a very important person indeed.

At the end of a curving three hundred feet, they stopped before a large door. Mudge inserted an ID tip into the code-hole. A few seconds later, a voice told them to come in. Mudge stepped behind Ohm again and told him to go in. Ohm pulled the door open and went in. He was in a large ante-room with plenty of comfortable-looking chairs and davenports. Obviously, he was to go into the next room. He opened the door to that and entered a very large room. Its windows gave him a view of the Hudson River and of the forest covering the part of New Jersey that he could see. There was a lot of furniture, though not too much for this room. On the wall, spaced among the activated strips, were paintings in the ancient Chinese manner. Ohm wondered if these were originals and not copies. The furnishings and the furniture were certainly

Chinese. One of the objets d'art that caught his eye was a big bronze Buddha in a niche.

The man sitting in a chair at the end of the room, near a window, was wearing scarlet pyjamas and slippers and a Kelly-green morning robe. He was large and dark-skinned and had prominent epicanthic folds. His nose was large and hawkish; his eyebrows, heavy; his chin, massive. He looked familiar, but it was not until Ohm was a few feet from him that Ohm realized why. Decrease the epicanthic folds by half. Change the blue eyes to brown. He would look much like Jeff Caird . . . Father Tom Zurvan . . . himself.

Mudge said, 'You may stop here.' Meaning, 'You must.' Ohm did so, and Mudge said, 'I'll take your bag.'

Reluctantly, Ohm handed it over. He had intended to see just where Mudge put it, but the man arose from the chair and bowed slightly, shaking hands with himself. That was Tuesday's greeting, which meant that this man could be that day's citizen. Or it could mean that he was indicating that he knew Ohm's primal persona. Or it could mean both.

The man smiled and said, 'Welcome, grandson.'

Ohm stared, felt his blood rushing from his head, and said, 'Grandson?'

'Also my great-great-grandson in your paternal and maternal lines.'

Though shaken, Ohm had recovered quickly. Aware that he had not returned the formal greeting, he did so. And he said, 'You have the advantage of me.'

That was not quite true. Only one man in the world could be his great-great-grandfather and still be living. But he had died.

That was what the vital statistics of the World Data Bank recorded. However, who knew better than Ohm that the data bank held many lies?

'Advantage?' the man said. He gestured that Ohm

should sit down. Ohm, as was proper, waited until the older man seated himself first. Before taking the chair offered, he glanced around. Mudge was standing by a table ten feet behind him. The shoulderbag was on the table but unopened. Mudge, of course, would know by its weight that it contained a gun.

Ohm also scanned the strips, each of which displayed some of the exhibits in the tower.

Ohm sat down, looked steadily into the man's eyes, and said, 'All right, no advantage. You did take me by surprise, I admit that. I had no idea . . . we've all been told that the founder was killed in a laboratory accident.'

'Blown to bits,' the man said. 'It was not difficult to grow skin and organs and bones from my own cells, even hands, which had, of course, my fingerprints, and one eyeball that was not destroyed by the explosion. By design, of course. There were a lot of *of courses*.'

'Your intimates were wondering why you looked so young,' Ohm said. 'You finally had to seem to die, and then you took a new ID.'

Gilbert Ching Immerman nodded and said, 'My permanent residence is not in this country. It won't hurt for you to know that. You may also know that Saturday is not my official citizenship day. I flew here to straighten this mess out.'

Whatever Immerman's name was now, it was that of a very high official, Ohm thought. Probably he was a world councillor. Only a man of that rank and influence could have a personal apartment – such a large one, too – that he rarely used. And only a very high official could break day when he pleased. Ohm wondered what his cover-up story was. Not that that mattered. What did matter was why Immerman was here.

'Grandfather,' Ohm said. He paused. 'May I call you Grandfather?'

'I'd like that,' Immerman said. 'No one has ever done

that. I had to deny myself the pleasure of my grandchildren's company. But, of course, I also did not have to be involved in the sometimes painful and distressing troubles that come with the joys of grandchildren. Yes, you may call me Grandfather.'

He stopped, smiled.

'But what do I call you?'

Ohm said, 'What . . . ? Oh! I see. Today's Saturday. Call me Charlie, please.'

Immerman shook his head slightly, then made a gesture. Mudge appeared by Ohm's side and said, 'Yes, sir.'

'Would you get us some tea. Our guest may be hungry, also. Would you like some food, Charlie?'

'Some protein cookies would be nice,' Ohm said. 'I had a very light breakfast.'

'I would imagine you would,' Immerman said. 'The way of life you lead . . . today, that is. You are amazing, Charlie. Not quite unique in being a daybreaker sanctioned as such by the immer council. But unique in your roles. And in the intensity with which you have adopted these roles . . . personae, rather. I believe that you actually become a new man each day. Admirable, in some respects. In others, dangerous.'

Here it comes, Ohm thought. Now we're getting to the reason I'm here. This is not meant to be a family reunion.

'May I walk around a little while we're waiting for the tea and cookies?' Charlie said. 'I didn't get my accustomed exercise. I'm tight and sluggish. I can think better with the muscles loose and the blood flowing.'

'Be my guest.'

Feeling somewhat self-conscious, Charlie got up and strode up and down the room. He stopped at the entrance, turned, and went as far as a few feet from Immerman before turning again. The old man – old man, he did not look more than five years older than his grandson! – sat with folded hands and watched. He was smiling very faintly. While Charlie paced back and forth, he saw a huge seal-point Siamese cat enter from a doorway. It paused, looked intently with enormous blue eyes at Ohm, then trotted to Immerman and leaped upon his lap. It curled down there while Immerman gently stroked it.

'Ming is my first and only pet,' Immerman said softly. 'Ming the Merciless. I doubt you know the reference. He's almost as old as I am. In obyears, that is. From time to time, I stone him.'

Charlie took his gaze away from the wall strips, though he had seen something in one that had startled him. He said, 'Even so, Ming must have been given the elixir for him to live so long. Right?'

'Right,' Immerman said. 'Only . . . it's not an elixir. It's a biological form, a genuine life form, though artificial in origin. It cleanses the plaque from the arteries, does many things. It also partially suppresses the inherent ageing agent in our cells. I don't know how it does it, though I've been trying to find out for a long time.'

Ohm was not pleased by the confidences. They could imply that his grandfather did not care what his grandson learned. Charlie Ohm was not going to be able to pass on the information. But could a man be so objective, so hard-hearted, that he would rid himself – and the family – of his own flesh and blood? The answer was, of course, that he could. The immer family had survived this long because its leaders had been objective and logical. It might grieve Immerman to dispose of his own grandson, but he would do it if he had to. The family came first; its individuals, a long second place behind.

'I've wondered about that,' Charlie said. A little hole in the blackness inside his brain seemed to open. A little light shone briefly through it. Wyatt Repp? Repp seemed to be telling him something. Then he knew, and he spoke it aloud before the knowledge vanished back into the darkness.

'Ming the Merciless,' he said. 'He was a character, the chief villain, in an ancient comic book and movie series. *Flash Gordon*. That was the name of the hero of the series.'

Immerman looked mildly surprised, then smiled. 'That originated in the twentieth century AD I didn't know that anybody but a few scholars knew of that. I've underestimated you, grandson.'

'I'm not just Charlie Ohm, a bartender, a weedie, and a drunk.'

'I know that.'

'I think you know everything about me,' Charlie said. 'I hope that you know me well enough, understand me well enough, that is, to know that I am not a danger to you . . . to the immers.'

Immerman smiled as if he were genuinely pleased.

'Then you realize fully why I have summoned you here. Good.'

Maybe not so good for me, Ohm thought.

He had been about to say something, but one face in a wallstrip display seemed to zoom out, to expand, and to crowd his mind. He trembled. That face could not be there. He looked away and then his head was turned as if it were clamped in a machine. Yes. It was.

The screen showed a large recess near the top of the tower, the third from the final. It contained figures from the past, EXTINCT TYPES OF HOMO SAPIENS. The face that had snagged him in his swift survey, caught him as a stump in shallow water caught the bottom of a boat (and threatened to rip out his guts), belonged to a figure in a seventeenth-century group. This, he thought, represented The King and The Queen and their Court. It could be, judging from the dress, the period of the Three Musketeers. The King would be Louis XIII; the Queen, Anne of Austria. The figure with a foxlike face and dressed in the red robes of a cardinal must be Richelieu.

Ohm struggled to quit shaking. He used one of the

techniques that had been successful many times. He visualized the king and queen and the court and the face that had alarmed him as just one of many. He shrank the scene, rolled it into a ball, and pitched it out of his mind through the top of his head.

It did not work. He could not keep from looking sideways at the face.

Trying to smile as if he were thinking of something pleasant, he returned to the chair and sat down. The scene was at his back. He could not see it unless he turned his neck far to the right, and he would not do that. Immerman would know that he had seen the face.

25

'That's interesting,' he said in a steady voice. 'I mean . . . it's puzzling. Why doesn't the age-slowing life form show up on blood tests?'

He did not, at that moment, care about the subject. But he had to make conversation and then steer it to the subject that just thinking about made his heart hammer.

'It hibernates,' Immerman said. 'A single organism sleeps, as it were, in a blood vessel, attached to the wall. Then, at a programmed interval, it fissions, and the resultant millions of cells do their work. Then all die but one until the time comes for fissioning again. The statistical chances of a blood test being taken when the life form is populous are very small. But the form has been detected four times. It's been recorded in medical tapes as a puzzling and seemingly nonpathogenic phenomenon.'

Mudge came with the tea and cookies. After Mudge had returned to the table on which was Ohm's bag, Immerman sipped his tea.

'Very good,' he said. 'Though I suppose you would rather have liquor?'

'Usually I would,' Ohm said coolly. 'But I am not quite myself just now. The shock . . .'

Immerman looked at Ohm over the rim of his teacup. 'Not yourself. Who are you, then?'

'I'm having no problem with my identity.'

'I hope not. There have been reports that you are showing signs of mental instability.'

'Those are lies!' Ohm said. 'Who reported that? The man who wanted to murder Snick?'

'It doesn't matter. I don't think you are mentally

unstable. Not any more than most people. You are to be commended, by the way, on your handling of the Castor business. However . . .'

Immerman sipped his tea. Ohm said, 'Yes?' and lifted the cup to his lips. He was pleased that his hand was steady.

Immerman put the cup down and said, 'The woman . . . Snick . . . has been taken care of.'

Ohm hoped that the shudder running over the upper part of his body was slight enough to be unnoticed. Those blue eyes seemed to be looking for some sign of reaction to the news.

He forced a smile and said, 'Snick. Already?'

'Early this morning. Her disappearance will eventually cause a hullabaloo, of course. But today's organics don't even know she's missing. She's a rather independent agent. She doesn't have to check in with the organics on any schedule. It may be that she'll not be missed until Sunday. She has to report in on her natal day, of course. But . . .'

'She hasn't been killed, has she?'

Immerman raised his eyebrows. 'I was told that you objected to her being killed. I'm glad you have such humane feelings, grandson, but the family's welfare comes first. Always, first. I don't hold with killing unless it's absolutely necessary. So far, it never has been necessary. If Garchar had killed Snick, I would've made sure that he was punished.'

'Garchar?'

'The man you . . . No, not you. It was Dunski.'

'Sure,' Ohm said. 'I know. Garchar. The man Dunski called "Gaunt".'

Immerman said, 'If you know that, you must remember being Dunski.'

'Just a few important things about him,' Ohm said.

Immerman shook his head while he smiled. 'You're a

unique phenomenon. Someday . . .'

He sipped tea instead of finishing his thought. Then he looked suddenly at Ohm and said, 'You aren't personally interested in the Snick woman, are you?'

'What makes you ask that?'

'Answer the question.'

'No, of course I'm not. You're talking to Charlie Ohm now, grandfather. Tingle and Dunski are the only ones who've seen her, as far as I know. I don't know how *they* feel about her. I doubt they could be physically attracted to her, if that's what you mean. After all, she was dangerous to them.'

He was not telling the exact truth. The unremitting pressure these last few days had pierced, though not broken, the walls of segregation of self from self. The memories of Caird, Tingle, Dunski and Repp were not his; they were secondhand memories. The most vivid of these were intertwined with the persons and events that most threatened all of them. Yet, he felt a trace, a ghost, of attraction to Snick, which could only be feelings that Tingle and Dunski somehow transmitted to him.

Ohm could not have explained just how he knew that Garchar was the man whom Dunski had called 'Gaunt.' Or that he would recognize Snick if he saw her.

Immerman said, 'It's unfortunate that your Wyatt Repp identity has been exposed. We do have a new one to plug into the data bank and are ready to arrange all that goes with that. But would it be better if all seven of you just seemed to disappear and re-emerged with seven new IDs? I doubt it. Some organic Sherlock Holmes might run a massive and detailed data bank search and comparison. You would be found, would be interrogated with truth mist, and you would tell all because you couldn't help it. And then . . .'

Ohm looked Immerman straight in the eye. 'Are you trying to convince me that logic demands one course of action? That I must be a sacrifice? I'm to be stoned and hidden away until some time later? Maybe much later? Or perhaps I won't be destoned *ever*?'

'Think about what you just said,' Immerman said. He sipped some more tea, then refilled his cup.

'You're not going to do that,' Ohm said. 'If you were, you wouldn't have bothered to bring me here to explain all this. You would've just had me snatched and stoned and buried.'

'Good! My children are not fools. Not all of them, anyway.'

Charlie Ohm did not *feel* as if he were a child of Immerman. Looking at him, Charlie had the same emotions that he would have had at looking at a photograph of an unknown grandfather. He knew that he was his flesh and blood, but he had had none of the frequent contacts nor the loving and caring from his grandfather that made loving and caring grow in the grandson. He was awed by the founder, and he had a huge respect and admiration for him. But did he love him or feel that he was truly his grandfather? No.

'What must I do, then?'

'You will abandon all your roles. You will assume a new identity. That will be confined to one day. You will no longer be a daybreaker . . . What's the matter?'

'We'll . . . they'll . . . die!' Charlie said.

'Good God, son, get hold of yourself! You look as if you'd been told that your best friend had died.'

Immerman paused while looking shrewdly at Charlie, then said, 'I see. It's even worse.'

He bit his lip and looked past Charlie as if he were trying to see into the future.

'I didn't know that you were . . . that far gone. Perhaps . . .'

Charlie said, 'Perhaps?'

Immerman sighed, and he said, 'We don't have much

time for this. I have hardly any at all. I can't personally supervise you, get you into your new persona. It *will* be a persona, not just a role, won't it?'

'I'll be all right,' Charlie said. 'It was such a shock. Maybe I have thrown myself into each day's ID too deeply. But I'm not a halfway person. I do it right or not at all. I can handle this, though. After all, I am very adaptable. How many people you know could make the transition so smoothly from one persona to another? How many could handle seven with ease? An eighth person'll be no trouble. In fact, I'm looking forward to a new ID. I was getting tired of the others.'

Had he gone too far in trying to convince Immerman that he could do it?

Voices were shouting in him. 'I don't want to die!' They were so loud and desperate that it seemed to him that Immerman must surely hear them. That was nonsense, of course, but he felt as if the room should be ringing with their cries.

Immerman said, 'You'll return to your job. As I said, a *friend* has made an excuse for your lateness at work. The friend called herself Amanda Thrush. Don't forget that. She said that you had hurt your back in a fall in the shower, but that you'd be in later. Got that? Good.

'I want you to think about your new identity and make sure it's a good one. You'll have to be an immigrant, and arrangements will have to be made to cover everything in the data bank. Mudge will see you early in the evening at your apartment; stay home after work. You'll tell him what and who you want to be. Then he'll do the necessary fixing up and leave a message for his Sunday colleague. The colleague will get in touch with you. You have one more day in your old character, Sunday's, unless something happens to prevent it.'

Charlie expected to be dismissed then. His grandfather, however, sat staring past him and chewing his lip. Charlie waited. The Siamese was also staring at him, and he was purring loudly while Immerman gently stroked him. His grandfather was using his left hand. Charlie thought, I must have inherited my sinistrality from him. On both sides of my family.

Though apparently delighted with his master's petting, Ming suddenly stood up, stretched, and leaped off Immerman's lap. He walked slowly out of the room, heading for whatever mysterious goal cats went to when they departed. Immerman watched him fondly, then said, 'Cats are like people. They're predictable in many respects, but just when you think you've got them completely analyzed, they do something you could never have anticipated. I like to think that that trait is free will.'

He looked at Charlie Ohm. 'I don't think you completely understand what's at stake, what we're trying to do. Perhaps, when I explain it, you'll get over your repugnance at the little violence necessary now and then in order to attain our goals.'

Ohm shifted uneasily in his chair. 'That was explained fully by my parents.'

'That was a long time ago,' Immerman said. 'Also, your case is peculiar. Living from day to day, horizontally, and being a new person each day, you've lost some of the intense feeling most of us have about being immers. Each of your personae has tried to repress as much connection with the others as possible. But that's a limited and qualified segregation because you've had to pass from one to the other, had to cover up your tracks, so to speak, and also you were reminded from time to time that you were seven, not one. That was during the rare occasions when you had to take a message from one day to the next. Recently, however, you have often been reminded that you are more than one person. You've been shaken up, put into a mixer, as it were. Each of your selves is threatened, each of your self-images clashes with the others.'

'The whole thing is just temporary,' Charlie said. 'I'll be all right.'

'You mean *we*, don't you?' Immerman said, smiling slightly. He leaned forward, his hands on his lap. The fingers of his left hand moved over his leg as if he were petting an invisible cat. 'You see, Jeff, I mean, Charlie, you're not the only daybreaker we have. There are at least a dozen others in large cities in the Western Hemisphere and several in China. But none of these have thrown themselves into their roles so completely. None have *become* the personae they adopted. They're just good actors. You are unique, the superdaybreaker.'

'I don't believe in half-measures,' Charlie said.

Immerman smiled and sat back, his fingers interlocked.

'Very good. A true Immerman. But this same intensity and drive in your personae-being should also be applied to your other role.'

'What's that?' Ohm said after a long silence.

Immerman's finger pointed accusingly at Ohm.

'Being an immer!'

Ohm's head jerked back as if the finger was close to his eye. 'But . . . I am!'

His grandfather put his hands together again, the fingers of the left seeming to tap a code on the back of the right hand.

'Not enough. You've betrayed some hesitation about following orders. You've allowed your personal feelings, your revulsion against violence, admirable enough in other situations, to interfere with your sense of the higher duty.'

'I think I know what that is,' Charlie said, 'but I'll ask anyway.'

'You were ordered to go home immediately after Snick was questioned. Yet you stayed outside the apartment building. Obviously, you were thinking about trying to keep Snick from being killed. You failed to consider the danger in which we were placed because she was alive.

Now, I don't think that in this case she really had to be killed. As it turned out, because of your interference, she wasn't killed.'

'Has she been killed?' Ohm said.

'No. She's in a safe place. But she may have to be killed. From time to time, we have to do things we don't like to do. We do that, Charlie, because we're working towards the greater good of all.'

'Which is . . . ?'

'Towards a greater freedom for all, towards a true democracy. A society where we're rid of this constant and close scrutiny by the government. It's bad enough now, but it's going to be far worse. The government has been considering for a long time doing something that would justify the actions of us immers if it was the only thing we opposed.'

He sipped more tea. Charlie leaned forward, intent.

'Some of my colleagues and I have been fighting against this indecent and undignified proposal. But we're losing.'

So, Charlie thought, he *is* a world councillor.

'The proposal is that every adult be implanted with a microtransmitter that will emit the individual's coded ID. Satellites and local stations will receive this whenever it's being transmitted, and that will be all the time except when the person is stoned. They'd like to have it transmitting then, but that's impossible.

'What this means is that the government can locate any person within a few inches of his position and can also identify that person immediately.'

Charlie tried to rock mentally with the punch, but he was nevertheless partly stunned.

'Why, that means that no one can daybreak without being found at once!'

'That's true,' Immerman said. 'However, putting your personal problem aside for the moment, the proposal robs all human beings of any dignity whatsoever. Strips them, makes them ciphers, zeros with numbers, you might say. We don't want that, and we don't want the monitoring we now have. It's better for humanity that we have the dangers of democracy along with the benefits. You can't have one without the other.

'But this is only one of our goals. We believe, we *know*, that there is more room on this planet than the government says there is. The population can be increased without any loss of the comfort and well-being we now have. It should be a gradual process, of course. That radical Wang wants to stop all methods of birth control, but he's crazy. You know whom I mean?'

Charlie nodded and said, 'He doesn't have a chance of being elected. He shouldn't be elected.'

'There are others like him in all the days,' Immerman said. 'All, of course, working for the government and acting on its orders.'

Charlie sat up and said, 'What?'

'Wang and the others are agents provocateurs. They propose these radical measures just to anger the population and to make themselves look ridiculous. Thus, more moderate and quite reasonable proposals are rejected. The people classify the radical with the moderate. They're manipulated by the government for the government's purposes. The government wants a status quo.'

'I shouldn't be surprised,' Charlie said.

'We intend to establish a government that won't use such underhanded and unethical methods.'

Immerman looked at the clock strip.

'We don't intend to do it through swift and violent means until the time is ripe for such means. We have been working slowly and subtly to get the family into high positions in the government. You'd be surprised if you knew how large the family is. But the bigger it becomes, the more danger there is of its being exposed. And the more danger there is, the tighter we have to control our members. It's unfortunate but necessary.'

Charlie thought, That's exactly the excuse the government has used since the beginning.

Immerman stood up, and Charlie also rose from his chair.

'I know what you're thinking. We won't be any better than the government we now have and possibly we'll be worse. Don't believe it. We've been working on the best system of government possible, given the human situation. Someday, that plan will be revealed. Meanwhile, remember this. It was Thomas Jefferson who said that the best government is that which governs least. You were named after him. Or didn't you know that?'

Charlie shook his head.

'I must be going now,' Immerman said.

'One thing,' Charlie said. 'I believe that there's only one situation in which killing is justified. That's when it's in self-defence.'

'Ah, but what is self-defence? Aren't there many kinds?'

'I won't be confused by all that,' Charlie said. 'My ethics are of being rather than of words. I know what's right.'

'Very admirable,' his grandfather said. 'Which one of you is saying that?'

Ohm was surprised when his grandfather stepped up to him and embraced him. While hugging Immerman, Ohm looked over his shoulder at the seventeenth-century tableau. Yes. He had no doubt now, and he hated Immerman for what he had done.

On his way out, he picked up his shoulderbag. It was noticeably lighter, but he said nothing. Immerman would wonder why his grandson wished to keep the weapon when there was no logical reason to do so.

The trip back was almost a complete reversal of the trip up. However, Ohm did not go to his apartment. Instead, he walked into The Isobar. The usual uproar and odour of beer and liquor greeted him. He waved at various patrons in various stages of drunkenness and went into the manager's office. After getting a mild chewing-out (no sympathy for his supposedly hurt back), Ohm put on an apron and went to work behind a long curving oak bar on which stood the statuettes of three patron saints: Fernand Petiot, creator of the Bloody Mary, W.C. Fields, and Sir John Falstaff. Only half the customers were local weedies. The rest were slummers or organic agents. The latter were hoping to catch someone making a barter deal for bootleg liquor.

Ohm was not a complete weedie in that he had not been satisfied to live off the minimum-income credit furnished by the government. His job, however, was not just to supply himself with extra goodies. He overheard much while behind the bar and in front of it after working hours. Sometimes, he picked up information that the immer council could use.

Today did not go as most. He drank very little, and he was so evidently wrapped in his thoughts that some of the patrons kidded him about it. Not sure that he was lying, he told them that he was in love. What he had seen on the screen in Immerman's room, the voices that shouted inside him, and his efforts to select the elements of a new personality beat at him like waves against a seawall. He was glad when quitting time came; he rushed out past his relief with a short good-bye and walked to his apartment. There he ate a light supper and then paced back and forth as if he would wear off the rug and reveal the coded answers to his problems on the floor beneath. He stopped when, at 7:35 PM, Mudge came to the door.

Bearer of a scowling face and bad news, Mudge told him that Immerman had changed his mind about his disposition of Ohm. It would be better, thus, imperative, that Ohm be stoned and shipped to Los Angeles in a box labelled as goods. The California city was due next week for an influx of ten thousand immigrants from Australia and Papua. Arrangements would be made so that Ohm would be listed among them. Tonight, Mudge and Ohm would work on the new ID. After Ohm got to Los Angeles, he could create the fine details of his persona.

Charlie sat down, breathed deeply, and said, 'I suppose there's no use protesting?'

'None,' Mudge said. 'Hetman Immerman said that you must get far away from Manhattan.'

'When?'

'Tomorrow night. A Sunday agent will take care of everything.'

Ohm thought, What guarantee is there that I'll ever be destoned? The logic of the situation demands that I just disappear from the living, be stuck someplace where I won't be found.

Mudge removed a tape from his bag and handed the tiny cube to Ohm. 'Here's the outline of the new persona, the really vital vital statistics and the outline of your background.'

'Already?'

'The council members are old hands at this sort of thing. They must have these in stock. A few changes, and they're ready. Study it tonight and then erase it. You'll be given another one when the time's right.'

Which may be never, Ohm thought. Or am I just too suspicious?

He needed a drink, but he would not allow himself to have one.

Mudge walked to the door and turned. Instead of saying good-bye and good luck, he said. 'You've sure been a lot of trouble. I hope you stay out of it in L.A.'

'I love you, too,' Ohm said, and he laughed.

Mudge scowled even deeper and closed the door behind him. Ohm turned on the hall and outside monitor strips to make sure that Mudge was not hanging around. Then he went to bed, applied the electrodes of a sleepwave machine to his temples, set and turned the unit on, and slept dreamlessly and compulsively. At 9:30 PM, he was awakened by the unit alarm.

'I have to do it,' he muttered. 'Maybe I shouldn't. But I have to.'

26

The loud voices had become whispers, perhaps because the *others* had hope now that they would not die. The quieting of that part of the inner tumult allowed Ohm to concentrate. Sitting in a chair, a cup of coffee on the table by him, he gave orders to a strip. One after the other, appearing or disappearing at his command, the diagrams of the Tower of Evolution and of the area beneath and around shone on the screen. At 10:15, he ordered any evidence of his viewing of the diagrams to be erased. He did not know that it would be done. It was possible that the Department of Building Construction and Maintenance had programmed a non-erasure command. However, he could think of no reason why the department should do that. Even if it had done so, the chances that anyone would note his request and ask for the identity of the requester were not high.

He left the apartment at 10:17 PM and walked as much under the tree cover as possible. The sky was clear, and it was still hot but cooler than in the daytime. The streets were almost empty of traffic, though the sidewalks were crowded with neighbourhood residents. Most of them were going home from the empathoria, the bowling alleys, or the taverns. In fifteen minutes, few would be outside. That would make him more conspicuous, but that could not be helped. Fear of consequences and desperation did not go hand in hand.

Ohm turned onto West Fourteenth Street and walked to the northwest corner of the Tower of Evolution. Here, as on every night at this time, an oblong of light shone up from a hole in the sidewalk. Ohm looked down into the hole and saw two men standing there. They were in the kilted blue uniform of Saturday's Civilian Corps of Transportation and Supply. Ohm pressed the UP button on the mobile cylindrical machine by the hole. As the platform began moving, the men looked up. Ohm nodded at them, got onto the platform when it stopped level with the sidewalk and pressed the DOWN button. Twenty feet below the sidewalk, the platform stopped. Ohm got off and said, 'How're things going?'

The two men looked at each other, and one said, 'Fine. Why?'

Ohm bounced the tip of a finger off his ID disc as if he was indicating that it contained his authority. 'I have to investigate a shipment. It's nothing illegal, just an error.'

He was at the first obstacle, the foremost of several ticklish crossroads. If the workers doubted him and asked for his ID, he would have to improvise an explanation. The workers, however, were not concerned, and his air of knowing what he was about convinced them.

He walked past them and into a tunnel, and soon he was around a bend and out of their sight. Below the grating on which he walked were well-lit levels on which belts or elevators carried boxes of stoned or unstoned supplies. These were part of the vast underground system that transported goods and food to computer-assigned destinations from the unloading depots at the ports or the Thirteen-Principles Towers. The individual belts and elevators moved with little sound, but their aggregation caused a low rumble like that of a distant cataract.

Ohm took an elevator reserved for personnel to the third level down. From there he passed over a narrow catwalk to a bank of personnel elevators, chose number three, and sent himself swiftly up to Exhibit No. 147, EXTINCT TYPES OF HOMO SAPIENS. He went down a short but wide and high hall and stopped at a door. The next ticklish crossroads would be when he entered the room beyond the door. There were hundreds of monitor strips inside the Tower, all active during visiting hours. Was there any reason for them to be on now? Vandalism and burglary were such uncommon crimes, especially in public buildings, that it seemed to him that active monitor strips and personnel to watch them would not be required. However, there might be someone in Immerman's apartment who was viewing the exhibit display strips. Mudge was a likely candidate.

He breathed in deeply and pushed the door open. Stepping through, he found himself at the rear of the seventeenth-century French court tableau. The vast interior of the tower was silent, the sightseers gone, the circling escalator stopped, the information screens turned off, the sounds of the robot beasts quelled. The workers that he had feared might be repairing or altering exhibits were not there. Or, if they were, he could not hear them. Certainly, there were none in this recess.

He moved from around the back of the dais and thrones past the sitting figures of The King and The Queen. He zigzagged through The Courtiers, the gentlemen in their finery and powdered wigs, the ladies in their silk, brocades, hooped skirts and high-piled wigs. They all looked very realistic. A smiling young woman displayed four teeth missing, the rest blackened by decay. A man's face was deeply scarred with smallpox. A fan held by a woman did not entirely conceal that part of her nose had been eaten away by syphilis. Missing, however, were other realistic elements. The stench of long-unwashed bodies and the perfume to cover the stench. The head lice infesting the wigs. Stains on the shoes spattered when their owners urinated in the corners of the palace halls.

He also noticed something that at another time would have made him laugh. Despite all the research and rechecking, the designer of these figures had forgotten that seventeenth-century people were much shorter than New

Era people. Every one of these figures would have towered above all in the court of the real Louis XIII.

Near the middle of the throng, he stopped. The silent and motionless woman in a scarlet and yellow gown and golden-yellow wig stared at him with large brown eyes. Her face was thickly powdered and rouged.

He said, 'God help us!'

He lifted the wig and saw, as he had expected, the short, straight, gleaming-brown hair that looked like the fur of a seal.

'The bastards! The old bastard! What arrogance!'

He stepped behind her and began dragging her backwards towards the elevator. Her high-heeled shoes made a slight rubbing noise, then came off. He stopped, held her upright with one hand, and bent down to pick up the shoes. He must not leave any evidence that an exhibit figure was missing. It was possible that her absence might not be noticed for a long time. All he wanted was a relatively short time.

'Ohm!'

The voice came from somewhere close, and it was Mudge's. Charlie dropped the shoes and the stoned body of Snick, which fell with a loud noise to the floor. He stared wildly around and saw two men, but he was so bewildered and surprised that he did not immediately recognize them. It took a second or two for him to bring them into the focus of reality. A dreamlike state washed over him, numbing him. Then he saw that the two cavaliers who had seemed to come to life were Mudge and a companion.

They had clad themselves in the clothes taken from two figures and had waited for him. They must have monitored him from the moment he entered the underground. They had assumed the stiffness of exhibit figures just before he came through the door.

'Traitor! Damn fool!' Mudge said as he walked slowly

towards Ohm. 'What do you care about the woman? She's an organic, a danger to us! What in hell is wrong with you?'

Ohm slipped off his shoulderbag and let it fall to the floor. He crouched and looked around as if he were about to run. Let them think that.

The other man, a tall thin fellow with burning black eyes, circled around to cut Ohm off. He was drawing the rapier from the scabbard at his belt and would be in the path to the exit door before Ohm could get past him.

'I told Hetman . . . the chief . . . that you'd fall for it,' Mudge said. He had stopped and was removing the long moustaches and the feathered hat and wig. His right hand was on the grip of the rapier at his left.

'Fall for it?' Ohm said.

Wyatt Repp's voice seemed to come faintly to him, telling him that this scene was right out of one of his dramatic – admittedly, corny – empathorium works. 'You're the hero,' the fading voice said.

'Yes. It wasn't any accident that you saw Snick. There was a subliminal flashing just above her head. You couldn't have missed her. Hetman Imm– . . . the chief . . . put her there to test you. He wanted to find out if you really were mentally unstable, if you could be a traitor. Now we know!'

'I wanted to find out if you killed her,' Ohm said. He moved towards a splendidly dressed male courtier on his right.

'What does it matter to you?' Mudge said. 'You were getting away free, and the family was safe.'

His rapier whispered as it was pulled from the scabbard.

'Come quietly with us, Ohm. There's no one else here, and you can't fight us. If you do, I'll have an excuse to kill you here and now.'

'Is she dead?'

Mudge smiled and said, 'You'll never know.'

'The hell I won't!' Charlie yelled. He sprang forward, reached across his stomach with his left hand, and snatched the blade from the scabbard of the courtier dummy. '*En garde*, you son of a bitch!'

Mudge's smile became even broader. 'You stupid weedie, it's two against one. You may be a pretty good fencer, Bela said you were, but you're a drunk and even a world champion couldn't stand against two good fencers. I'm not bad, and Bela . . . he's an Olympic silver medallist Put the sword down, Ohm, and take your medicine like a man.'

Mudge looked as if he were enjoying the coming attraction of combat to the death. The other man also seemed to be relishing it. So much for seven generations of government conditioning against the impulses and use of violence.

It would take five seconds, maybe more, for Bela to reach him. By that time, his intended victim should be even further away. Yelling, his voice seemingly reinforced by the shouts of the others in him – especially Jim Dunski and Jeff Caird – he pushed over the figure from which he had taken the sword. It fell towards Mudge, causing him to step back. Then Ohm had leaped over the figure and was on Mudge. Moving swiftly in the position required, he thrust for Mudge's face. This was a target forbidden in fencing, but he hoped that Mudge, not being used to such an attack, would not react in time. Mudge, however, parried and then thrust for his enemy's upper sword arm. Ohm riposted and leaped back out of the seventeenth-century exhibit area. Mudge advanced. With his right arm, Ohm toppled another figure, The Stockbroker, at Mudge.

He ran towards the railing and vaulted over it with his right arm to the escalator. Bela Wang Horvath and Janos Ananda Mudge stood side by side for a moment. Horvath said something to his partner, who nodded, turned, and ran towards the corner of the recess. Horvath ran towards the opposite corner. They were going to cut him off and move in on him from his front and back.

He went over the railing back into the recess and ran towards Mudge past the figures of The Mail Carrier, The Bald Man and The Diplomat. Mudge stopped, whirled, and assumed a defensive position.

Mudge was grinning. Ohm grinned back at him. From the moment he had yelled, he had lost all doubts and fears. He seemed to have the strength of seven, a hallucination, no doubt, but his adrenalin was pumping through him. And he wanted to kill. Not just anybody. Mudge.

Their blades clashed and rang again and again. Though the rapier was heavier and stiffer than the foil, it felt to Ohm as light as balsa and as supple as a feather. Cold fury and the combined self-survival drive of seven men powered him. Mudge was an excellent fencer. But he had several disadvantages, one being that it was difficult for a right-handed fencer to duel with a left-handed fencer. The lines of target were changed, making it hard to aim at them. The sinister-handed fencer was also in the same reversed position, but he was more used to it.

After a brief engagement, Ohm leaped back, transferred the rapier to his right hand to confuse Mudge, attacked, was beaten back, was nicked in the shoulder, and transferred the rapier to his left hand. Mudge attacked. Ohm parried with a slight movement of the bell guard, deflecting Mudge's point. At the same time, Ohm directed his point so that Mudge, who kept moving forward, received the point in his right forearm. It slid under the ulna, or outer bone, and came out beyond it.

Ohm stepped back, yanking the sword from the wound. Mudge's hand opened. His rapier dropped. Ohm moved forward. Mudge staggered back into the figure of The Senator. It toppled over, and Mudge fell backwards over it. He started to get up, but Ohm stepped up to him and ran his sword through Mudge's other forearm.

Hearing the sounds of boots behind him, Ohm whirled. He brought the tip of the sword up and then down into a defensive position, ready to meet Horvath's attack. He had turned so swiftly and whipped his rapier around so fast that it acted like a whip. A drop of blood was flicked from its end into Horvath's right eye, disorienting him for a split-second. That was enough for Ohm, who seemed to see everything as if it were in a slow-motion film. He noted every meaningful detail; he was prepared by years of training to take advantage of every weakness or off-balance of his opponent. His rapier beat Horvath's aside just far enough and long enough for him to send his blade through the man's thigh.

Horvath jumped back, Ohm's blade withdrawing from the flesh, followed by a gush of blood. Ohm attacked but could not for a moment get past Horvath's desperate but effective parries. Coolly, knowing that Horvath was weakening with every pump of blood, Ohm pressed him. Horvath, as was inevitable, bumped into a figure. The Soldier fell over, causing Horvath to fall onto the floor on his back. The Soldier knocked over The Oil Driller, which toppled The Insurance Salesperson, which knocked over The Mafia Gangster, which felled The Publisher, which toppled The Loan Shark, which knocked over The Marxist. The last in the domino series to crash to the floor was The Capitalist.

The wound in the thigh and the injury to his elbow in the fall seemed to put Horvath out of the combat. Ohm had thought that Mudge would be helpless, too, but the clomping of boots and a deep sobbing told him that that was not so. Howling, Ohm whirled just in time to meet Mudge's attack. It was weak, however, and especially ineffective because Mudge was using his left hand to hold the rapier. He was brave – Ohm had to give him credit for that – but he was also stupid. He did not have a chance. Ohm's point drove through Mudge's left shoulder, sticking out behind it for at least three inches.

Mudge crumpled. Ohm whirled again. But Horvath was not making another incredible attack. He was crawling, groaning, trailing much blood, towards the elevator. Charlie watched him until he collapsed, face down, on the floor. His arms and legs moved, responding only partly to his will to get up and go.

Ohm turned and walked, breathing hard but feeling exultant, to Mudge. The man sat on the floor, holding his shoulders with his hands and glaring at Ohm.

'You were lucky, you bastard!'

'Don't whine,' Ohm said, grinning. 'Now . . . I want the star that opens the door to Immerman's apartment.'

'I don't have it!'

'Just how were you planning to get back into the place?' Ohm said. 'Come on. Hand it over, or I'll kill you and search your clothes.'

'You'll never get away with this,' Mudge said. 'You can't outrun us, and you know that.'

'So what am I supposed to do? Go along meekly to the execution? Hand it over! Now!'

Mudge let loose of his shoulder, which pumped blood, felt in the pocket of his splendid coat, and held out a disc-star attached to a long chain. Ohm took it and said, 'This had better be the right one.'

He had to act swiftly but was unable to do so because the two men could not carry Snick for him. He rejected the idea of transporting her himself at the same time that he went with the men. Though wounded badly – Horvath was becoming grey – they could still be dangerous. He would have to leave Snick here while he took care of the men.

As it was, he had to drag the now near-unconscious Horvath into the elevator cage and then support Mudge into it. When the two were lying on the floor, Ohm took the cage up to the top level. The star admitted him into the end of the apartment opposite that which he had entered that morning. Fortunately, the stoner room was close to this end. There were only two cylinders, which forced him to prop Horvath, the closest to dying, into one first. He turned the power on at the switchboard behind a panel, reluctantly revealed by Mudge. Then he shoved Mudge into the other one. The man had enough blood and spirit left to spit in his face before Ohm could close the door. A few seconds later, Ohm dragged Mudge's stiff and heavy form out. He returned to the elevator and, in three minutes, had Snick into the apartment. After he had put her into a cylinder, he turned the power on. He opened the cylinder door and dragged her out onto the floor. After laying her down, he felt for her pulse. It was fluttering weakly, but it was there.

He stripped her and looked for wounds. Though he could find none, he knew that that did not mean that she might not be dying. She could have been injected with a slow poison as insurance that, if she were found, she would die shortly after being destoned. Or she might have been given an overdose of an anaesthetic. Whatever had been done to her, she should go to a hospital immediately. He could not get her to one without putting himself in danger, and he did not want to call in. He had to have plenty of time to get away from the Tower.

He put her back into the cylinder and stoned her. After looking through the apartment, he found a compacter and jammed her clothes into that. Then he dragged her to the elevator and went down with her to the level that exhibited ancient sea creatures. One of these was a gigantic carnivorous whale which was frozen in the act of shooting out of the sea. Its enormous and open toothed mouth was a few feet below the level of the fence by the spiralling escalator.

Puffing, Ohm hauled her to the railing and balanced her stiff body on it, her head pointing inward towards the now quiet sea.

'In a way, Snick,' he said, 'you've been my Jonah.'

He laughed hysterically, the echoes bouncing back from the far walls of the Tower. When he had managed to get control of himself, he said, gasping, 'I'm doing this because you're a human being and because I just won't murder. To hell with the greater good!'.

He tilted her and then shoved. She slid over the railing and fell into the mouth of the whale and into its belly.

'They'll find you someday,' he said, sobbing. 'By then . . . by then . . .'

No matter what happened to him by then, he would not regret having saved her. He would pay whatever price was required.

Sunday-World
VARIETY, Second Month of the Year
D6-W1 (Day-Six, Week-One)

27

Thomas Tu Zurvan, 'Father Tom,' priest unlicensed by the government, licensed by God, awoke. He did not curse, though most men would have done so. He, who never drank liquor, had a hell of a hangover. (How else describe a hangover than as a 'hell'?) Saturday's sinner had escaped punishment by passing on his headache to Sunday's saint. Father Tom did not mind. He gloried in the pain perhaps too much. His shoulders were big enough to bear the bad karma of others, and so was his head.

Nevertheless, when he got up and passed the cylinder from which Saturday stared, Father Tom omitted the sign of blessing that he made to the other five occupants.

What Father Tom did not know was that Charlie Ohm did not elude the consequences of his guzzling. Ohm always awoke with a hangover because he thought he should have one. By the time that he realized that someone else had taken it over for him, he was rid of his hangover or had submerged it with the hair of the dog that bit him. Thus, in this strictly economic, budget-keeping universe there was one extra hangover not down in the books.

After his sojourn to the bathroom, Zurvan ate a light breakfast. Then, naked, he got down on his knees by the bed and prayed aloud for every creature in the cosmos. Rising, he set swiftly to the things that needed doing, the changing of the bedclothes, the picking up of items left by Saturday's slob (bless him!), and the washing and putting away of things that needed such. After that, he went to his personal possessions closet, removed the items he used in his battle against evil, and arranged them as required. That two of them were a wig and a long thick beard did not cause him to wonder why. At this time of day, he accepted everything as always having been ordained, no reason to ask for reasons. He had forgotten that he had deflated the dummy that looked so much like him. He was, by the time he awoke, one man only. That is, except for the rare times when he had to pass on a message to the immer council. That period of knowing that he was not quite Father Tom quickly evaporated. In the evening, ah, that was different. Then voices and visions and thoughts that he did not know while the sun shone strongly crept in like shadows.

He dressed and went into the bathroom to paint and dye. Ten minutes later, he was striding towards the door to the hall, a long oaken shaft that curled at the upper end in his right hand. It was seldom that he remembered that he was born left-handed but had grown right-handedness into the Zurvan persona.

His wig was auburn and wild and fell to the back of his waist. The end of his nose was painted blue; his lips, green. The waist-long beard was decorated with many small butterfly-shaped cutouts of various dazzling designs. Broad red circles enclosing blue six-pointed stars decorated his white ankle-length robe. His ID disc-star bore a flattened figure eight lying on its side and slightly open at the end.

A big orange *S* was painted on his forehead.

His feet were, as every prophet's and holy man's should be, bare.

He carried no shoulderbag, an omission that made Manhattanites stare at him.

The door opened and gushed a light that very few other than he ever saw.

'God's good morning!' he shouted at the five adults in the hall. 'Bless you, brothers and sisters! May your selves strive to overcome your selves! May you respect your mortal bodies and your immortal souls and each day take one more step upwards to genuine humanhood and to Godhood!'

Holding the staff with three fingers, he made a flattened oval of the thumb and first finger. With the other hand, he passed his long finger three times through the oval. The oval was for eternity and immortality, hence, for God. The finger sliding three times through the oval represented the act of spiritual intercourse of humankind with The Eternal. The thumb and the two fingers stood for God, the human body and the human soul. They also symbolized God, all creatures and Mother Nature, God's consort. Thrice symbolic, they also stood for love, empathy and knowledge of self and the universe.

Some of the loungers said, 'God bless you, too, Father Tom!' Others grinned broadly or also made the sign of blessing, though not in the sense he intended.

He strode by them, his nose wrinkling, in spite of himself, at the odour of tobacco smoke, booze and unwashed bodies. 'Let them discover, God, what they are doing to themselves. Show these children the light so that they may follow it if they would!'

'Give it to them, Father!' a man shouted. 'Scorch them with hellfire and brimstone!' He laughed uproariously.

Father Tom stopped, turned, and said, 'I don't preach hellfire, my son. I preach love, peace and harmony.'

The man got to his knees and stretched out his arms in mock-repentance. 'Forgive me, Father! I know not what I do!'

'A prophet is not without honour save in his own block building,' Zurvan said. 'I don't have the power to forgive you. You forgive yourself, and then God will forgive you.'

He stepped out into Shinbone Alley under a cloudless sky and a steadily warming sun. The light of day was not as bright as that which came from everywhere in the world, from the distant stars invisible even to radio astronomers, from the trees and the grass, from the rocks in the garden, and from the centre of the Earth. Brightest of all, though, was that which shone from the centre of Father Tom Zurvan.

Thus the day passed with Father Tom standing on the street corners and preaching to whomever would listen or standing outside the doors of block buildings or private residences and shouting that he had The Word and the tenants should come out and listen to It. At 1:00 PM, he went to the door of a restaurant and rapped on the window until a waiter came. He gave his order for a light lunch and passed his ID disc-star to the waiter. Presently, the waiter came with the star, which he had used to register the purchase, and he handed the platter of food and glass of water to the priest.

The organics watched him closely, ready to arrest him if he went into a restaurant with bare feet. Father Tom, grinning, usually went to them and asked if they cared to share his meal. They always refused. To accept would have made them open to a charge of bribe-taking. The priest could also have been arrested for offering a bribe, but the organics had orders just to observe and record. The only act so far that had upset them during the past subyear was his conversion of an organic who had been shadowing him. That had been entirely unexpected, had been done without coercion by Zurvan, and was not illegal. However, the convert had been discharged from the force on grounds of religiousness and adherence to superstition.

At 3:00 PM, Father Tom was standing on a box in Washington Square. Around him were two hundred members of the Cosmic Church of Confession, about a hundred of the curious, and a hundred who had nothing better to do. There were other soapboxers scattered through the park, but they did not draw such large crowds.

Here Father Tom began preaching. His voice blared out deeply and richly. His timing and phraseology were suited to his message and appreciated by most of the hearers, even those who rejected The Word. Father Tom, having studied the great black preachers of the past who had also been on fire with The Word, knew how to deliver it.

'Bless you, citizens of Sunday. Whether or not you are here to hear a voice of God – not *the* voice, *a* voice – bless you. May your virtues swell and your weaknesses shrink. Bless you, my children, sons and daughters of God all!'

'Amen, Father!'

'You're telling the truth, Father!'

'God bless you and us, Father!'

'The hound of heaven is baying at your heels, Father!'

'Yes, brothers and sisters!' Zurvan cried. 'The hound of heaven is barking! Ba-a-arking, I say!'

'Yeah, Father, barking!'

'It has been sent out by the great hunter to bring you in, my children!'

'Bring us in! Yeah, bring us in! You speak the truth, Father!'

Eyes wide and seeming to flash, his shepherd's staff held high, Father Tom thundered, 'Barking, I say!'

'Barking, Father! We hear him!'

'But!'

Father Tom paused and glared at the crowd. 'But . . . is the hound of heaven barking up the wrong tree?'

'What tree, Father?'

'The wrong tree, I say! Is the hound barking up the wrong tree?'

'Never!' a woman screamed out. 'Never!'

'You said it, sister!' Father Tom said. 'Never! God never makes mistakes, and His hound wouldn't ever lose the quarry! His hound . . . and our hound . . . is us.'

'Us, Father!'

'When the hound of heaven has treed its quarry . . . *who* is that creature up in the tree?'

'It's us, Father!'

'And them, too!' Zurvan cried, waving his staff to

indicate the nonbelievers. 'Everybody!'

'Everybody, Father!'

He was improvising, yet he spoke as if he had long rehearsed his speech and his disciples responded as if they knew the exact timing and phrasing expected from him. He praised the government for all the many benefits it had ensured for the people, and he listed the great ills that had plagued the world and had made so many suffer in the past. These, he said, were gone. This was indeed the best government the world had ever had.

'Now children . . . children, I say, who will someday be adults in God . . .'

'How about adulterers in God!' a man on the fringe of the crowd shouted.

'Bless you, brother, and bless your big mouth and hard heart, too! Saint Francis of Assisi, a true saint, greeted whatever donkey he met on the road as Brother Ass! May I call you Brother Ass? May I address you as a fellow Assisian?'

Zurvan paused, smiled, and looked around until the crowd's laughter had ceased. He shouted, 'Yet the government is not perfect, my children! It could change many things for the betterment of its citizens. But has it changed now for, lo, five generations? Has it not ceased to seek change for the better because it claims that there is no need for change? Did it not cease? I ask you, did it not cease!'

'Yes, Father! It has ceased!'

'Thus! Thus! Thus! Thus, my children! The hound of heaven does not bark up the wrong tree! But, thus, my children, the hound of the government barks up the wrong tree! O, how it barks! Day and night, from every side, it barks! We hear that it is perfect! The millennium has come, and all is right in this world! The government discourages any talk of change for the better! "We are perfect!" the government says!

'Is it perfect? Is the government, like God, perfect?'
'No, no, no, Father!'
Zurvan stepped down from the box then. Shouting, continuing to speak, his disciples trooping after him, moaning, crying and yelling, he walked to a place one hundred and sixty feet away. The other speakers were also moving. Zurvan occupied a spot just vacated, and he mounted the box again. The law had been observed, and the place of meeting had been moved within the legal time to a legal distance away.
'The government permits the practice of religion! Yet . . . the government allows no believer in God to hold a government office! Is that the truth?'
'That's the truth, Father!'
'Who says that only those who believe in fact, in reality, in the truth . . . T . . . R . . . U . . . T . . . H . . . are fit to hold government office?'
'The government, Father!'
'And who defines fact, reality and truth?'
'The government, Father!'
'Who defines religion as superstition?'
'The government, Father!'
'Who says there is no need for change, for betterment?'
'The government, Father!'
'Do not we deny that? Do not we know that there is a great, a crying, need for betterment?'
'Yes, Father!'
'Does not the government say that it has a contract with the people, a social contract?'
'It does, Father.'
'Then tell me, children, what good is a contract if, of the two parties who agree to the contract, only one can enforce it?'
'None, Father!'
That was as far as he dared to go today on that subject. He was not yet ready for martyrdom. He now switched to

his 'cooling-off' stage. He asked for a few questions from non-members of the church, and, as always, he was asked why he daubed his nose, what the *S* on his forehead stood for, and what the butterfly shapes on his beard symbolized.

Zurvan said that he and his disciples had been reviled and mocked as 'bluenoses' because of their high moral standards. So, he had adopted the pejorative literally to show his pride in his belief and his indifference to the revilers and mockers. When he preached, he showed his 'bluenose' to all who would see.

As for the butterflies, they represented the last stage of becoming a believer. Just as butterflies, once ugly caterpillars, wrapped themselves in a cocoon and burst forth in the metamorphosis of lovely creatures, just so the souls of himself and his followers had burst forth.

'The big *S* on my forehead,' he thundered, 'does not represent Saint or Sinner! Nor does it stand for Simpleton, as our enemies claim! It stands for Symbol! It is not *a* symbol, but *the* symbol! The *S* absorbs all symbols, all symbols of good, that is! Someday, so we hope, do we not, children, this *S* will be as instantly recognizable, and far more respected and valued, than the cross, hexagram and crescent I spoke of earlier. Is that not our hope and trust, children?'

'Amen to that, Father!'

Zurvan then began the slow-paced approach to the calling for public confession. As the minutes went by, he sped up his delivery, his gestures, his intensity, his passion. Before five o'clock, when all lecturers and preachers had to stop, he had heard the detailed confessions of twenty, one of them an on-the-spot convert. That this part of the programme attracted many more from the park than his preaching did not dim his joy. He knew that nonmembers loved to hear the confessions because of the sometimes sordid, humiliating and salacious details.

Never mind. Sometimes, some who came to be titillated were overcome – imploded with the light of God – and they converted and confessed.

The organics were taking all this in and might use the confessions against the confessors if they found reason to. Martyrdom, however, was the price paid for faith.

At five, Zurvan went home, tired but exuberant and exultant. He was riding high on the saddle of God's light. After a low-calorie supper, he prayed. Later, he listened in the privacy of his apartment to people who had not had time to finish their confessions. At nine, he held a short service for those who crowded into his apartment. It was against the law for people to stand in the hall and watch the ceremonies on the hall strips. But organics were not usually around at that time, and the other tenants did not object. Some of them liked to watch, too, though not to share in the light.

All of this had taken place on Day-Five, Week-One, last Sunday.

Today, Day-Six, Week-One of Sunday, Father Tom Zurvan had not appeared in Washington Square. His followers, after waiting for fifteen minutes, during which they failed to get him on the strip, had gone to the apartment building on Shinbone Alley. The block chief rightly refused to use his code-key to enter Father Tom's apartment until the organics had been notified. After another long delay, two organics showed up. These went in with the block chief, the throng of disciples, and some curious tenants.

A search revealed that Father Tom was not at home. His stoner was empty. His staff was leaning against a wall strip on which was a cryptic message:

I HAVE GONE TO A HIGHER PLACE.

28

Tom Zurvan had not lied.

He was indeed in a higher place, the Tao Towers, in Tony Horn's sixth-floor apartment at the corner of West Eleventh Street and the Kropotkin Canal. He was not altogether himself nor altogether any of his selves.

Normally, he would have gone through the ritual of becoming Father Tom and then sleeping. The nightmare of Saturday had, however, stopped the flow of customary events as an avalanche would dam up a river. It had goosed his soul and sent it screaming down paths that he did not wish to take. It had shotgunned the cocoon of Zurvan and was letting the voices and faces and even the hands of *those others* through the holes. They were mumbling at him, staring at him, groping him.

This had not started until he had got himself, much less smoothly than usual, through the mental mantra of metamorphosis. (Was that Bob Tingle speaking that thought, the Alley Oop of alliteration? Wyatt Repp who voiced the metaphors of 'goosing' and 'shotgunned'? Charlie Ohm who suggested they were 'groping' him?)

He was aware but did not want to be aware that the winds of the recent past were blowing through him as if he were a shredded sail, as if fragments of the others were coming through him like pepper from a shaker.

'Stop that! Stop that!' he screamed in his mind.

Though, possibly excepting Jeff Caird, he had the strongest personality of all, he could not fight back with all his powers. They had been let, as it were, to other tenants who were moving in with court orders. And he was being shorn, his strength drained out just as Samson's had drained when his hair was cut by Delilah, the delicious daughter of false-faced Philistines, the buxom barber of Beelzebub.

'Stop that!' he screamed. 'This is serious!'

('Damn right, it's serious!' Caird said in a faraway voice that, however, was getting nearer. 'Tingle, shut up! We're about to die, and you joke!')

Aloud, his voice ringing in his apartment, Zurvan said, 'By the light of God, I command you to go back into the darkness from which you came!'

('Bullshit,' Charlie Ohm said.)

('Smile when you say that,' Wyatt Repp said. 'Come on, men. Give him a break. The lynching party is coming. If we don't hang together, we'll be hung separately on sour apple trees. He's the ramrod today. Shut up and let him save our skin. Then we can have the big powwow, see who's the big mugwump. The only way . . .')

('Tony Horn's apartment,' Caird said. 'Go there! It's the only place we'll be safe! For a while, anyway!')

'Tony Horn?' Zurvan said aloud.

('Yes. You remember. Don't you?')

('I remember,' Jim Dunski said. 'If I can, you can. Caird was given permission, remember. His . . . our . . . friend, Commissioner-General Anthony Horn. She said he could use it in case of emergency. And this is it!')

('She's an immer,' Bob Tingle said. 'Once an immer, always an immer, no pun intended even if you know German. She'll betray me . . . I mean, us.')

('She won't know anything until Tuesday,' Caird said. 'Come on, Zurvan, get going! Hightail it!')

Only Will Isharashvili had not spoken. Was that because he did not know yet what was going on? Or because, being the last in line, if Tuesday was the beginning, he was the weakest? His voice would not be added until he was awakened tomorrow? If so, he would never speak. He was not going to be awakened. He would die in his sleep.

That roiled Zurvan even more. If he was not Isharashvili

tomorrow, who would he be? Could he keep on being himself, Tom Zurvan? He had to. He, at least, would not perish.

'Oh, Lord, forgive me!' he cried. 'I am thinking only of myself! I am abandoning my brothers! I am a coward, a Peter denying his Lord before the cock has crowed three times!'

('Peter! Cock! You big prick!' Charlie Ohm said. 'Cut out the holy bullshit, man! Get going! Save our asses!')

('I wouldn't say it that way,' Jeff Caird said, 'but the minnie is right. Hide out! Now! Get to Horn's place! For God's sake, man, the organics may be at the door now! Or the immers may be there! Get rid of everything that'll tie you in with us! Go!')

The voices had stilled, for the moment, anyway. As he stared at the traffic on the street and the canal, he felt a little stronger and more confident. He had no rational cause to be so, but confidence often welled not from long experience so much as from the inborn belief in one's self.

He had had to struggle hard to do what reason said he must do. Grief and a hard-quelled resistance had shaken him as he bustled about gathering up items to be compacted and stoned for the garbage collectors. The wig, beard and robes had to go. With them went the dummy of himself. He considered destroying Ohm's also, but the chances were good that his dummy would not be discovered until next Saturday. He did get into Ohm's PP closet with the ID star from Ohm's cylinder, and he dressed in Ohm's clothes. They would make him stand out because Sunday did not wear the neck-ruff on the blouse nor kilts. That, however, could not be helped.

It hurt him to deceive the followers. Part of his grief was caused by this, but it was better that he not shatter their faith. Yes, it was, he told himself again and again. Far better. But he could not help wondering how many leaders of the faithful in the past had been forced to practise such fraud.

'If I were only I, Father Tom', he muttered, 'I would stay and take the consequences. The blood of the martyrs is the seed of the faith. But I am not the only one involved. And if I were just Father Tom, I wouldn't be in this horrible mess.'

Nevertheless, when he had propped his staff against the wall and the message was displayed, he weakened.

'It isn't right!' he cried. 'I am betraying my people, my self, and my God!'

('*Theokaka*!' Charlie Ohm said.)

('You are just one of many,' Jeff Caird said. Then, after a pause, 'There may be a solution, a good way out.')

'What is it?'

('Don't know just yet.')

Turning at the door, Zurvan said, 'Farewell, Father Tom!'

('This guy is just too much,' Charlie Ohm said. 'But really not enough.')

('A fine sense of the dramatic,' Wyatt Repp said. 'Or is it of the melodramatic? I'm not sure he knows the difference between pathos and bathos.')

('Were those two of the Three Musketeers?' Bob Tingle said.)

'Shut up!' Zurvan shouted as he swung the door open, startling two loafers in the hall.

Who was this strangely dressed crazy man charging out of Father Tom's apartment?

Zurvan was also startled. He had not expected anyone to be out this early in the morning. Muttering something unintelligible even to him, he slammed the door behind him. At 3:12 AM, he strode out of the building and headed for Womanway Boulevard. The sky was still clear. The air was hot but cooler than earlier in the day. A few cyclers and pedestrians were out, which made him feel less conspicuous. He passed several State Cleaning Corps vehicles and one organic car. This slowed down when it got opposite him but did not stop. He had no idea what he would do if he was stopped and questioned.

Having crossed Womanway, he went west on Bleecker Street. He passed Caird's house, which seemed to make Caird stronger. At least, his voice was louder than the others.

('I loved you,' Caird cried.)

Zurvan did not know whom Caird was calling to, but the sorrow in the voice troubled him. He walked faster, then slowed down. If any more organics came by, they would wonder why he was in a near-run.

Reaching the street alongside the canal, he went north. He looked over the railing from time to time and stopped when he saw a small jetboat tied to a floating dock. He went down the steps and back along the canal on the narrow path until he came to the boat. It probably belonged to the tenants of a house by the canal, and Sunday had not bestirred himself or herself to get up this early to fish. He got into the boat, untied the line to the dock, started the electrically powered jet, and steered it north up the canal. He passed about a dozen small boats occupied by men and women fishing and several cargo boats. He took the boat to the west side of the canal at West Eleventh Street, got onto the pathway, and shoved the boat out to drift. One more of many crimes.

The trees along the street would hide him from the sky-eyes. They would not observe which building he went into. Anyway, unless someone inspected the recordings, his disappearance under the trees was of no importance.

Before entering the building, he thought briefly of Isharashvili. Tomorrow, the ranger's wife would wonder why he had not left the cylinder. She would open the door, thinking that something had gone wrong with the power. She would touch him, and she would not feel the expected cold hardness, she would touch the soft warm flexible plastic of the dummy.

Her scream sounded in him.

Isharashvili's voice was there, though it, too, was far off, somewhere just past the horizon of his mind.

After getting into Horn's apartment, he went through every room. They were more numerous and larger than his and far more luxurious. Since she shared them with only one other tenant, Thursday's, she did not have to put her many personal possessions, bric-a-brac, jewellery, paintings, figurines and ashtrays, in the PP closet. The ashtray surprised and disgusted him – Caird, that is – since he had not had the slightest suspicion that she used the illegal drug. Which meant that, if she did, so did Thursday.

He looked at the faces in the cylinder windows. The face of the Thursday resident of Horn's apartment was framed in the first cylinder's oval.

He moved to the next cylinder and looked into its window. Tony Horn stared back at him with huge unblinking eyes. Good old Tony. She was his good friend and had always been big-hearted and sympathetic. Perhaps he should destone her and tell her about his situation. She could help him as no one else he knew could help.

('Are you crazy?' Ohm said. 'She's an immer!')

('That wasn't Zurvan thinking,' Caird said. 'He doesn't even know her. I was thinking for him. But you're right, Charlie. She'd turn us in.')

While the voices tore at him and faces sprang like jack-in-the-boxes before him and hands tapped on his mind as if it were a window, Zurvan paced back and forth in the living room. When he reached one end, he turned and strode back to the other.

('Like a tiger in his cage,' Repp said. 'It's good exercise, but it won't get us out of the cage.')

('If he leaves the apartment,' Ohm said, 'he'll just be in a bigger cage.')

Zurvan ignored the voices as best he could. They were

an itch he wanted to scratch, but scratching would only make them itch more.

'Jacob, he whose name became Israel and whose descendants were as numerous as the grains of sand on the beach,' Zurvan muttered, 'Jacob saw a ladder. Its ends rested on Earth, and its other ends ascended into Heaven. Angels went up and down it, doing the bidding of the Lord. I need a ladder, Lord! Let it down so that I may climb up it to the promised abode!'

('He's cracking up!' Ohm said. 'He'll become a raving madman, and we'll all die with him!')

'No!' Zurvan shouted. 'I am not mad, and there is no ladder for me! I do not deserve it!'

If a ladder was lowered for him, he would have to climb on rotten rungs. There were seven rungs, and the last, himself, would surely break.

Monday-World
VARIETY, Second Month of the Year
D6-W1 (Day-Six, Week-One)

29

Monday was not blue. It was grey with heavy low clouds blown in from the east.

One of the few things permitted to be transmitted from one day to the next was the weather forecast. The meteorology of NE 1330 was far superior to that of the early ages, which had been often baffled and fooled by the exceedingly complex forces that made up the weather. Now, over one thousand and five hundred years of research had enabled the forecasters to predict with 99.9 percent accuracy. But Mother Nature, as if determined to show man that he could never have that one-tenth percent in his grasp, sometimes pulled a reverse on him.

Today was an example of her trickery. The meteorologists had smugly announced that it would be clear and hot. But the wind had shifted, and the cloud continent over the mid-Atlantic was charging westwards, its forefront now over eastern New Jersey.

Tom Zurvan had resumed his pacing. Will Isharashvili, the Central Park ranger, the gentle soul and henpecked husband, had protested feebly against being barred from the day that was rightfully his. Jeff Caird, in growing Will's persona, had made a mistake. He had gone too far in shaping a nonviolent and passive man. He had, however, given Isharashvili a great stubbornness and courage in refusing to act violently, and it was these that were causing the death of Isharashvili. Though not quite deceased, he was fading away. Rather than use force, as the others were, he would cling to his principles and so slide back on them into the elements from which he had come.

Not so Jeff Caird and the others. Though Zurvan had slammed and locked the doors on them, he saw them creep out of holes that he had not known existed. When he shoved them back in and cemented the holes, he found them oozing out through the walls in a sort of osmosis.

('This isn't like you, Zurvan,' Jeff Caird said. 'You're supposed to be religious and noble. Highly moral. A true son of God. You should be glad to be a martyr, to sacrifice yourself for others. But you're not. You're hard and ruthless, as godless as those you preach against. What happened?')

('He's a hypocrite, that's what,' Charles Ohm said.)

('Of course, he is,' Wyatt Repp said. 'He was never fully what he claimed to be. Here he was, preaching absolute truthfulness and honesty. Confess your sins! Confess! Free yourself of all guilt and shame! Become the round man, the round woman! Be complete! Yet he was concealing from his disciples and from the public that he was an immer. He had a gift that he was denying them, the gift of a much longer life. He was and is a criminal, this righteous man. He belongs to a secret and illegal organization. He is indeed a hypocrite!')

'Shut up! Shut up!' Zurvan cried.

('Yes. Lie down whimpering and die,' Jim Dunski said. 'Make it easy for the hypocrite.')

('Whimper, whimpish, whelp, hard-hearted hound of heaven,' Bob Tingle said. 'You're barking up the wrong tree, Preacher Tom. The dog of deity is following a sour scent.')

'What do you expect me to do?' Zurvan shouted.

That quieted them for a while. Anything that he did would not help them. Or him. He could not resume the habit of the past and be one man one day and another the next. There was no place to go to where they could be themselves again. There was also no place where he could be Father Tom again. He was facing death as surely as they were. If the immers caught him, they would kill him. If the organics caught him, they would, after the trial, send him to an institution for the mentally unbalanced. If the therapy succeeded, he, Zurvan, would dissolve. So would all of them, Jeff Caird included. The man that walked out of the institution might be named Caird, but he would not be the same persona.

If the therapy failed, he would be stoned and put away until such time as psychic science found a sure cure for him. Inevitably, he would be forgotten. He would gather dust in some vast warehouse along with the millions now there and the billions that would be there.

'Yes, I am a hypocrite,' he muttered. 'I have failed. Why? I thought that I was a true son of God, that I believed what I urged others to believe. I did believe! I did! But my Maker made me flawed!'

He chewed his lip and stroked a beard that was no longer there.

'Don't put the blame on Him! He gave you free will! You had the power to heal the flaws! You did not have to blind yourself to them! You blinded yourself! Your Maker didn't blind you!'

(Jeff Caird said, quietly though very near, 'But you forget that *I* am your *maker*.')

Zurvan yelled and fell to the floor. He rolled back and forth on the carpet crying, 'No! No! No!'

When he stopped rolling and shouting, he lay for a long while on his back staring at the ceiling.

('Hell, why don't we quit prolonging this agony?' Charlie Ohm said. 'Let's turn ourselves in. They're going to catch us, anyway. And we'll be safe from the immers.')

('Too many organics are immers,' Jim Dunski said. 'They'll get to us, find some reason to kill us before we can talk. Anyway, I don't like to quit.')

('It's shootout time at the Psychic Corral,' Wyatt Repp said. 'May the best man win. Get off the floor and be a man, Zurvan. Fight! If you lose, go down trying to win! Fight! Don't listen to that loser, the lush!')

Zurvan walked to the kitchen as if he were pushing through cotton candy. He drank a tall glass of water, went to the toilet, relieved himself, and put cold water on his face. After drying off, he picked up his shoulderbag and walked to the hallway door.

('Hey, where you going?' Ohm said.)

('He's going to turn us in,' Bob Tingle said. 'By the time the organics get through with us, no stone will be left unturned. We'll be turned inside out and then turned to stone. Think about it, man!')

('I didn't mean it,' Ohm said. 'I was only kidding you, pushing you to see if you really were crazy.')

('Don't do it!' Caird said. 'There may be a way out!')

Zurvan closed the door behind him and walked towards the elevator. 'I'm not going to turn myself in,' he said. 'I'm going for a long walk. I can't stand being caged in the apartment. I need to think. I need . . .'

What did he need? A possibility where all was impossible.

('When the rat in the laboratory can't find the way out of the labyrinth,' Caird said, 'when the rat runs up against an insoluble problem, when the rat is hopelessly confused, it lies down and dies.')

'I am not a rat!' Zurvan said.

('No,' Caird said, 'you're not. You're not even a rat. You're a fiction! Remember, I am your maker! I, the real, made you, a fiction!')

('Then that means the rest of us, too, are fictions,' Repp said. '*You* made *us*. But so what? You're a fiction, too, Caird. The government and the immers made you.')

('Fiction can become reality,' Dunski said. 'We're as real as Caird. After all, he made us from parts of him. He grew us as surely as a mother grows the embryo in the womb. And he gave birth to us. Now he wants to kill us.

His children!')

('For Chrissake!' Ohm said. 'We all want to kill each other! God, I need a drink!')

('I am your maker,' Caird said over and over again. 'The maker of all of you. What I can make, I can unmake. I am your maker and your unmaker.')

('Bullshit!' Charlie Ohm cried. 'You're not Aladdin, and we're not genies you can put back into the bottle!')

('You *would* think of a bottle,' Bob Tingle said. 'Lush, loser, lessening Lazarus! Think of yourself as a hangover we all want to get rid of. You're all hangovers!')

('*En garde*, you son of a bitch!')

('Play your hand!')

('All fictions. I made you. I now unmake you.')

('Ohm-mani-padme-hum!')

('Humbug, you alcoholic hummingbird!')

('I made you. I am unmaking you. Do you think for one moment that I didn't foresee this. I made the rituals that admitted you each day into your day. I also made the reverse ritual, the undoing ritual, the no-entrance ritual. I knew that I'd need it some day. And today is the day!')

('Liar!')

('Fictions calling the fiction-maker a liar? Living lies calling the one who made you truths, though temporary truths, a liar? I am your maker. I made you. I am unmaking you. Can't you feel everything slipping away? Go back to where you came from!')

The wind that blew across Waverly Place was not strong enough as yet to blow off a hat. But the winds howling inside Zurvan seemed to lift him up and carry him away into the clouds. The light grew dim; the pedestrians around him were looking at him because he was staggering. When they saw him drop to his knees and lift his hands high, they backed away.

Far in the east, thunder stomped its feet in a war dance and lightning flashed its many lances.

Zurvan sped whirling through the whirling greyness. He tried to grab the dark wetness to keep himself from falling. Up? Or down?

'O Lord,' he bellowed, 'I'm lost! Snatch me from this doom! Take me away from this grey world to your glory!'

The people on the sidewalk backed even farther away or hurried off as Zurvan clapped his hands to his eyes and screamed, 'The light! The light!'

He fell forwards on his arms and lay still for a moment.

'Call an ambulance,' someone said.

He rolled over, staring and blinking, and got unsteadily to his feet. 'That won't be necessary,' he said. 'I'm all right. Just a bit dizzy. I'll go home. It's near. Just leave me alone.'

Jeff Caird, whispering, 'The light! The light!' walked across the bridge over the canal. By the time that he was a block away from Washington Square, he felt steady and strong.

('He's gone?' Tingle said.)

('Like the Indian that folded his tepee and stole away into the night,' Wyatt Repp said.)

('He almost took me with him,' Charlie Ohm said. 'God! The light!')

('It was sword-shaped,' Jim Dunski said. 'It came down and lifted him on its blade and tossed him up into blazing sky.')

Their voices were faint. They became a little louder when they discovered that Caird was now in control of the body.

('Oh, my God,' Ohm said, 'we're sunk!')

('Look at it this way,' Repp said. 'Zurvan's bit the dust. Now . . . it's Caird's last stand. We'll have his scalp before this is over.')

Zurvan had not been sure that he had not been making up the voices of the others. Caird was equally unsure. It did not matter that they might be imaginary. Nor did it matter that the voices might be those of personae as real as his. What mattered was that he was master. And he knew what he was going to do.

He walked against the increasing wind towards the tall yellow vertical tube on the northwest corner of the park. This was one of the entrances to the underground system of transportation belts and power and water lines. A strip by its side warned that only SCC workers could use it. There were no workers or uniformed organics in sight, and the few people who had lingered in the park were leaving it.

He stopped. Under the branches of an oak tree in the distance sat a lone figure. The man who had been playing chess with Gril was walking away, shaking his head. Apparently, Gril had asked his partner to finish the game. The man, however, would rather forfeit.

Caird stopped by the entrance to the tube.

('What now?' Ohm said faintly.)

A few leaves blown from the trees whirled by. The wind, cool with the promise of rain, lifted his hair. A bicycler, bent over, feet pumping, sped by.

Gril stood up. His red beard and long red hair were ruffled by the wind. He gathered up the pieces, put them in a case, folded the chessboard, and slid it into the case. Caird began running towards him. He shouted, but the wind carried his words over his shoulder as if they were confetti.

Gril turned and saw Caird running at him. He crouched and looked to both sides as if he wanted to find the best way to flee. Then he drew himself up and waited.

30

Caird slowed down and smiled to show Gril that he meant no harm. When he got within speaking distance, he said, 'I'm not an organic. Not now, anyway. I just wanted to talk to you for a minute, Yankev Gad Gril. No longer than that, I swear it. I have urgent business; I won't detain you long.'

Gril was regaining his colour. He said in a deep rich voice, 'You know my name. I don't know yours.'

'No need to know it,' Caird said. 'Let's sit down for a minute. Too bad you put the board away. We could have finished our game.'

Gril frowned and said, 'Our game?'

Caird considered saying, 'I make the first move: 1 BL-WC-4. Then you make the second, BL-WC SG.'

That would be enough to tell Gril that this was his Tuesday's opponent. Last Tuesday's ex-opponent. But Caird wanted him to know as little as possible about his identity.

('You don't know much about it, either,' Ohm said.)

Instead, Jeff Caird said, 'I know you're a daybreaker. No, don't be alarmed. I'm not going to turn you in . . .'

He looked around. There were even fewer pedestrians and cyclists. A taxi, two people in the back seat, went by. The rumbling was getting closer. The storm was flashing open its dark overcoat to expose lightning.

Gril's small green eyes became smaller, and his thin lips squeezed even thinner. He said, 'What do you want?'

'I want to satisfy my overwhelming curiosity. That's all. I just want an answer to a question.'

('Are you nuts?' Charlie Ohm said. 'What if the organics

come while you're indulging your craziness? For Chrissakes, Caird!')

'If I can answer it,' Gril said.

Perhaps Ohm was right, and he was crazy. Or perhaps he was indulging the Tuesday organic in him. Whatever the reason, he had to know the man's motive.

'From what I know of your case,' Caird said, 'you had no apparent reason to daybreak. Why did you?'

Gril smiled and said, 'If I told you, I don't think you'd understand.'

('Any second now,' Repp said, 'any second now, the organics will be coming around the corner. Maybe they won't wonder why you two are sitting under a tree that might get struck by lightning. Maybe they won't come over and ask you why. And then maybe they won't ask for your ID. Maybe they won't already have your description.')

'Try me,' Caird said.

'How much do you know about Orthodox Judaism?'

'Probably enough. I know your name, remember? I know who you are.'

Gril looked across the table at Caird. He clutched the case so hard that his knuckles whitened. 'Then you know how important keeping the Shabbos, the Sabbath, is to us?'

Caird nodded.

'You know that the government does not forbid us to observe the Sabbath? It won't let us have a synagogue, but it doesn't play favourites. No religion has a church or temple or mosque or synagogue.'

'The people need the space those would occupy for housing and factories,' Caird said. 'Also, religions are a form of malignant superstition, contrary to all . . .'

Gril held up a big red-haired hand.

'I don't want to get into an argument about the reasons.'

'I don't either,' Caird said, looking around. 'It was

just that . . .'

'Never mind. As I said, we are permitted to do what God enjoined us to do. We observe the Sabbath. That is on the seventh day of the week, beginning with dusk on Friday and ending with the dusk on Saturday evening.'

'I understand,' Caird said.

'Yes, but you don't understand how important it is that we do observe the ancient practice, the ancient law. The law. Not the government's law. Ours. A much more ancient law.'

'But you have your Sabbaths.'

Gril raised a hand from the case and lifted a finger.

'Yes. But we do not go by the ancient and sacred calendar. Instead of travelling horizontally on the calendar, we travel vertically. Last Monday was the Sabbath, not Saturday. That is, it was if we obey the law of the state.'

'I think I know what you're going to say,' Caird said. 'It's hard –'

'Please. It's going to rain very soon. Since I've been courteous to you, a stranger who came in from nowhere and will probably go nowhere . . .'

('Ain't that the truth!' Charlie Ohm said.)

'. . . without telling me who you are and why you're here, I'm not asking too much of you to refrain from interrupting.'

'Right,' Caird said.

('The organics!' Ohm whispered.)

Caird looked around quickly, but Ohm was just warning him to watch for organics.

'I did not like the idea of observing the Sabbath on the wrong day, on Monday instead of as it should be and has long been decreed . . .'

('The man's as windy as you, Caird,' Ohm said.)

'. . . but I obeyed the state and the rabbis. After all, they reasoned that, regardless of whether it was Saturday or not, the Sabbath still fell on the seventh day. But I was not happy with this reasoning. Then, one day, while reading the book of a very wise man, though he was sometimes mistaken and prejudiced, I came across a passage that affected me deeply.'

'Cerinthus?'

Gril's only sign of being startled was a rapid blinking. 'How did you know that?'

'Never mind. I'm sorry I interrupted again.'

'Actually, the author was Pseudo-Cerinthus. The scholars had established that some books supposedly by Cerinthus were by another man, name unknown, called, for the sake of convenience, Pseudo-Cerinthus. I, however . . .' – Gril looked very pleased – '. . . I was able to prove that Cerinthus and Pseudo-Cerinthus were actually the same person. His style as Pseudo-Cerinthus was different from Cerinthus' because, when he wrote as Pseudo-Cerinthus, he was possessed by the *Shekinah* or *Doxa* . . .'

'By what?'

'God's presence or the light that His presence shed. The Targumists used that term . . .'

'Never mind,' Caird said. 'What was this passage that affected you so deeply?'

('Cerinthus and Pseudo-Cerinthus,' Bob Tingle said. 'Another schizophrenic. Do you think we have room for him, too? Come on in, sibling sage, seer and psychotic.')

('I can't believe that we're standing out in the open discussing theology and stylistics while the storm and the organics are closing in,' Ohm said.)

'Cerinthus,' Gril said, 'believed that the angels created the world. And an angel gave the Jews their law, which was imperfect. He was wrong about that, of course. The *Shekinah* gave the law to the Jews, and the *Shekinah* cannot give imperfect laws. Not to His chosen people.

'But Pseudo-Cerinthus, inspired by the *Shekinah*, wrote that, even if the law had been imperfect in the beginning, it was made perfect by the Jews. Their stubbornness in clinging to their law despite all persecutions and misfortunes and their survival despite everything that should have wiped them from the face of Earth proved that they were obeying the perfect law. After this passage, Pseudo-Cerinthus denounced Cerinthus as being in grave error and, indeed, not too bright. He mentions several letters he sent to Cerinthus explaining the error. These have not been found . . .'

The first rain fell, large but scattered drops. The wind tried to pry Caird's hat loose. Thunder stomped. Lightning raced towards them on many glowing legs.

'What you're saying,' Caird said loudly so he could be heard, 'is that you broke day just so you could obey the letter of the law?'

'The letter is the soul of the spirit!' Gril cried.

He paused and he glared.

'Also, there was another reason. It was strong, though not strong enough to have made me a daybreaker if it had not been coupled with my desire to observe, even if only once, only once, the Shabbos as it should be observed.

'I am a human being. I am the son of a species that has always been one with the rhythm of Nature as decreed by God. Countless generations from the beginning of the species have enjoyed the slow unfolding of the seasons, a phenomenon that they took for granted though it was one of God's many gifts. But the New Era . . . the New Era! . . . they did away with the seasons, man! They've ruined them, shrunk them!

'Spring is an explosion of green, come and gone in a few days! Summer . . . summer is a hot flash! Too many summers. I'll get only the searing days and none of the cool! Autumn doesn't slowly change into its beautiful colours! It doesn't slip into one colour after the other like a woman trying out clothes! It's green one day and a burst of fully realized colours the next and then it's all dead, dead! and you may miss the snow, God's blanket, entirely!'

'That's true,' Caird said. 'On the other hand, the racing-by of the seasons can be exhilarating, and think how many more seasons you get to see than if you lived like our ancestors did. There's always something gained when you give up something and vice versa.'

'No,' Gril said, shaking his head violently. 'I want it as God said it should be. I will not . . .'

Caird did not hear what else he said. He rose swiftly, staring past Gril's shoulder at the patrol car that had appeared from around the corner of the building on the street by the canal. It would be past the underground access tube at the northwest corner of the park long before he could get to it. He was cut off.

Gril turned his head, looked once, and said, 'Perhaps they are headed elsewhere.' He sounded calm.

There was another access tube at the northeast corner of the park. He must not run now, though. Wait and see if the car went on.

It was going fast, headlights spearing the dim light and bouncing off the raindrops. Several feet from the junction of Fifth Avenue and Washington Square North, however, it slowed and then it came to a stop.

Gril had quit talking for a moment. Now, seeing the car, he said, 'Our destiny is here.' He closed his eyes, and his lips moved.

'Yours, maybe. Not mine,' Caird said.

Gril opened his eyes just as the car doors opened. The clouds also opened up, the rain coming down as if it were ambitious to become Niagara Falls. It bent the leaves above the two and dumped a cascade on them. They were soaked and chilled, though the rain was only partly responsible for the coldness.

Two men and a woman got out of the vehicle. The driver came around the front of the car, revealing the green-and-brown uniform in the headlights. His belt held a holster, from which stuck the butt of a gun.

The woman screamed something and ran towards Gril and Caird. The two organics shouted after her. Caird thought that he heard, 'Stop!' Lightning struck immediately thereafter, seeming so close that Caird thought that a nearby tree must have been hit. The flash showed him Ruth Zog Dinsdale, his . . . no . . . Isharashvili's wife. Her face was distorted; her screeching cut through the rumble of thunder.

Her block building was across the canal almost directly opposite the Tao Towers. He had been reckless to walk so boldly down the street in front of the building. Since he knew that she might look out her window and see him, he should have gone to the back street. But the probability of her seeing him had been low, and he had not been himself. Zurvan had been in no shape to think of such details.

He turned and ran south. Flight towards the access tube he had planned to take was too dangerous. He could be intercepted too easily. There was another tube located at the corner of La Guardia Place and Washington Square South.

Gril called, 'Good luck, man!' and said something in an unintelligible language. A Yiddish blessing?

'I need it!' Caird said, and he ran.

31

He zigzagged, trying to keep trees between him and his pursuer. A glance behind during a lightning flash had shown his wife standing still and one organic running after him. Gril was gone. He probably had just walked away. Another glance in the dimness told him that the driver had gone back to the car. Outlined against the streetlight, which had just come on, the car was moving eastwards towards Washington Square East. Its driver was following organic procedures. While one man chased the fugitive, the other would drive the car to head the fugitive off.

Caird thought that he could get to the tube before the car did. He also had a good head start on the other organic. But he could not outrun the beam from a gun. By the time that he reached the tube, however, he had not been shot at. Or, if he had been, he was not aware of it.

The car was sixty feet away when Caird got to the tube. The man on foot was about a hundred feet back. Caird went around the tube to the side by the street, Washington Square South. The entrance was oblong; the interior, half-lit by the streetlights. He put his hand on a plaque on the back wall six inches above his head. This was a globe with superimposed letters, MSUTS (Manhattan State Underground Transportation System). He pressed the *M* and then the *T*. The seemingly immovable plaque responded to his hand on its lower edge, swinging up to the left. He reached within the exposed recess and felt the two buttons there. Monday's code was left button, one short press, right button, one long press, one short press. He was fortunate that Isharashvili, as a Central Park ranger, knew the code and that enough of the ranger was still in him to remember that.

Having released the locking mechanism on the person-hole cover, he bent down, lifted the handle inset in its middle, and pulled. The cover came up, but only because he was heavy enough to register as an adult on the security sensor plate around it.

Light had come on in the tube and from the hole as he had raised the lid. Below the hole was an irradiated plastic ladder inside a plastic framework. He let himself down, stopped, reached up, and pulled the cover down with the handle on its underside. It came down easily, restrained by a hydraulic mechanism from falling. Just before the lid closed, Caird saw the organic's feet. A hoarse voice said, 'Stop in the name of the law!'

'Whose law?' Caird muttered.

His pursuers were organics, but they were also immers. There had not been time for them to go to a precinct station and withdraw charged-particle beam weapons. These two must have been in the neighbourhood or close to it, and they must have been looking for him. They were lucky – unlucky for him – to be the nearest to Ruth Dinsdale when she had called in. They had brought out the illegal weapons, their own property, from a hidden place in the car, and they meant to use them.

Caird went down the ladder for thirty feet before stepping off onto the rubbery plastic walkway. It extended east and west as far as he could see, which was not more than a hundred feet either way. Whichever way he went, the lights would travel with him and darkness would follow and precede him.

The walkway was bounded on one side by a thick plastic wall and on the other by a guardrail. Beyond it were two goods transportation belts, each fifteen feet wide. At the moment, they were not moving. Beyond them, against the wall, were two huge pipes. One was a water main; the other was for sewage.

Because he was both an organic and an immer, Caird had studied the systems. Every three hundred feet the rock wall bore tunnel and belt identification signs and diagrams of the local system. By each was a communication strip. These could also be used to monitor the tunnel. If the men after him took time to call in to an immer at the monitor control centre, they could check with the monitor through the tunnel strips. The monitor could tell them exactly where their quarry was.

He did not know if the immers had anybody at the control centre. He could not take the chance they might not have one. He had to get to a place where there were no monitors. Though he knew of such a place and was running towards it, he would encounter dangers there of which his pursuers would be only one.

He ran, his feet slapping the walk and his breathing the only sounds. When he looked back, he saw another light following him. The two men were tiny figures inside a worm of light. They were about six hundred feet behind him, too far for effective range of their guns. He had to keep that distance. So far, they had not stopped to call in and they would have if they had someone at the monitor control centre.

The tunnel sloped down so gradually that he would not have been aware of it if he had not studied the system. It would pass under the Kropotkin Canal, but, before it got there, he would come to two tunnels crossing this tunnel at right angles. He took the first one and ran north. The belt by the walkway was lower than the previous one and was carrying a few boxes of goods. The belt plates, two microns thick, were not joined but moved silently like a caravan of caterpillars, one behind the other. They slid on the lubricant provided by the continuous strip beneath them and were propelled by magnetic impulses.

Jogging, looking back often to make sure that his pursuers had not broken into a run, Caird kept on until he came to a three-level tunnel intersection. Just off the walkway was a large room cut out of the dirt, rocks and cement blocks forming the first level under the streets of Manhattan. The room was walled, floored and ceilinged with thick plastic. He went into it, the lights turning on as he entered. This was a tool and recreation room and toilet for the workers. After looking hurriedly around, he ran to a table and picked up a flashlight, two batteries, a hammer and a screwdriver with a long thin shaft. He tested the flashlight and put the five artifacts in his shoulderbag. On the way out, he stopped to drink from a fountain.

Coming out of the room, he saw that the two had gained on him. One raised his weapon and fired. Caird ducked even though the movement was useless. The ray struck close to him but did not damage the wall. He jogged faster than before. The two were gaining on him at the rate of about ten feet every ten seconds. He increased his speed so that he could get to the previous six-hundred-foot distance from them.

Beginning to pant now, he ran towards his first goal, a yellow enclosure of uprights circled by two horizontal rails. He was running so fast that he had to stop himself by grabbing the top railing. He went around it and let himself swiftly down another plastic ladder. Just as his head disappeared into the hole, the light above him went out. An angry yell reached him before he was halfway down the ladder.

'You won't go so fast now, you bastards,' he muttered. At the foot of the ladder, hc groped in the bag and brought out the flashlight. Its ray, poking here and there, showed him what was left of the old transportation belts. This system had been abandoned seven hundred obyears ago when the second great earthquake had struck Manhattan. The plates were thick aluminium alloy, many of them torn off or buckled. The gaps exposed the rusty and dislodged rollers beneath. The system had been obsolete long before it, along with three-fourths of the buildings on the island, had been destroyed by the temblor.

That catastrophe had been terrible, though not as difficult to recover from as the even greater quake of NE 498. On this level, however, the quick-drying plastic sprayed thickly to enclose the tunnels had not been as twisted as that on the first level. It was bad enough. Here and there, the plastic had been bent out past its strength to withstand the shock. Dirt had spilled through the cracks, and seepage had brought more dirt through. The flashlight showed no complete blockage trapping him. Not in this area.

The light had come on above him. The two were getting closer. He hesitated. He could get away as fast as possible from here or he could wait and try to knock out or kill the first one to come down the ladder. To do that, he would have to retreat beyond the range of their flashlights while they played the beams from the entrance above. Then he must run in after the first man began the descent, and somehow . . . No. If he threw the hammer, it might miss or only slightly hurt the immer. Both men would have their guns in their hands, and the one above would be directing his flashlight into the area below.

Just as he decided not to attack, the expected light beam came down through the entrance hole past the ladder. Caird turned and walked swiftly away, hoping that he was going in the right direction for him. There was enough light from the hole for him to see dimly for some distance ahead of him, though he had rough footing. The walkway was buckled and bent, and once he almost stepped into a gap.

Knowing that the man to first come down would stop on the ladder and explore the area with his light, Caird stepped up his pace. He did look back once. Seeing the beam dart around, he got down behind a pile of wet dirt that had fallen through a hole in the wall. He was just in time. The light played on the mound and then went away.

Caird's second goal, if he remembered correctly, was about four hundred feet away. He got up and stumbled on, feeling his way by the walkway railing, walking crouched over, afraid that he would fall. And then he did tumble, sprawling forward when he stepped onto a part of the walkway that was not there. He repressed a shout and shot his arms out and across to avoid injury if he struck something. He landed unhurt in a small hole. He did not get up at once because the beam shot above him. If he had been upright, he would have been caught in it.

The tunnel amplified sounds. He heard one of the men say, in a low tone, 'Where'd he go so fast? We shouldn't split up!'

'You're talking too . . .' the other man said. His voice died down so that Caird could hear only a muttering.

'Too loud,' Caird finished for him. They would probably stay together and explore the areas in both directions for a hundred or so yards. Watching from the edge of the broken walkway, he saw them turn away from him. He breathed easier. He crawled back onto the runway and continued on hands and knees. When a beam flashed near him, he flattened out. They would be turning from time to time to try to catch him with the beam.

They also would be looking at the numerous piles of dirt. It would not take them long to know that he had not gone in the direction they had taken. Though he might jump over some of the dirt, he would eventually step in some. Blundering through the darkness, he could not avoid leaving prints.

Which meant that, when they came back this way, they would see his tracks.

As fast as he could crawl, he followed the walkway. He had estimated that he must be very close to his goal. A few more yards, and he would be there. He was near to the wall so that he would not miss it. Once he got down it, he could use his light. For a while, at least.

Groaning softly, he stopped crawling. Something had driven into his face just below the right cheekbone. It came loose when he jerked his head back, and his cheek burned. He put his hand to it and felt blood flowing. Cursing, though softly, he slipped off his shoulderbag, opened it, felt around, and came out with some tissue paper. After sticking it on the wound, he felt carefully around until he got hold of the thing that had gouged his face. It was the broken end of a pipe or a railing.

He put the shoulderbag back on and slid between the wall and the pipe. The walkway twisted so that he tended to slide into the wall. Wriggling, he got by the railing. He had to stand up then because he kept sliding back. His feet slipped out from under him, but his wildly flailing hand grabbed a railing.

He crouched down at the peak of the bent walkway and slid down on his feet into the next upward slope. Just beyond it, he bumped his head against another railing. He cursed at the pain, then smiled. His hands told him that he had found his second goal.

It had been a protective enclosure around the entrance to the next level down. It was, however, squeezed in at the top. He had to take off the bag and drop it into the entrance hole before he could get his body into the narrow aperture. For a tense few seconds, it threatened to hold him.

Just as he scraped through, feeling that the skin on his ribs had come off, he was speared by light. The men shouted. He dropped and caught hold of the edge of the entrance. His feet groped for and found the ladder rungs. He scrambled down the ladder, which was twisted and at a slant. Halfway down, he had to let his feet dangle while he gripped the junction of the uprights and the rungs. He wished that he had taken the flashlight out of the bag so that he could see how far the end of the ladder was above the ground. Then his feet touched the earth, and he let loose. After groping around, he found the bag. The flashlight in his hand, he turned it on.

The place looked just as he remembered it. He had never been here, but, three Wednesdays ago, he had seen a strip show about it. This was Wednesday's allotted share of the early New Era archaeological dig. It was mostly the old sewage and water and power systems, not very interesting. He went forward on the dirt past bent and broken mains and pipes and snapped cables. The beam shone on the quick-drying plastic the archaeologists had sprayed to keep the walls and ceiling of dirt and debris from falling in. He walked fifty feet and found another safety enclosure around the entrance hole to the level below. This was new and had been put in by the archaeologists.

The old goods transportation and water-sewage level had been filled with dirt and cement and stone blocks and other debris after the second great earthquake. Because the ocean waters were rising as a result of the melting of polar ice, the authorities wanted the ground level to be higher. The present underground system had been built on top of the old one.

The level in which Caird was now standing had been excavated some years ago. During the digging, the archaeologists had found the bent safety enclosure to the ladder. It had not been removed but had been preserved as an historical site. When the level below had been excavated, the ladder had also been left as it was. Though the darkness had kept Caird from seeing the plaque that indicated the historical site, he had remembered it from the show.

Caird went down the ladder into the next level, the flashlight in one hand so that he could see the rungs. He got off the ladder and directed the beam around the immense cavern. The upper part of the cavern had once been dirt and the sewage and water system under the old transportation level. After this had been thoroughly studied and everything measured and photographed, the artifacts had been removed. The level beneath, that which had been the ruins of the city after the first great earthquake, had then been exposed. The cavern in which he now stood had once been occupied by two layers of archaeological treasure.

To the west, a hundred feet beyond the ladder, was a solid wall of dirt from which projected parts of stone and cement blocks and unrecognizable artifacts. Near it were two digging machines, looking like metal elephants on treads, two plastic-spraying machines looking like praying mantises, piles of temporary shoring material, and machines for carrying the dirt away.

Caird had to go the other way. If the two immers knew that, they could go through the level above and try to get to the next exit before he did. Or one could come down to drive him ahead while the other waited above for him.

Today was, however, Monday. The immers might have seen Monday's show about Monday's digs. But that would not be about this area. They had to be ignorant of the layout in this area. Not until they got down here would they realize that Caird had made for the exit and would beat them to it.

He hoped that that was the situation. It was possible that the two, carrying out their organic duties, had once pursued an outlaw down here. If so, they would know the area.

His light stabbing the gigantic hollow, veering to pass by plastic-walled blocks of earth on top of which were artifacts, sidestepping trenches in which were artifacts not yet completely uncovered, he trotted swiftly. The air-conditioning machines were not turned on; the air was dead and heavy. It was also warmer than he had thought it would be. He was sweating and getting thirsty.

It was unfortunate, he thought, that the floors were soft wet dirt. If the floor had been hard, its lack of prints would have slowed down the immers. They would have been forced to look into the huge pipes above to make sure that he was not hiding in one.

He went around a crushed and rusty automobile, an ancient internal combustion vehicle. Its occupants were now pieces of bone. Past that was another obstacle, a tangled mass of steel that the strip-show mentor had said was the ruins of a Ferris wheel. Another detour was around a tangled mess the identification of which he did not remember. It was roped off like all the other artifacts and was marked with a sign. He did not have time to stop and read it.

He came around a block of earth on top of which was a huge mirror which had miraculously not been shattered. He stopped, and, despite the extreme need not to do so, he yelled.

Centred in the beam was a gigantic monster, a thing with a colossal head, enormous many-faceted eyes gleaming a vicious red, dripping mandibles, and a body with many legs. It was crouched, ready to spring upon him.

32

His yell bounced back from the far walls.

He swore at himself and muttered, 'I forgot about it.'

His terror was gone, but his heart was still beating hard.

The plastic monster had once been part of a 'house of horrors.' Most of that had been destroyed during the earthquake, but there were some exhibits or 'monsters' here and there, roped off and labelled.

Hoping that the gigantic spider would give his pursuers heart attacks, he ran on. His beam played on some of the artifacts, one of which was the severed head of a woman with tangled snakes where her hair should have been. Medusa. The unhappy woman of ancient Greek myth whose look turned all she saw into stone statues. He ran on, passing many other remnants of the fun fair until, panting and thirsty again, he stopped. There were four vertical tubes here, shafts for elevators. Two were very large, containing cages for bringing down machinery and supplies and taking up dirt and debris. The smaller cages were for use by personnel. A half-mile east was another bank of elevators.

Caird's flashlight shone on the control panel by the elevators. It had OVERRIDE buttons that permitted remote control of the cages. According to the indicator panel, these were all on the level of the new transportation system. Caird pressed three of the DOWN buttons and then the corresponding LL (lowest level) buttons. Presently, the doors to three of the tubes opened, and light flooded out from the cages.

He hoped that the immers, when they got here, would believe that he had taken the one still at the top transportation level.

When the cages got to the bottom, he stepped outside of the light that shone from them when their doors opened. He stood in the darkness and looked towards the west. A few seconds later, a flashlight shone from the ceiling, illuminating the ladder. A man climbed down in the beam directed by his colleague in the next level above.

When the two men had reached the ground, Caird turned and sped towards the next bank. He tried to run as softly as he could because the cavern amplified sounds. He did not turn his light on until he was beyond the paleness shed by the cage lights. He kept the flashlight at belly level and directed straight ahead. There were many blocks of earth and artifacts between him and his pursuers. These, he hoped, would prevent them from seeing his light. When the light struck an obstacle, he turned it off and detoured, letting his memory carry him past the blocks and objects for a few steps. After which he turned the light on.

Though he had rested a minute and had drunk from a fountain by the elevators, he was still tired. The air seemed to thicken. It was dead, rising from dead earth and dead things. It suggested slowness, sluggishness and an eventual motionlessness. The half-mile to the bank seemed to stretch to a mile and a half. Just as he arrived, panting and sweating heavily, he was surrounded by light.

He groaned. The immers had found the switch to turn on all the illumination in the cavern.

Had they seen him?

That was answered quickly. Here they came running, their guns in their hands. They were so far away that they looked small, but they would become large sooner than he wanted.

He jabbed the OVERRIDE, the number-one cage, and the DOWN and the LL buttons. He had been wrong in trying to fool them. He should have taken the elevator at the first bank. He would gain nothing by attempting to beat them to the next bank, another half-mile away. He would have to wait until the cage here got to the bottom. But would they be here before then? Or, if he did get into the cage and its door shut before they got to it, could they stop his cage?

They could. Not only could the cage be stopped at any level but a control also permitted it to be halted halfway between levels. Which, of course, it would be. They would trap him and then leisurely take him.

He could run and try to hide. That would only put off the end.

Though the immers were getting closer, they were slowing down. Their faces were agonized with the strain of pushing their dead legs and heaving lungs to the limit of speed. Within a minute or so, though, they would be shooting at him at the same time as they ran.

The elevator doors opened.

Caird jumped into the cage, turned, and punched the UP button and then the button for the third level, the next one above. He might get to it before the immers realized that they could stop him. Trying for any floor above that was suicidal. Trying for the next level might be suicidal, too.

The doors were closing when a ray struck the edge of one. The metal hissed and pooled, but the door closed, and the cage moved up.

Four seconds later, the cage stopped. The doors began sliding back. He grabbed their edges and pushed. He fell out through the narrow opening. The doors opened all the way and then slid back shut. Total darkness closed in on him. Somewhere on this level was a panel with a button to turn on all the lights in this area. He had been lucky that the immers had not found it when he was escaping from them. He did not have time to look for one now. Using the flashlight to light the floor before him, he ran.

They would expect him to take the next bank of

elevators. But which bank? The one to the east or the one to the west? And which level would he go to?

If he had breath to spare, he would have laughed. One would have to go back to the first bank and the other would have to run on to the eastern bank. Both would then go to the top level, the transportation system tunnel just below the street. From the cages there, they would head towards each other, expecting, hoping, anyway, to catch him between them.

But what if one of them took the elevator in the middle? He could go to the same level as Caird, and he could see Caird's flashlight. He would go after him while his quarry was running again as fast as he could to beat the other immer striving for the western bank. Then they would know that Caird was heading for the ladder down which he had come.

He stopped, breathing hard, his heart thudding. Some of his tiredness was lost in a surge of delight. His flashlight had shone on another ladder.

He went up that and had no trouble with a bent enclosure. He was in the tunnel of the old transportation system. He walked as swiftly as he could, too fatigued to run anymore, until he came to the first ladder down which he had sunk into the buried and ancient darkness. At the top of the ladder, he raised his head until his eyes were just above the edge of the hole. The light would not come until he had emerged to his waist.

As far as he could see, there was darkness.

When he climbed out, light blooming around him, he found that the belts, which had been inactive, were now moving. A large green plastic box moved swiftly from the blackness, through the light he had caused, and into the blackness. Before he had turned to walk westwards, another box was squeezed out by the artificial night. And two more, going eastwards, were carried to their destination.

He walked until another westering box approached. He

climbed over the railing and jumped onto the belt. The light filled the belt area for a hundred feet in each direction. There was nothing he could do about that, but he could rest. At the same time, he would be going faster than if he walked. He sat down on the cool plate, his back against the box, and watched the east for a sudden glow in the night. It might be caused by workers, but the probability was that it would announce the two killers.

Three minutes later, his box was snatched from him. Aware that it would be, he had risen and leaped to the railing. Here was an intersection where the belt passed beneath a northward belt. The sensors of the pair of mechanical arms stationed here had read the coded plaque on the box, had determined that its route should be changed, and had lifted it and deposited it on a belt in a recess. Caird climbed up a short ladder and got onto the north-going belt. For a moment, he thought about switching to the south-going belt. In a little more than a quarter-mile, he could get onto an east-going belt. The immers would not know where he was because they could not see his light. However, that would be the longer route to his destination. He could take the chance that the immers would not catch up. How would they know when they got to the intersection – if they got to it – that he had taken this belt? They would not know unless they arrived quickly enough to see the light wrapping him like a photonic shroud. He was gambling that he could switch to an east-going belt before then.

His back against another box, he passed quietly under the Kropotkin Canal. Above him was rock, metal, water, fish and the storm. He was, at the moment, both subterranean and subaqueous. And he was passing from darkness into darkness, his presence birthing new light. In the darkness behind were known terrors. Who knew what unknowns faced him?

('Corny,' Repp said.)

('It's life,' Dunski said.)

('Clinched, cloistered, and cloyed by clichés,' Tingle said.)

The next voice startled Caird. He had thought that it was gone forever.

('I was wrong,' Will Isharashvili said. 'I've wrestled with the ethics of the situation, and I've decided that I shouldn't just give up to avoid violence. What I think –')

('My God! Isharashvili rides again!' Repp said.)

('You can't keep a good man down,' Dunski said. 'And Will is *good*!')

('What I think,' Isharashvili said gently, 'is that –')

'Quiet!' Caird said more loudly than he intended. 'Shut up, you fools! They've found me! I can't think with you chattering away at me!'

Far down the tunnel, the darkness had opened like a fist to let light out. Two Lilliputian figures were climbing over a box. He watched as they got down from the box and started trotting.

He was tired and desperate, but so were they. He climbed over the box, got down on the other side, and trotted. Sooner or later, he would pass SCC workers. If he had been alone, he would, probably, be reported. The workers would assume, however, that the two organics had reported to HQ that they were chasing the criminal. Those who asked the two officers if they wanted help would be told that none was needed. The immers did not want other organics involved.

When he saw an envelope of light in the darkness, he forced himself to run faster, and to climb over the boxes more vigorously. Fortunately, there were only three to get over before he got to the light. This came from an office in a recess at the intersection of north-south and east-west belts.

He leaped out when he approached the steps and grabbed the railing. His chest heaving, breath sawing, he ran up the steps. The light accompanying him would merge with the light from the office windows. But that would not keep the pursuers from seeing him leave the belt.

He went past the windows. A man was sitting at a desk and watching a strip show while he drank from an unlabelled bottle.

If there was another worker around, he or she could be in the toilet or sleeping in the back room. Caird did not hesitate to take his chances. He ran around the corner, through the door, and at the man behind the desk. The man had just put the bottle down when Caird charged in, and he did not see Caird until he was almost on him. The man rose from the chair, saying, 'What the . . . ?' Caird grabbed the bottle by the neck and brought it down on the man's forehead. He just wanted to stun him, not severely injure or kill him. The man fell backwards over the chair and sprawled out, his eyes closed and his mouth hanging open. Whisky fumes rose from it.

Caird glanced at the half-closed door to the back room. A woman's head and the cot on which she lay were visible. Her mouth was open, and she was snoring as heavily as the unconscious man. He assumed that she had also been drinking the bootleg whisky.

The man on the floor groaned, and his eyelids fluttered. Caird groaned, too, though not for the same reason. He had to make sure that the man was unconscious for at least five minutes.

Gritting his teeth, disliking what he had to do, Caird lifted the man, propped him against the desk, and hit him on the jaw with the bottle. The man fell over on his side.

33

Caird dragged the body by the feet through the doorway. Forty feet eastwards was one of the huge mechanical arms that removed boxes from one belt to another. He dropped the man's legs and switched the controls on the panel at its base to MANUAL. He slipped his hand into a metal-mesh glove and moved it as he wished the arm and its 'fingers' to move.

The man, his waist gripped by the 'fingers,' his body arched, head and arms and legs dangling, was placed in front of a box on the east-going belt.

Caird brought the arm back to the upright position – it would not do for the immers to notice it sticking out over the belts – and he ran back to the office. By then, his heavy breathing had become light. He went back into the office and got behind the door of the back room. The woman was still snoring. Caird pushed the door so that it was an inch open, and he turned the back room light off. He put his shoulderbag on the floor and took out the screwdriver and hammer.

A few seconds later, he heard the rasping breathing of the two men. Through the opening, he saw one enter the office, gun in hand, stop and look around. The other walked past the windows and out of sight. The first man waited until his partner came back.

'He's on the east belt,' the second man said. 'I saw his light.'

'Where in hell're the workers?' the man who had entered first said. His thick eyebrows made his face even tougher-looking.

The second man had a very short and upturned nose.

He looked like a picture of the ancient extinct bulldog. Pointing at the open whisky bottle which Caird had put back on the desk, he said, 'They're probably passed out in the back room.'

'I'd sure like to turn those slobs in!' Eyebrows said.

Bulldog walked to the fountain and drank deeply. Still gasping, he straightened up. 'Drink up. We can't just stand here while he's riding away from us. He can see there's no light following him. He'll be resting.'

Eyebrows drank deeply, too. When he had his fill, he wiped the sweat from his eyes with his arm and said, 'You think we should call in for help?'

'I sure wish we could,' Bulldog said. 'But it's too risky. We got to get that son of a bitch soon.'

'What happens if we don't?'

Bulldog looked disgustedly at Eyebrows. 'You know what'll happen.'

'If I could just get in range!'

'You won't standing here. Come on.'

As soon as they left, Caird went to the fountain, which he had been too pressed to use before then. He drank more sparingly than the immers, though he wanted more. Before going out of the door, he got down on his knees and stuck his head out just far enough to see his pursuers. Who were now the pursued. They were not trotting, just walking fast. They assumed that, since they could not see Caird, he was hidden behind a box. Undoubtedly, they were hoping that he was so exhausted that he would rest long enough for them to catch up with him.

He had to take the chance that they might look back. He rose and ran from the door, the screwdriver and the handle of the hammer in his belt. He went up the steps to the walkway over the east-west belts, climbed over the railing, and dropped onto a box. He got down quickly from it and crouched between two boxes. Now, if they looked back, they would think that his light was theirs unless they noticed that their light was much longer than it should be. He prayed that they would not.

When he stuck his head up over the edge of the box, he saw them climbing over a box. He waited until they had gotten off it and then went over his box. He ran while they walked. He overtook them when they were going over another box. His hammer and screwdriver were in his hands when he slid off the edge of the box.

Just as he came up behind the man in the rear, Eyebrows, the man started to turn his head to look behind him. Caird brought the hammer down on the side of his head harder than he had intended. He dropped the hammer and the screwdriver, not caring how much noise he made now. Bulldog, on getting ready to slide off the box, had turned his head when he heard the thud of the hammer. Caird caught Eyebrows' body with one hand. With the other, he snatched Eyebrows' weapon from his holster.

'Hold it!' Caird said, and he let Eyebrows fall. The gun was set for full power. Bulldog knew that.

'I don't want to kill you,' Caird said, 'though I should. You were going to kill me.'

('Take them out, anyway,' Repp said. 'They're vermin, and a dead enemy is one less enemy.')

('Don't!' Isharashvili cried.)

'Your left hand up in the air. High. OK. Now, slowly, very slowly, ease the gun out with the right hand. Drop it on the box by you. Turn your head away; don't look at me. Hold it until I tell you different.'

Bulldog's neck quivered, but he looked straight ahead. After a slight hesitation, he took the butt of the weapon by two fingers and placed it on the box by him. His right hand joined the left one above his head.

'Now slide off the box and walk about twenty feet away. Keep your hands high. Don't turn around. I know how to use this. I'm a crack shot.'

Bulldog obeyed. Caird got swiftly onto the box and stuck the gun into his shoulderbag. He got down off the box, walked to Bulldog, reversed the weapon, and struck the man hard on the crown of his head. Bulldog crumpled.

('Don't!' Isharashvili cried again.)

'Go back where you came from,' Caird muttered. He removed the ID disc-star from Bulldog's neck and put it in his shoulderbag. He might be able to use it, though he doubted it. He rolled the body onto the west-going belt and climbed back over the box. After putting Eyebrows' ID in the bag, Caird rolled the body onto the west-going belt. Since there might be a use for the hammer and screwdriver, he placed them in the bag. It was bulging and was very heavy, but he did not plan to carry it for some time. He stood watching the light and the two unconscious men in it for a minute. Then he lay down. He did not think he had closed his eyes, but a man shouting at him woke him up.

The man's eyes were level with the belt. Caird shouted, 'Surprise inspection! You should be glad I found you awake!'

Caird sat up and grinned at him until the man turned and walked into the office. Caird did not have time to worry about what the worker meant to do. He had to change belts soon. If he kept going much longer, he would be under the East River and on his way to Brooklyn.

By the time that he had gotten to his goal, he had switched belts nine times. A few times, he had been forced to travel for a while in the opposite direction. He had stolen a worker's lunch. He had gotten off four times to drink from a fountain and had twice had to go down an access ladder to the lower level. He had washed off the tissue from his cheek wound and the dirt from his face and hands.

When he got out of an elevator in an access tube, he was tired. The events of today and the six days before, the tension, the uncertainty, the battles, the running and the warring voices within him had punished him. He had been stretched to his outer limits on a rack and squeezed to his inner limits in a compacter.

Nevertheless, when he stepped out into Central Park near the Alice in Wonderland statue, he at once felt stronger and more hopeful. Alice, after falling down a hole, had survived her many perils. He hoped that there was no mirror he had to pass through in his future.

He planned to hole up somewhere in the park overnight. As a ranger, that is, drawing on Isharashvili's memory, he knew several good hiding places. Tomorrow, he would try for the wilds of New Jersey. The great forest that covered most of the state's eastern part sheltered some outlaws. They might accept him. If he was rejected, he would starve. He knew nothing of noncity survival. Even if he was taken in, he would live hunted and harried.

At least, he would be living. Someday, he might get back into a city and there insert a new ID into the data bank. That idea, at the moment, tasted like he imagined cockroach droppings would taste.

The sight of Central Park cleansed him of such thoughts. Amazingly, the storm had passed and was now only low black clouds in the west. The air was exhilarating; the wind, a mere five miles an hour. The world looked as it always does after a good rain. It seemed to have been remade by God to His better liking. A male cardinal's *Toowheert – Toowheert – Toowheert – Twock – Twock – Twock – Twock* rang from an oak branch. A squirrel was scold-barking from an Osage orange tree branch at a big black cat that had braved the wet grass.

The clear sky also meant that the satellites had their eyes on Central Park.

This did not bother Caird. He walked along a winding, up-and-down flower-lined path past bushes and trees, past statues of Frodo and Smaug, Lenin, the Cowardly Lion and Dorothy, Gandhi, Don Quixote, Spinoza, Rip van Winkle, Woody Allen and John Henry. He went by a few people who had taken shelter from the storm and were out again. So far, no rangers or organics, but they would be somewhere near.

After going for several hundred feet on a path covered by interlocking tree branches, he left it. He plunged into an area that was not off-limits to the public but was seldom ventured into. It stood out like a green thumb, a patch of bright and poisonous-looking vegetation. The stone statues of the animals crouching in the very thick ranks of fronds and huge elephant's-ear plants looked slightly misshapen. He was walking in a landscaper's reproduction of an Amazon jungle by the ancient French painter Henri Rousseau. Yellow eyes framed in spotted faces gleamed from behind heavy nightmarish bushes. A proboscis monkey, resembling a politician whom the landscaper disliked, stared down foolishly from a branch.

Caird pushed through the forbidding growth, struggled uphill, skirted a black-painted granite god, squat, massive, crouching on frog legs, its half-human, half-jaguar face snarling, and came to the ridge of the hill. He crossed into the vegetation on the other side, descending abruptly into a land of pines and birches. The statues here were of folk-tale monsters of the far north, baba-yagas, cernobogs, chudo-yudos, hiisis, koshcheis, lyeshies and veshtitzes. At the bottom of the hill, he walked, ankle-deep in mud, around a swamp from which protruded the heads of rusalkas, female water-spirits with long wavy green hair.

This was a fenced area the public could visit only during guided tours. Between the fence and a creek flowing under it into the swamp was a gap of two feet. He got down on his knees in the water, pushed the fence up, and, bent over, went beneath the fence. Trees growing thickly along the creek banks shielded him from the sky-eyes.

Another half-mile would get him to a small cave well

hidden by bushes near the foot of a hill.

After wading for several hundred yards in the winding stream, he came to a bridge. All had gone well so far. He needed only a few more minutes to get to his haven.

He froze.

There, like a troll under a bridge, was an organic.

She was standing, half-hidden behind a bush, on the right bank. The only good thing about the situation was that she was facing away from him.

('Hide!' Ohm said.)

('Go for it!' Repp said fiercely. 'Take her! Don't pay any attention to that cowardly coyote!')

('You don't know that she's looking for you,' Tingle said. 'Maybe she's waiting there for her lover.')

('True,' Dunski said. 'She could be here for any of a dozen reasons. Maybe she just took a pee.')

Caird paid as little attention as possible to the voices whispering inside him. He turned and slowly climbed onto the bank and pushed gently through the bushes and high grass on the slope. Once, he startled a dragonfly. He became motionless until it was long gone, then went on. He came up on the walk that led to the bridge. For a moment, he would be exposed to the sky-eyes, but he would cross the path quickly into the dense vegetation on the other side. Unless the organic had by now come up from under the bridge, he would be safe.

Before leaving the bushes, he looked both ways down the path. No one was in sight.

He started to walk across the path.

A voice rang out, 'Hold it!'

He whirled around to his right. A male organic with a holstered gun had just come around the bend in the path. The weapon told him that the two officers were looking for a fugitive and that the fugitive was probably Isharashvili.

Not wanting to lead the organic into the woods and straight to his hiding place, desperate, panicky, he turned and ran down the path. He crossed the bridge, hearing the man shouting to his partner to come up and help him. A glance behind showed Caird that the organic had not yet drawn his weapon. But he soon would.

He passed something lying in the path, a reminder of what seemed to be the far distant past. The name associated with it flashed through his mind and was forgotten.

Just as he had decided to leap into the bushes, he heard another shout behind him. It was not the stern command or warning he had expected. It was a yell of surprise. He turned just in time to see the organic stretched out a few feet above and parallel with the ground. His legs were spread wide; his arms were flailing. Then he struck the path hard on his back, and he was silent and unmoving.

Just beyond the man's head was a banana peel.

'Rootenbeak!'

That was the name that had darted across his mind.

The peel had probably not been dropped by Rootenbeak – what would he be doing so far north of Washington Square? – but it had certainly been dropped by someone like him.

And that inconsiderate slobbishness was helping him escape.

He ran into the woods. Looking to one side, he saw the conical helmet and auburn hair of the female organic who had been under the bridge. Then the heavy bushes and trees screened her. He slowed down, not wanting her to hear him, until he was several hundred feet from the path. Zigzagging through the growth, he headed for the creek. When he was close to it, he got down on all fours and looked from behind a bush that grew close to the bank of the stream. At first, he could hear loud voices but could see no one. Then a man appeared in a break between two trees. He was an organic and had a large green pack on his back. A thick wire ran from the pack to a small square plate he held in one hand. Another wire ran to a long tube with a disc at its end that he held in the other hand. This was being moved from side to side and then up and down.

Caird groaned quietly. The tube held equipment that would probe for the heat of his body, sniff for his odour, and listen for his breathing and the beating of his heart.

If only he could have crossed the stream and gotten to the cave. If only he could have gotten here before the rain.

('If only, hell!' Repp said. 'You got two guns! Fight, man, fight! Go down with guns blazing!')

('No! No!' Isharashvili said.)

Light suddenly appeared in him and swept across, followed by a shadow. The light seemed to spill out of his eyes, blinding him, and then the blindness was made even darker by the shadow. He shook. What was happening? Was he at last falling apart, taking refuge in disintegration?

('I am back,' a voice said.)

Caird bit his lip to keep quiet.

('You?' Ohm said.)

('I was taken up by God, and He weighed me in the balance and found me wanting.')

('Father Tom!' Dunski said.)

('How in hell can a fictional God reject a fictional soul?' Ohm said.)

('He told me to go back to my maker,' Zurvan said. His voice was as deep and muffled as the bell of a sunken ship swayed by a current. 'He hurled me out of the kingdom of glory back into the nothingness from which I came.')

Caird wanted to yell at the voices. If he did so, he would be located immediately, and he would be done for. But what difference did it make if he was silent or screamed? He was going to be caught. The only question just now was whether he would surrender quietly or shoot to kill until he was killed.

('Killing is not the right path,' Isharashvili said. 'You . . . I . . . we, I mean, have taken many wrong paths.

Don't take this most evil of all.')

('Hypocrite!' Ohm screamed. 'Hypocrite! Hypocrites all! But just this once, Isharashvili, you're right!')

The voices babbled on while he lay prone, his chin on his arm. The blindness had passed, but he seemed to be seeing through a veil of heat. The tall grass before him wavered.

A grasshopper ended its leap upon the stem of a weed. It swayed back and forth with the weed, clinging to it. It was a brightly coloured metronome, back and forth, back and forth.

And in and out. His eyes focused, then unfocused. The insect became clear, then fuzzy. But he could make out the purple-painted antennae, the Kelly-green head, the golden eyes, the orange legs and the green-and-black-checked body.

He groaned, 'Ozma!'

He began weeping, and the grasshopper dissolved in the tears.

He had turned into a river of tears shaken by an earthquake. He could not control himself even if he had wanted to. He sobbed and stretched his arms out and clawed at the earth.

He had betrayed the state, the immers, his lovers, his friends and himself.

The voices within him screamed, roared, and tore at him.

He rolled over to look up into the trees. He was dimly aware that two men were looking down at him.

Tuesday-World
FREEDOM, Seventh Month of the Year
D6-W4 (Day-Six, Week-Four)

34

Today was Tuesday's Christmas.

Jeff Caird looked out the window down at the huge yard surrounding the institution. It was on West 121st Street, near the junction of Frederick Douglass and St Nicholas avenues. A light snow, which was quickly melting, formed patches of white and green. It was the first of the winter and might be the last. There were no holiday decorations in the yard or on the trees, but many of the windows of the apartment building across the street displayed holly or figures of Santa Claus and his reindeer.

'Saint Nicholas,' Caird said. 'The great giver of gifts. The state.'

He turned and walked across the large room past the desk of the psychicist and sat down in an easy chair.

'Frederick Douglass, the slave who led his people out of bondage. Me.'

'Your people are dead,' the psychicist said.

'The immers?' Caird said, looking startled.

'No,' the psychicist said, smiling. 'I didn't meant the immers, and you know it. I referred to the others. Your personae.'

Caird was silent. The psychicist said, 'You still feel a sense of great loss?'

Caird nodded and said, 'The big wringout. The grasshopper was the key, the stimulus, the trigger, the catalyst.'

'The funny thing, the peculiar phenomenon, I mean,' the psychicist said, 'is that you grew new nerve paths when you grew your personae. They should be dying, you know, since you no longer use them. There's no sign of shrinkage in the neural circuits. Yet, you've been cured. Cured, I mean, of your multiple personality disorder.'

'You know that for sure?'

'Don't you? Of course, you do. Just as we know. That is, unless you've found some way of cheating the truth mist. If you have, you're the first, and I'm one hundred percent sure that you haven't.'

'You even know that I haven't once, not once, thought of an escape plan.'

The psychicist frowned. She said, 'That's an even more puzzling phenomenon, I don't mind telling you. Even though you had no desire to escape, you still should think about it now and then. You should at least fantasize about it. Fantasizing is part of your nature. I don't understand it.'

'Maybe I'm completely cured. The state finally has its perfect citizen.'

The psychicist smiled again. 'There is no such creature, any more than there is or ever will be a perfect state. Our society *is* as close to perfection as it can be. It's a benevolent despotism, but that has to be. You know something of history. You know that no other government has provided plenty of food, good housing, luxuries, free education, free medical treatment . . .'

'Spare me,' Caird said, lifting his hand. 'What I want to hear is that someday I'll walk out of this place and take my place in society again.'

'That can be. I am confident that you have the potentiality to be cured. But . . .'

'But . . . ?'

'There are political considerations. I don't want to upset you. Still, the world councillors are very upset, and the people are demanding punishment.'

Caird sighed, and he said, 'So, even in this near-perfect society, politics can override the strict interpretation and practice of the law.'

The psychicist made a face. 'There are situations where . . . never mind. The truth is, Jeff, that you, and all of you immers, were fortunate that you were not immediately stoned after the trial. You were lucky to have a trial.

'Of course, you could have saved the state the expense of a trial if you had killed yourselves before you were arrested. You all had the means. Yet very few of you used them. You all wanted to live too much.'

'Another betrayal,' Caird said.

He did not feel guilt. That had been washed out by the tears along with much else. *Water wears out stone.*

There was a long silence. Then the psychicist, looking as if she did not want to say what she had to say, spoke.

'I've been authorized, ordered, I mean, to tell you that Detective-Major Panthea Snick requested that she be allowed to speak to you personally. She wanted to thank you for having saved her life. The request was denied, of course.'

Caird smiled and said, 'Snick? She actually said that?'

'Why would I lie to you?'

'It was just a rhetorical question,' he said. 'Well, well! Do you know, for some reason, I have a feeling, a hunch, that I'll see her again.'

'That seems to make you happy,' the psychicist said, 'though I don't know why. You must know that there is not the remotest possibility that you'll ever see her again. Hunches . . . sheer superstition.'

'Perhaps hunches are the output of a sort of biological computer inside a person,' Caird said. 'The computer calculates all future probabilities and their chances of happening. And it comes up with a high probability for an event that a human-made computer would rate as low. But the flesh-and-blood computer has more data than the human-made one.'

'The human-made doesn't have hope in its circuitry,' the psychicist said. 'Hope isn't data. It's an irrelevant electromagnetic field.'

'Irrelevant? Nothing is irrelevant in this tightly interconnected universe. However . . .'

He was silent for a few seconds, then said, 'I heard, don't ask me from whom, your efforts to keep me incommunicado have not been completely successful . . . I heard that the news shows said nothing about the age-slowing bacteria when they reported the trials.'

The psychicist betrayed nothing on her face, but she paled slightly. She said, 'How could you have heard anything? And what bacteria are you talking about? Is this some more of your nonsense?'

He smiled and said, 'No one told me. I just made that up about hearing it from someone. I wanted to see your reaction. I wanted to find out if what I've suspected is true. You might as well tell me the truth. I can't pass it on to anybody. I know that every immer who was questioned told all about the elixir. That revelation would have to be passed on to the higher-ups. But I believe that it got no further than the interrogators and their superiors, and, of course, the world council. The news about it was suppressed.'

The psychicist, who had become even paler, told the monitoring strip to back up the display. Having stopped it at the point where he had asked her about the bacteria, she erased all of the recording from that point forward. Then she turned the strip off.

'You think you're so clever!' she said. 'You fool! You're asking to be stoned immediately!'

'What's the difference?' he said. 'I've known all along that I will never be released as cured. None of us immers will be. The government will go through the legal procedures, keep us long enough to fulfil the law, then announce that we're incurable, and stone us. We'll be put away where we'll never be found.

'The government has to do that. It can't release us when

it knows that we know all about the elixir. At the end of the minimum period for us "mentally unbalanced" to be "cured," we go into the stoners. I've got two more submonths to live, if you can call this near-solitary confinement living. Two more months, unless the government gets uneasy and decides to stone us at once. It could do that. It could easily cover up its illegal action.'

'You don't know what you're talking about!'

'Sure, I do. You know I do. You must also know, if you've any intelligence, that you're in almost as much danger as I am. The best way for the government officials who know about this to keep you silent is to offer you the elixir, too. But they must be wondering if you can keep it to yourself. Won't you want your husband, your children, all whom you love to age as slowly as you will? Won't you be strongly tempted to get it for them? Won't you ask for it for them? And what will you do if you're refused?

'They can't afford to take a chance with you. They want the elixir for themselves, a very select group, I imagine. They haven't told the public, and they won't. The social and political and you-name-it consequences would be too great. No, they're keeping it a secret, making the same mistake that Immerman did. And you and all those others who interrogated the immers and are now their keepers are dangerous to the elite, the new immers!

'The main difference between the old and the new was that my people, at least, wanted to change the government for the better!'

The psychicist sat down and looked past Caird as if she were trying to see the future. Caird felt sorry for her, but he had had to test her to determine if his suspicions were valid. That they were was evident.

'Maybe we'd better talk about both of us getting out of here,' he said.

The psychicist stood up. Her voice shaking slightly, she said, 'I don't deal with traitors.' She called to a strip, and the door opened at once. Two huge male attendants entered.

'Take him to his room,' she said. 'And make sure that he doesn't talk to anybody on the way. Make sure!'

'I'll go quietly,' Caird said. 'But think about what I've said. You may not have much time to do that.'

When he returned to his small but comfortably furnished room, Caird sat down. He stared at the blank wall strips as if he was trying to conjure displays of the future on them. Probably, the psychicist was doing the same in her office. But he could not depend upon her to do anything that might help him. She would be thinking of her own self-survival. Meanwhile, she would be going through the routine of therapy sessions with him. He would be going through the same mechanical business until she disappeared, having been taken away by the organics or having broken day in a frenzied effort to escape.

Next Tuesday, if events went as on many Tuesdays, he would breathe the truth mist. And he would be asked if he had thought of any way to escape.

He would reply that he had. He was hoping that he could get the psychicist to help him. That was all. He had no other plan, and that one was almost hopeless.

He sighed. Why hadn't he thought of many ways to get out of here? Any prisoner would have concocted a score of plans for escape. Any prisoner. But he had thought of only one and that had been this morning before he went to the psychicist and he had expected nothing from it. It had seemed to him more of an amusement than anything.

The psychicist had said that his lack of escape plans was puzzling her.

He was also puzzled.

35

There was a place where there was no illumination but there was light. Yet it could be said that there was no light but that there was illumination.

There was no time there unless a clock with one hand could be said to mark time. That hand did not move. It was waiting for time to strike it. Not just time. *The* time.

There was in that place which was many places a creature that had no shape. Yet it looked exactly like Jeff Caird and exactly like the *others*.

It had no name. It was waiting for the right time to choose one.

It could be said that it had no parts yet was a sum.

Formed on Tuesday, it had lived its short life in Tuesday only. Yet it looked forward to moving through seven weekdays in a row again.

It had all the thoughts about escape that Caird should have had. It knew how to break out from the escape-proof institution and how it would get to the forests across the Hudson River.

Yet Caird had grown it and had encysted it except for one channel. Through this channel, it had siphoned off thoughts of escape as swiftly as they had come to Caird. It cut off the channel when Caird was subjected to the truth drug, and it switched the channel back on when the drug had worn off.

It had also siphoned off, neurally speaking, all the thoughts that Caird had had when, long ago, he was planning this thing of no time, no shape, and no name.

The government would sound the alarm and notify all relevant authorities when it discovered that he had escaped. But its identification of the fugitive would be wrong. The thing, which had become a man, would not be the prisoner known as Jefferson Cervantes Caird.